"THERE'S BEEN ANOTHER MURDER!"

Everyone stopped talking and froze at the words. All eyes went from the aide to Chkarad, who bowed his head, lost in thought.

A moment later, he looked up and said, "What happened?"

"One of the members of the media, the ones who covered the quarantine, killed a farmer on Fith."

"How?"

"He used some implement, not a weapon from the reports."

"And where is he?"

"Being held by the local officers. But, sir…"

Chkarad looked at the aide warily, worried about what was to be added.

"Riker was seen at the farm as well."

Picard, already trying to process the information quickly, was alarmed to hear that Will's father was now present at the only murders to occur on the planet in a century….

Current books in this series:

A Time to Be Born by John Vornholt
A Time to Die by John Vornholt
A Time to Sow by Dayton Ward & Kevin Dilmore
A Time to Harvest by Dayton Ward & Kevin Dilmore
A Time to Love by Robert Greenberger

Forthcoming books in this series:

A Time to Hate by Robert Greenberger
A Time to Kill by David Mack
A Time to Heal by David Mack
A Time for War, A Time for Peace
   by Keith R.A. DeCandido

STAR TREK®
A Time to Love

ROBERT GREENBERGER

Based on
STAR TREK: THE NEXT GENERATION®
created by Gene Roddenberry

POCKET BOOKS
New York   London   Toronto   Sydney

This book is a work of fiction. Names, characters, places and incidents are products of the author's imagination or are used fictitiously. Any resemblance to actual events or locales or persons, living or dead, is entirely coincidental.

An *Original* Publication of POCKET BOOKS

POCKET BOOKS, a division of Simon & Schuster, Inc.
1230 Avenue of the Americas, New York, NY 10020

Copyright © 2004 by Paramount Pictures. All Rights Reserved.

STAR TREK is a Registered Trademark of
A VIACOM COMPANY   Paramount Pictures.

This book is published by Pocket Books, a division of
Simon & Schuster, Inc., under exclusive license from
Paramount Pictures.

ISBN: 0-7434-6285-8

First Pocket Books printing June 2004

10 9 8 7 6 5 4 3 2 1

POCKET and colophon are registered trademarks of
Simon & Schuster, Inc.

Manufactured in the United States of America

For information regarding special discounts for bulk purchases,
please contact Simon & Schuster Special Sales at 1-800-456-6798
or business@simonandschuster.com

Once more, for my wife, Deb, who has always found the time to love me, regardless of whether or not I've deserved it or her.

A Time to Love

Chapter One

"THREE MORE?"

William Riker, first officer of the *Starship Enterprise,* bolted out of his seat, his eyes wide. Across the table sat Deanna Troi, the ship's counselor. Her deep brown eyes normally showed great empathy for the plight of others, but now they just looked tired.

Riker's hand rubbed his chin, stroking the freshly grown beard that had been the subject of much debate between them. A few short years ago, he agreed to shave it as he and Troi renewed their romance. However, after the last few months, he felt the need to change something, and growing the beard back was the easiest solution. She had playfully refused to kiss him since then, and had held out a surprisingly long time. But at the moment neither one of them felt particularly playful about anything.

With a shake of his head, he looked at the padd she had pushed his way. He already knew what it said, but still, to see three more requests for transfer rankled.

Crain from engineering, Nybakken from environmental sciences, and Kawasaki from the technology group—all solid career officers, and certainly not the type Riker ever expected to see request a transfer off the *Enterprise*.

"They want to be on the best starship in the fleet . . ." Troi began, her voice soft and understanding.

"Which we are," he said emphatically.

"Which we are, yes," she echoed. "But the *Enterprise*'s prestige has been damaged, its crew's reputation tarnished. These three want to avoid having their own careers derailed."

"Kawasaki was up for promotion, too," Riker said, sounding deflated. He was past being angry, but the hurt was still there, and he allowed it to creep into his voice. Around Troi he could be himself, slipping off the professional mask he wore among the crew.

"How many is that now?"

Troi shook her head sadly. "Seventeen in the last three months." The transfer requests had begun trickling in right after the encounter with the "demon ship."

The entire crew of the *Enterprise* was aware that the ship Picard had ordered to be destroyed was not a Federation vessel, but a "demon ship" masquerading as one.

What galled Riker the most was the notion that despite everything Picard had done for Starfleet, Command tallied up only the black marks, never bothering to weigh them against the successful missions.

To the admirals, Picard was increasingly a liability—an inconvenient reminder of the ideals they too had sworn to uphold. When the Borg invaded Sector 001, the admirals sent the *Enterprise* to the Romulan Neutral

Zone rather than let the flagship defend the Federation's birthplace. But Riker saw the expression on Picard's face when the audio reports came through, of how a single Borg cube was decimating the fleet. The *Enterprise*, in violation of orders, arrived on the scene, took command of the remaining ships, and destroyed the Borg cube.

Picard continued to embarrass the admirals by cherishing their principles while another one of their own—Admiral Dougherty—seemed to lose sight of them, almost causing the annihilation of the Bak'u.

And now this. Banishment to the hinterlands was Picard's only reward for steadfast courage and integrity. No wonder people wanted off the ship. Riker had privately hoped that the crew would remain intact, thumbing their collective noses at the faulty reasoning of their superiors, but with hundreds of people aboard the starship, unanimity was virtually impossible. He had to take comfort in the knowledge that those closest to Picard remained unfailing in their loyalty.

"How quickly do they want off? Is it worth my time talking to them?" Riker asked.

"You might have a chance with Kawasaki, since this will delay her chances at promotion. You just need to assess which is more important to her: advancement on a tainted ship or a fresh start."

"We're not tainted," he said with some heat.

"To us that's true," she agreed. "But not to everyone."

Riker held the padd, his thumb rubbing against the smooth metallic side. He pondered the choice, trying to imagine the thoughts in the younger woman's head. It occurred to him he didn't know Kawasaki all that well, just that she was petite and had an outsized laugh. Of course, he couldn't possibly know each crewman equally well, but he was having trouble coming up with details on this crewman, only that she was due for promotion within the year.

He quickly accessed her service record. Scanning her accomplishments, he was reminded why she had been placed on the recommendation list. She had helped write new programming for enhanced long-range sensors in addition to coming up with new safety systems to protect the core during red alert situations. Her initiative and wide-ranging talents had caught everyone's eye. The reviews were quite good, which Riker had come to expect from the entire crew under his watch.

"She's worth a shot," he mused.

"Oh?" Riker immediately detected the playful tone in Troi's voice. He grinned at her, stroking his beard once more.

"Well, she is single and kind of cute," he continued, rising to her challenge.

"And that's enough for you?" Troi teased. "That laugh of hers is a bit much, isn't it?"

"Well, it might get annoying in a closed space," Riker admitted, leaning closer to her. She leaned back against him, and her touch warmed him a bit.

"Annoying? Deafening is more like it," she said.

"You could sway me away from her," he offered, his hand reaching out for hers. She took it, and their fingers intertwined.

"I thought we were past the beginning," she said, the flirtatious tone suddenly gone. Her eyes glittered bright.

"Oh we are, *Imzadi*," he said softly. "We haven't been at the beginning since I first met you on Betazed."

"And where are we now?"

"Day twelve," he said, the twinkle back in his eye. "I think you're holding out just to vex me. You're determined and ready to make a point." Riker sat down and added, "I *will* speak with Kawasaki and try to convince her to stay. But for the sake of my ears, I'll talk to her in Ten-Forward."

Troi gave his hand a sympathetic squeeze. Riker returned his attention to the padd and frowned as he scrolled down to the next set of names. He studied them intently, his eyes narrowing.

Finally, Troi asked what else was wrong.

"We've been assigned more crew," he said in a flat, disapproving tone.

"They do that, you know," she said.

"When has Starfleet ever had to assign us crew? In all these years, people used to compete for assignments. And now we're getting castoffs. Look at the first officer's note on Nafir's file."

He pushed the padd toward her, and she quickly thumbed to the transporter technician's file. She read a few lines, and her frown began to match Riker's. The padd fell to the tabletop with a loud clatter, and she looked across to her friend. "Two disciplinary reports in a year, and all they can say is he has a difficult time following protocol. There's more to it than that."

"And we get him."

"I'd like to say they sent him here because they knew

we could turn him around, and maybe a year ago that would have been true."

"But today," Riker continued, annoyed, "we get him because Captain Chen'farth doesn't want the headache."

"We can still work to make him better than he is. We can still do good work," Troi said emphatically.

"Sure, we can work with him. Geordi and Chief T'Bonz won't put up with Nafir's attitude, so he'll either do it our way or he won't be on any starship in the future. The point is, we can't afford to become the prime dumping ground for Starfleet's entire population of malcontents."

"And we haven't," Troi insisted. "Most of them will still go to the *Excalibur.*" She rose and moved to the replicator for a fresh cup of tea. After all her years on the *Enterprise,* she had finally developed a taste for certain blends. "Anyway, not everyone coming to us is a troublemaker. Some have genuine problems. The Dominion War's effects have been deeper than first suspected, Will. People no longer seem as interested in facing the unknown or being out near the borders. Some planets have turned positively xenophobic."

"Fighting a vicious army led by shape changers will do that to some people," Riker noted, concerned but unsurprised by the summation.

She returned to her seat, blowing across the top of the steaming mug.

"We're all stretched so thin in terms of personnel, materiel . . . well, everything."

"Someone in particular you're concerned about?" he asked, hearing genuine curiosity in his own voice.

"There is one new member of Geordi's team that

seems to have some issues. I don't think you've met her yet. Anh Hoang, a plasma specialist. She transferred here about two months ago, right before we went to Dokaal. She lost her husband and daughter when the Breen attacked San Francisco."

He thought about the attack almost four years earlier and how many lives it altered. Earth had been struck by enemy forces in the past, the first being the Borg in the early twenty-first century, although the *Enterprise* thwarted that effort. Hoang's story was just one of millions, he knew, and immediately he felt sympathy for the woman.

"What's the issue?" he asked softly.

"We met only once," Troi admitted. "But my impression is that she took this posting to run away from the memories. She does her job well, from all indications, but she isn't making connections with the rest of the crew."

"And you're worried."

"And I'm worried. I intend to spend some time with her while we're not going anywhere." Immediately she regretted the words, he could see from the expression that flitted across her face. He hadn't become a successful cardplayer without learning how to read others. Still, he winced at the notion that he was serving aboard a technological marvel that was merely updating stellar cartography charts.

"We'll finish this tomorrow," he said shortly.

He strode out of Troi's office and immediately quickened his pace to keep up with the hustle caused by the approaching shift change. The first officer never ceased to marvel at how busy the *Enterprise* could be even when there was no meaningful mission to perform. The starship was truly a small town filled with every type of inhabitant. Its people might be caught up in their own lives and careers, but they still served their captain. They were never less than professional, and even though there were grumblings about the galactic politics in play, they were in this together.

Well, mostly, he considered, remembering he had just approved the departure of two crew members from this town. And he was still uncertain if he could convince the third to remain.

Geordi La Forge finished scanning codes for a supply requisition, looked over the figures on the screen, and hit the submit button. Despite the size of the universe, he noted, there was some comfort in knowing the starbases and supply depots all worked from a common framework of parts and corresponding numbers. Normally, the starship could count on receiving the supplies from a nearby runabout along its patrol route since they were not critically required. At least, not yet.

He surveyed the staff arriving and handing off assignments. Like the engines that thrummed beneath his feet, La Forge took pride in how well his staff operated as a team. When he took over engineering well over a decade earlier, he had seen to it that his people learned how to perform several functions and could work together both when things were calm and during a crisis. Being the son of a captain will teach you a few tricks. As a result, whenever the *Enterprise,* either the current ship or its predecessor, had trouble, his crew knew what to do without panic. In fact, after the *Enterprise*-D crashed on

Veridian III, he was asked to lecture at a symposium on crisis management. While he expected the room to be filled with fellow engineers, there were as many captains and first officers in attendance.

The *Enterprise*-E had been in operation for seven years, and it had been through some tough battles, so it didn't surprise La Forge that certain critical systems had worn out ahead of specs and needed early replacement. As the flagship of the fleet, the *Enterprise* covered more space and suffered more wear and tear than the average ship. Its missions were more important, more dangerous . . . until recently.

These last few months had weighed on the veteran officers, the ones used to running from assignment to assignment, coming to live as much on coffee and adrenaline as on well-balanced meals. The stultifying routine was harder still on the newer crew. They had graduated from the Academy with their heads filled with stories of glory and action, and then they arrive and . . . patrol. La Forge had been in space long enough to understand why things were the way they were, but no one expected him—or the others—to like it.

"Here are the inventory reports you requested." Taurik answered. Now a lieutenant, the Vulcan had served in Starfleet for nearly a decade, including an earlier stint aboard *Enterprise,* and Geordi was glad to have him back. He was gifted in propulsion theory and seemed always to find ways to coax more power from the impulse engines.

La Forge took the padd and frowned at seeing how low replacement inventory had fallen. He had a feeling there was a growing problem, and these figures confirmed it. Nodding thanks to his assistant chief, La Forge returned to his station, ready to call the regional quartermaster rather than send another request.

On the bridge, watching his officers leave and arrive, Jean-Luc Picard sat in the command chair and fought the impulse to fidget. Normally he walked freely about on the bridge, but recently he had started forcing himself to spend longer periods of time in the chair as a visible symbol that he was not cowed by the indignities heaped on his crew—and himself—by Command. Instead, he would be seen by all who had business on the bridge and wouldn't let his frustration show.

But he was frustrated, and he disliked the gnawing feeling. Starfleet Command had as much as admitted that the *Enterprise* would not take on high-profile assignments until tensions throughout the Federation cooled and the incident with the Ontailians faded from memory. Never before had his career been so affected by public opinion, but during the strenuous rebuilding efforts in the wake of the Dominion War, Command needed to make sure support remained strong while the Federation struggled to stay united.

And right now, support was lacking for both him and the *Enterprise*. A student of history, Picard knew full well how quickly a cheering crowd could turn into riotous rabble. Before that could happen, Starfleet Command had effectively banished the *Enterprise,* sending it off on errands that smaller and less prestigious vessels usually handled. He was afraid their next assignment would be to provide escort for an S.C.E. ship on a routine repair mission.

Gripping the armrests of his chair a bit more tightly, Picard mentally replayed the incidents with the demon ship once more. He went through each command decision and projected what would have happened had he done things differently. As always, the imagined results were disastrous, even more disastrous than they turned out to be in reality. At least he had saved his crew and prevented a situation from turning into a new war. But there were still prices to pay, more tangible ones beyond the bruises on Picard's ego.

Data had to surrender his emotion chip to Command.

Ever since his android friend first inserted the chip some years before, Picard had watched him struggle and then finally master the myriad emotions that had flooded his positronic brain. Data was no longer an outsider to the close relationships that had formed among the ship's senior staff. At last he could return in full measure the caring of friends who had become family.

Then the chip had been removed, and Data was once again orienting himself to an emotionless existence. Picard wondered how well the adjustment was going. He made a note to invite the android to his quarters for a frank talk in the next day or so. If nothing else, Data would see that his captain was concerned for his well-being and know he could count on his help. Even if receiving emotional support no longer mattered to Data, offering that support mattered to Picard.

He had watched Data's early adjustments as the weeks passed on the *Enterprise*'s trip to the Dokaalan colony.

If anyone could still touch Data's heart, it was the Dokaalan. Picard himself was impressed by how a society managed to flourish living only on asteroids, after their planet no longer could harbor life. What started out as a minor errand turned into an opportunity to do some significant good, and briefly Picard's hopes rose. Perhaps their success with the Dokaalan would end *Enterprise's* exile. . . .

Those hopes were dashed by the missions that followed, which proved to be short and unmemorable. He realized his log entries were brief, bordering on terse, and they clearly reflected his mood. While he would rather not have to be called to defend the Federation against some galactic threat, Picard still wanted a challenge worthy of the ship and its crew. The captain longed to be released once more to explore, but such missions had to wait until the fleet was rebuilt. He also recognized that on a personal level, he needed something to make himself feel he was still making a difference. He had seen to it that the majority of their assignments were important ones. It was why he defied Admiral Dougherty's orders and went into the Briar Patch, the region of space where Data had been assigned and subsequently damaged. That decision worked out for the best since it prevented the Son'a from subjugating their homeworld out of a twisted desire for vengeance.

But now . . .

Picard's dark thoughts were abruptly banished by a chime coming from the right arm of his chair. A flashing light indicated a communication from Starfleet Command, so by the time Christine Vale announced a message was coming in, Picard was already out of his chair.

He crossed the bridge and headed for his ready room, his pace increasing with every step.

Once at his desk, he adjusted the angle of the desktop viewer and activated the screen. The blue field with the UFP symbol was quickly replaced by the visage of Admiral Upton, a balding, gruff officer Picard could barely remember. Quickly, he mentally sifted through the organizational chart and remembered that Upton was with cultural affairs.

"Picard," Upton said by way of greeting.

"Admiral Upton, good to see you," Picard said, a professional smile playing on his face.

"Are you familiar with Delta Sigma IV?"

"Yes, sir," Picard responded, unfazed by the lack of pleasantries. "It's a few parsecs from our position. I believe they're celebrating their centennial as a successful colony world." That was all he recalled, and that only because it was mentioned on one of the newsfeeds he had read during recent downtime between missions.

"Well, they've just experienced their first murder in a century, and it's our fault," Upton said, his expression grim. His bushy, gray-streaked eyebrows looked like storm clouds over his blue eyes.

Picard frowned as the admiral elaborated on the nature of the mission. It was important, to be sure, but it would be personally trying as well, for one member of his crew in particular.

"You do realize the position this puts Commander Riker in," Picard said, when he finally could get a word in.

"I'm not worried about Riker. His issues have been considered," was all Upton would say.

Knowing it would be unwise to press the point, Picard changed the subject. "This is a higher profile mission than the last few," he noted. "Are we being unleashed?"

Upton paused before replying. *"Actually, this is a lousy mission. We're going to look bad regardless of how it turns out. Just how bad we look is in your hands."*

"Very well, Admiral," Picard replied neutrally. "We'll lay in a course immediately."

"Starfleet out," was the only reply, and the screen shifted back to its standby image. Picard sat back for a moment and let everything sink in. He reached for his viewer, entered a few quick commands, and then rose.

Moving to the replicator for a cup of Earl Grey tea, Picard tapped his combadge. "Picard to Data."

Instantly, the android responded.

"Mr. Data, I've just routed our latest mission packet to you. Please prepare to give senior staff a presentation in thirty minutes."

"Acknowledged."

That accomplished, the captain once again tapped his badge and summoned Riker to the ready room. This was not a conversation he was looking forward to, but one that he wanted to handle in private, before the rest of the crew learned of the new mission. Seating himself on the couch near a tome of his beloved Shakespeare, Picard sipped the hot liquid and tried to figure how much time had elapsed since he last longed for a new mission. Certainly less than thirty minutes, and he was reminded once more that one needed to be careful about what one wished for.

* * *

Upton left his office and took the turbolift to the floor housing a private room. Only admirals were given access to the space, filled with antique furniture salvaged from around the globe. The gleaming wood and brass always had a faint smell of polish, and voices were muted by the plush carpet found nowhere else in the headquarters building. It was a refuge away from staff, from cadets, even from captains light-years away.

The room was capable of holding only two dozen people at most, and usually had less than half that at any one time. However, it was a much desired refuge, and during the worst of times, it was where admirals could be found collecting their thoughts or just grabbing a quick nap when time permitted. The tradition began over a hundred years earlier when the building was repaired after an alien probe nearly destroyed the planet.

He entered the sanctuary and moved with practiced ease past three other admirals seated in a semicircle. He went straight to a sideboard, where he poured a generous amount of amber liquid into a cut crystal glass and then swirled it around three times. Traditional Scotch, there was nothing like it, as his father always used to say.

He took one small sip, let it rest in his mouth for a full ten seconds, and then swallowed. The ritual complete, he turned to face the others, who were debating some point of legislation that had just been passed by the Federation Council. Upton lowered himself into a comfortable wing chair and sipped in silence. The others—Admirals Janeway, Nechayev, and Stek—continued their discussion, with mere nods of their heads in acknowledgment of Upton's presence.

Finally, Stek, a senior Vulcan responsible for technological development, asked Upton, "How was the mission received?"

"Picard's a career man. He knows better than to complain."

"It's a pretty bad assignment. I wouldn't want it," Janeway admitted.

Upton smiled coldly at her. "That's about what he deserves right now."

"So, if he didn't complain, what did he say?" asked Nechayev, the smallest of the four, but the one with perhaps the most forceful personality.

"What do you think? He brought up Riker's issues."

"I'm sorry, I don't follow," said Janeway, recently promoted after successfully returning the *U.S.S. Voyager*, which had been lost in the Delta Quadrant for seven years. She was by far the youngest admiral in attendance.

"With Kyle Riker missing, there are questions we need answered, and Will Riker is his son."

Janeway's look of surprise amused the older admiral. He took another small sip of the aged Scotch and enjoyed feeling it travel down to his stomach.

"Do you know Riker?"

"Actually, Alynna, we had one date at the Academy," Janeway admitted, shifting uncomfortably in her chair. "Nothing came of it, and we never stayed in touch."

"Well," Alynna Nechayev added, "there's little love lost between those two. They've barely spoken over the years, from what I understand."

"But I do know Will helped his dad once years ago,"

Janeway added. "When the father was suspected of some crime."

"The reunion was brief and of little consequence, it seems," the Vulcan noted. "However, personal conflicts aside, Riker has proven to be a capable man. I do not fully understand why he has refused command."

"Never felt ready, or didn't want something less prestigious than the *Enterprise*," Nechayev guessed.

"Well, now Picard's holding him back. Maybe we need to force his hand," Upton said. He ignored Nechayev's look and admired the light reflecting off the crystal glass in his hand.

"If you feel that strongly, Jack, should the *Enterprise* be the one for this mission?"

"Kathryn, I know you've taken Picard's side in this," Upton said, "but trust me, any officer who has been through what he has, needs to be watched. But yes, he's closest, and he's come through for us repeatedly on these diplomatic fiascos. He just needs to know we're watching closely to make sure he doesn't get himself into trouble. Again."

Upton stifled the urge to roll his eyes at the disapproving glares that greeted his comments. Was he the only one there who could face the truth?

"All command officers get thoroughly evaluated," Stek said. "Those found underperforming get reassigned."

Et tu, Stek? Upton thought with disgust. "Oh for pity's sake, the man is reckless. Look how he lost *Stargazer* and crashed the *Enterprise*."

"Actually," Nechayev interrupted, "he's always put the Federation first. We might disagree with how he has handled his assignments—I certainly have—but in the end, he and his crew uphold our ideals. Better than most."

"Good as Picard has been in the past," Upton said unhappily, "right now we have to face the fact that he's a liability. Member worlds have raised concerns with the Council, and it's damaged our ability to function. At the first sign of trouble, we need to act decisively. I already have Braddock readying a squadron, just in case."

"With or without all the facts," Janeway noted archly.

"We let the facts speak for themselves," Upton replied.

"Yet, you let him keep the *Enterprise*," Janeway said, her voice deepening. "You kept his senior crew intact, and you've given him this diplomatic assignment. If the Council has concerns, why give him this? Especially with Kyle Riker in the mix?"

"Ever meet Riker the elder?"

"Yes, briefly, when I was an ensign," she said.

"Stubborn and pigheaded," Upton said. "A man of such virtue as Picard should be the one to rein him in. It's also a chance to see if Picard's learned anything these last few months."

He purposely ignored the frown that marred Janeway's features.

Chapter Two

PICARD AND RIKER WALKED into the briefing room off the bridge to find the senior officers already in place. As usual, Troi was seated to the left of the captain's chair, with Geordi right beside her. Opposite him was security chief Christine Vale, and beside her was Dr. Beverly Crusher, her hands stuffed into the big pockets of her blue lab jacket. Standing by the viewscreen, looking alert as always, was Data. Picard nodded to acknowledge them all and then took his seat.

Data at once activated the screen and a colorful star chart appeared, with the sector containing the planet Delta Sigma IV already highlighted. Data then zoomed in to show the planet in close-up.

"Delta Sigma IV was discovered by the Bader some one hundred thirty years ago. They were quite good at colonizing worlds and even took contracts to help other races perform the same function. It made sense that after their initial promising surveys, they would seek to colonize this one as well.

"Shortly after the Bader arrived, an exploratory team from Dorset also arrived on the planet. Both the Bader and the Dorset had a history of antagonism that stretched back three centuries, to shortly after both races developed spaceflight. They quarreled over asteroid belts, moons, planets, and even a rogue satellite that once flew through both solar systems. The skirmishes never led to full war, but harsh feelings have continued to cause conflict between the two planets.

"By contrast, the leaders of both colonizing parties chose to cooperate and built the colony together. It was an unprecedented display that must have been intended to influence both governments. If that was their intent, however, they failed, since hostilities between the home planets continue to this day."

"If I recall," Crusher said, "the Bader are pretty hostile to everyone."

"True, Doctor," Data acknowledged with a short jerk of his head. "They have antagonized a fair number of Federation worlds as well as unaligned governments."

"How did the joint venture turn out?" La Forge asked.

"Surprisingly well. Contrary to all expectations, the joint colony grew prosperous. At first there was conflict, but that almost immediately gave way to social and political harmony. Sociologists considered this a perfect example of interspecies cooperation."

"What allowed them to buck the trend?" Riker inquired.

Troi broke into a smile of recognition. "Wait, I read about this a few years ago. There have been many conflicting theories among sociologists. The leading hypothesis focuses on colonization as a bonding experience. In any case, the people of Delta Sigma IV now credit the wisdom of their pioneer leaders." They say it's thanks to these elders that theirs became a mutually supportive society, one based on peace, and totally at odds with their respective homeworlds."

"Correct," Data said. He paused to see if there were other comments and then forged ahead. "After such cooperation, they declared their independence from the Bader and Dorset homeworlds and managed to gain admittance to the Federation. That independence kept them out of the small wars between the colonizing races."

Picard nodded and gestured for Data to take his seat. "Thank you, Mr. Data. Some time ago, a Federation team was dispatched to the planet to study the new society to see if there were lessons that could be learned and then applied elsewhere in the Federation. Heading that delegation was Kyle Riker, whom most of you have met." As he paused, all eyes focused on Riker, who seemed to fixate on a point on the viewscreen.

"Representing the Federation, he worked with medical, educational, and anthropological research teams from the colony. He discovered a disturbing trend."

"They were living shorter life spans," Crusher said, snapping her fingers. "I read that same report! The researchers had only a few generations to work with, but their studies showed a steady and chartable trend. If things remain unchanged, the colonists won't live long enough to reach puberty and reproduce, let alone run the planet."

"Luckily the Federation was able to help," Picard

added, smiling at her. "Kyle Riker informed Starfleet Medical and the Federation. A counteragent was developed, then tested for some time on five volunteers from the planet. When things looked promising, the volunteers were returned to Delta Sigma IV and placed in final-stage quarantine.

"Riker returned to the planet recently to represent the Federation at its centennial celebration. The quarantine was scheduled to end as a part of the festivities. However, before the first event, one of the test subjects murdered another and escaped from confinement. Logs show Riker following the murderer out of the building, and he has not been seen since."

Everyone reacted to that. Everyone except Will, who seemed to have been replaced by a statue.

"The Dorset have formally complained to the Federation that Riker and the Federation are behind the murder. Our job is to go there, find Riker, and determine what is truly going on."

"Captain," Troi broke in quietly, obviously respecting Riker's feelings. "Is there any evidence that the Federation harmed the test subjects, however inadvertently?"

"Nothing concrete that we've been shown. The other three test subjects appear fine, according to the reports from the Federation ambassador."

"Does anyone have a clue where Kyle might be?"

"No, Counselor," Picard said. "It's assumed he's still on the planet, but that's all we know."

"Could Riker actually be after the murderer?" Christine Vale asked. "Acting when the locals didn't?"

Picard paused and thought about the question, measuring it against what he knew of the man. "Kyle Riker is a brilliant tactician and Starfleet adviser, but he is not known for directly interfacing with local civilians. Instead, he'd be more likely to advise their peace officers."

"I agree with your assessment," Troi added.

"Have the Bader also complained?" La Forge asked.

"Not yet. While we're en route, I want you, Counselor, to read up on the planet and its people. Dr. Crusher, please review the medical findings. Lieutenant Vale, I want your people drilled in planetary procedure. We're going to need them to help maintain the peace.

"Number One, you'll beam down and begin the search for your father. Counselor, I'll want you to join me as we speak to the planetary leadership. We'll plan further once we arrive. Mr. Data, have the bridge lay in a course and get us under way at warp five."

Everyone around the table acknowledged the orders and, out of respect for Riker, remained subdued as they left the briefing room. He stayed in his seat, not meeting anyone's gaze. Picard sat with him until the room emptied.

"Will, you can still ask to be relieved from the assignment," Picard said gently.

"No, sir," Riker said, his voice tight. He was clearly trying to control his emotions. The relationship between his father and him was a complicated one since the death of Will's mother. Kyle was left to raise the youngster alone. Riker had turned out well, but it was clear Kyle could take little credit for his son's success.

"Very well," the captain said. "We can always adjust the assignments once we learn more."

"I'm not the diplomat you are, sir."

"You are better than you think you are, Number One. After all, it was your diplomatic skills that got you the *Aries* offer."

Picard rose and returned to the bridge, leaving his first officer in the conference room. He could sense the increase in propulsion and knew they were nearing the desired speed. The bridge crew was at work as usual, but there was a slight change in the tenor of their voices, and more intraship communication. It happened every time they began a new mission and this time, it brought an overdue smile to the captain's face.

Riker strolled through the corridors and barely noticed the various greetings he received. Given the acknowledged speed of gossip, he assumed most of the crew already knew they were on their way to hunt down his father. He wanted to avoid discussing it with his subordinates. Well, with all but one.

He found his way to the ship's library and sure enough, he sensed Troi before he saw her. While not a full telepath, given her half-human, half-Betazoid heritage, she had empathic abilities and made an excellent counselor. Her abilities also meant that someone as deeply attached to her as Riker was had a subtle connection. Not that they could communicate telepathically like Vulcans or full Betazoids, but he took comfort in the connection. He liked knowing he was not alone.

Troi was seated at her favorite work station and had already called up the reports on Delta Sigma IV. Riker could tell by the way her head turned that despite her concentration, she knew he was in the room. Still, she remained focused on the data before her.

"Anything interesting?" he asked in a soft voice. The ship's librarian enforced the age-old belief in keeping quiet in libraries, allowing others to concentrate. Riker preferred keeping his voice low rather than risk one of her withering stares.

"I'm just getting started," Troi admitted. "There's a lot of information to sift through. I do know this is the first capital crime in nearly a century." She turned in her seat and looked up at him, and he could sense her concern for him. Part of him wanted it, and another part still didn't want to deal with the feelings Kyle's involvement brought up.

"I completely lost track of him," Riker said, taking the seat beside her. His terminal remained offline, so his fingers drummed along the edge of the station. "I can't even think of the last time we spoke. Possibly after Thomas showed up." Several years ago a freak transporter accident had created a duplicate of Riker, who took Riker's middle name of Thomas to help keep them distinct. He had tried to take Troi for himself, but wound up leaving the starship. He later joined the Maquis and wound up in a Cardassian prison. Will had lost track of Thomas, too.

"He seemed annoyed at Thomas's arrival," she said. Riker recalled the conversation in which he had explained the situation to Kyle. Instead of wanting to meet this new member of the family, Kyle had more pressing concerns over the brewing Cardassian conflict. Riker always wondered if Kyle, having recognized his utter failure at raising one son, did not want to disappoint another. Or, Riker mused, he just didn't care.

"Will you be okay with this assignment?"

"I'm as suited to the assignment as anyone," he said.

"Better, since you know him best among the crew."

"No, I don't," Riker said, surprised at the anger slipping into his voice. He swallowed and forced his voice lower. "I knew him once, but not anymore. Don't expect too much from me. Or him."

"Will, do you want to really get into this here?"

Looking around the library, he realized they were alone and so actually had the option. But did he want to get into a deep discussion and dredge up the feelings of anger and abandonment all over again? The last time he had faced those feelings was when his father was aboard the old *Enterprise,* thirteen years before. He knew it would all come up eventually, whenever Kyle was found. He decided it could wait.

"No, I guess I don't." And he left the worried-looking Troi in the library.

Chapter Three

DATA ENTERED ENGINEERING and walked directly to La Forge, who was standing over the broad tabletop diagram of the starship. The chief engineer appeared intent on studying various power outputs, so Data waited patiently. Finally, La Forge sensed the android's presence and looked up with a smile.

"Geordi, do you have a moment?"

"Of course, Data, how can I help?"

"The animosity Commander Riker feels toward his father is not something I had time to comprehend before giving up my chip. And now without it, I am afraid this is confusing to me."

La Forge sighed, in part because he despaired over his friend's loss, but also because explaining human relationships was never easy for him. He'd gotten a lot more comfortable with the topic since finally reconnecting with Leah Brahms. Still, describing complicated emotions to a digital man was a challenge.

"Near as I can figure it, the two never got along after the commander's mother died while he was still young. Even when they were both in San Francisco, while the commander was at the Academy, they never kept in contact. I have to admit, it's a different relationship than the one I had with my parents."

"You had both your parents," Data interjected.

"That's part of it, yes," the engineer admitted. "But they always believed in me and made sure I had every chance."

"Commander Riker seems perfectly capable," Data said, clearly trying to find a correlation between upbringing and personality.

"True," Geordi said. "But that has more to do with his own strength of character, something that his father's absence might have even helped create."

A sound from the console drew the engineer's attention.

"This isn't good," Geordi said. "Not at all."

In a different section of engineering, Anh Hoang worked at her station, monitoring the plasma injection system. The eighteen valved injectors required constant maintenance and adjustment. As Troi approached, the counselor studied the woman. She was petite, barely over five feet, with jet black hair that was fashioned into a tight ponytail down her back, ending between her shoulder blades. There was a slight frown on her round face above her black eyes and her lips were pursed in concentration. If anything was out of place, it was the short, ragged fingernails. She'd been biting them, a common enough habit for those suffering from stress.

"Taurik, you've got everything purring. You're the

Maintenance Maestro," called Crain, the older crewman who had put in for transfer.

Taurik stiffly ignored the compliment, but another engineer called out, "Okay, if he's the Maintenance Maestro, who's the King of Swing?"

"Benny Goodman," Anh said to herself as someone else called out the same answer.

Crain, rising to the challenge, then asked, "And who's the Sultan of Swat?"

"George Herman Ruth," Anh said softly, while another engineer called out, "Babe Ruth!"

Troi's brow knit in concern, seeing that Anh could hold her own with her peers but was choosing not to participate.

"And who obliterated his final remaining baseball record?"

"Buck Bokai," Hoang and Taurik both said, although the others heard only the Vulcan's steady tone.

"Why, Lieutenant, I had no idea you liked baseball," Crain said, sidling over.

"A former classmate of mine is serving with Captain Solok aboard the *T'Kumbra*. He is apparently fascinated by the game."

Troi moved away from the sports chatter and continued to observe in silence, enough of a distance away so as not to disturb the younger woman's concentration. She observed often enough during duty shifts that the crew paid little attention to her presence. As the minutes passed, Troi concluded that Anh's on-duty performance was fine, possibly even exceptional. But she did note that Anh barely spoke to a fellow crewman other than to provide information. No casual conversation, not even any of the typical byplay common to all ships. That was cause for concern.

Finally, Troi approached Anh and stood at her right side. The engineer looked up in surprise and then greeted the counselor.

"Hello, Anh, how is everything?"

"Fine, thank you," she replied in a soft voice. "May I help you?"

"Are you enjoying your time aboard the *Enterprise?*"

The question seemed to surprise Anh, who blinked a few times and then nodded in the affirmative.

"Making friends?"

"Some, I guess," came the tepid rely. "Is there something I can do for you, Counselor? Surely you didn't come all the way down here just to ask about my social life."

"In fact, I did. It's part of my job to make sure all of the crew is functioning well both on and off duty. The two are not mutually exclusive, you know."

"So you're telling me I have to make an appointment with you?"

"I don't want to toss orders around," Troi said gently. "But I do think you could benefit from spending some time talking with me, and I'd like to set up a time for us to have a good, long conversation."

"Are you trying to be my friend because you think I don't have any?" Anh was sounding more defensive than Troi expected, but she couldn't sense any hostility, just trepidation.

"I'm doing my job, which I think will help you do yours. Can you stop by my office around fourteen hundred? We'll have time before we reach the planet."

"If you insist," Anh said with a tone of resignation.

"I don't insist, but I do encourage you to keep the appointment, and we'll see how it goes from there." Troi gave Anh her warmest smile and left the woman alone at her post. On her way out of the section, she noticed that La Forge seemed unusually agitated but decided to let him work on the problem rather than interfere at the moment. *One engineer at a time,* she mused.

Dr. Crusher sat at her desk in sickbay, studying Starfleet Medical's report on Delta Sigma IV. It was grim reading, describing a virtual death sentence for the local people. She sat back, fingers drumming along the desktop, and let her thoughts wander, hoping her subconscious could take over for her poor, overworked, barely functioning conscious mind.

Bet Wesley never gets so punchy he can't think straight, she mused with a mixture of irritation and wistful pride. Her son had returned from the mysterious Traveler's dimension and proved instrumental in helping with the demon ship. Despite her practically begging him to stay with her, Wesley chose instead to continue living with the Travelers. He seemed so certain of his decision; the look in his eyes told her everything. On her better days she thought of Wes as determined; on her less charitable days she considered him mulish. Just like Jack had been. And for that matter, just like Jean-Luc still was. What was it with her and stubborn men?

The Travelers as a species fascinated her, and she genuinely liked the one she had met, posing as an engineer's aide. When he revealed himself and Wesley eventually left with him, she was a little frightened but figured she would be that way regardless of where her son went—his first post-Academy posting or another dimension. It took her a while to get past the emptiness that surrounded her off-hours with Wesley gone. She didn't date much, instead throwing herself into shipboard theater productions, and worked hard at staying on top of all the new medical advances.

She hadn't minded staying aboard the *Enterprise* because it had become her home and the senior crew her surrogate family. But they had begun to move on. First, O'Brien and his wife Keiko left for Deep Space 9, and they were soon followed by Worf, now an ambassador. Data had gone on extended missions on behalf of Starfleet, but without the *Enterprise*'s support. She imagined it would only be a matter of time before Riker finally got his own ship—he had had temporary command of enough other vessels to prove he could handle the responsibility.

Crusher thought about having her own command. She enjoyed taking gamma shift command as part of the rotation and was intrigued when Picard said a potential future had her commanding a medical ship. And then she flashed on all the times the captain dealt with reports, problems, politics, and distractions that kept him from leading the ship. "Does anyone remember when we used to be explorers?" he asked only a few years earlier. She remembered, thinking back to the earlier days of his command.

And of him.

Everyone else expected a romance to blossom between them, and there were times she expected it as well.

But they were warm, deep friends, with shared experiences spanning decades. Clearly, Picard was not going to marry and settle down, nor was he going to be comfortable married to a fellow officer. Not that he was cold to romance; Anij was proof enough of that. Crusher herself didn't shun romance when it presented itself, but it was clear it never would ignite between her and Picard.

Too much history, what with him being Jack Crusher's commanding officer and friend, being there when he died and having to be the one to tell her Jack was gone.

No, she was going to go forward and find her way. The question was, though, would she take the offer that Yerbi Fandau had made to her a few months back to take over Starfleet Medical when he retired?

Shaking her head to clear it, she returned her attention to the report. The counteragent positively altered the subjects' metabolism, returning their genetics to that of their native species prior to colonization. What went wrong?

She put out a call to Fandau. Given the distance, it would be a little while before a proper connection could be made. Meantime, she figured she could study the exact chemical composition of the before and after blood work.

"This is not good," La Forge kept repeating to himself.

Data stood patiently at his friend's side. La Forge didn't seem to notice as he stared at the communiqué displayed on his screen.

"Our supply request has been rejected," he grumbled.

"Do you mean we are being denied our replacement parts? That seems to run counter to Starfleet protocols."

"No, it's nothing like that," La Forge said in exasperation. "They'd send them if there were any in the region. We're a little off the beaten track, and restocking all the starbases is still an ongoing process."

"Has this not happened before?"

"Twice before, just in the last month." He slapped an open palm against a bulkhead in frustration.

"Then it would be safe to assume that Starfleet is having difficulty manufacturing or procuring the equipment required."

"Exactly. I've been nursing a balky manifold and I just replaced one RCS quad and we need at least one spare quad to be safe and none of the starbases anywhere near here or Delta Sigma IV have any to spare."

"Do you anticipate needing to replace more than one?"

"Nope. And don't tell me to get used to it. I have no intention of letting this situation continue."

Data opened his mouth, ready to rebut, but then reconsidered. After a few seconds he added, "It seems that you could let this continue to trouble you or find a creative solution to the problem. If you treat this as an engineering problem, a solution may present itself."

La Forge was quiet for a few moments and then nodded slowly to himself. "You just may have something there, Data."

Anh was only a few minutes late, arriving at Troi's office just after 1400. She remained in uniform despite her off-duty status, a fact not lost on the counselor.

"Please, sit," Troi offered, gesturing toward one of the comfortable, plush chairs angled to face her own chair. She kept the lighting just below full intensity, achieving a softer feel to the surroundings. The engineer refused a beverage while Troi nursed a cup of tea.

"How bad will the mission be?"

Interesting, Troi thought. Anh mentioned the danger first and was radiating concern.

"I'm not sure," Troi admitted, holding her cup. "The population is slowly dying."

Anh sat back, hands gripping the arms of her chair. She was anything but comfortable.

"From what I gather, the ship won't be endangered," Troi added.

"That's something," Anh admitted. "As you can imagine, I just don't like the idea of anyone losing their life needlessly."

"You're not alone in that feeling. In fact, I'm sure we all feel that way. So, tell me, what do you like best about serving on the *Enterprise?*"

"I guess I like working with Commander La Forge. He's a bright guy, and certainly cares for the engines. And he's not all spit-and-polish."

Troi nodded and waited patiently.

"I like my work with warp propulsion," she said with some pride. The emotion suited the woman, Troi noted. "There's an art in creating the right warp bubble and then maintaining it when all the universe wants to do is pop it." Anh fell silent, thinking for more to say.

"What about the *Enterprise* itself?"

"It's a fine ship," Hoang responded without hesitation.

"I like that we're on a newer model so we can continue to shake it down and make improvements. We move through space so effortlessly, you sometimes forget how complicated it gets making that possible."

"And the recent missions?"

"They've been okay, I guess. I wish there was more we could have done for the Dokaalan."

"Are you at all concerned about the rumors regarding the captain?"

"Not really. I haven't met the captain, but everything I've seen since I signed on has been positive. Commander La Forge thinks the stars of him. I try not to believe the scuttlebutt—never have been much for gossip."

"If only there were more like you," Troi said, and drank from her cup. They sat in silence for several long moments.

"Counselor," Anh began, shifting uncomfortably in her chair, "I appreciate your efforts, but if you're trying to be my friend, well, I'm doing fine on my own."

Troi sat and waited, seeing if there'd be anything else.

"I know I've had a rough time, but I'm not alone. The counselors on Earth saw to that. I know it looks like I've run away from my problems, but I've run away from nothing. That's just it: there was nothing to leave behind. There was just me, and I'm starting over."

Another silence stretched out.

"Look, I know you're concerned, but I guess I'm just not fast to make friends."

Deanna considered the woman, sensing the conversation had established a few things, and she might have to let it go at that for now.

"That may well be," Troi said, standing to let Anh know their time was over. "But you've been here long enough that some relationships should be established. And that has me concerned. We'll talk again."

"I do appreciate your effort, Counselor," Anh said, rising. All Troi sensed was relief that the conversation was over. No doubt the woman would need more time and attention.

Vale wore white, Riker red. Their entire bodies were covered in flexible, lightweight body armor with Japanese characters on the chest—*ataru, ram, urusai, yatsura*. In their gloved hands, they each held a staff with a red light at one end and a fatter, padded base at the other. They faced each other, comfortable in their surroundings, although Riker saw familiar intensity in Vale's eyes. She didn't do this often, he realized, and she knew he had been doing it since he was eight. Well, he hadn't practiced much in the last few years, and that would even things out a bit.

But just a bit.

They exchanged the standard greeting and then flipped down their visors. Now blind, they began to move atop the circular platform. Riker went to his left, Vale went to her left. They moved with small steps, straining their ears to pick up the other's movements. The soft buzz of the red tip helped mask sounds, complicating matters.

The first officer thought back to his boyhood, when he often performed anbo-jytsu, a modern form of an ancient martial art. He stood opposite his father countless times during their years in Alaska. He could still conjure up the emotions he felt when he learned that in all the years they sparred, the elder Riker had cheated. Kyle insisted that it was to keep his son coming back for more, that it was one of the few ways they connected. Instead, the deception fueled Will's anger and resentment.

Riker stopped practicing anbo-jytsu after that incident. Today, it was thoughts of his father that had led him to challenge Vale to spar during their off hours. He didn't need Deanna to analyze him to understand why he was suddenly wearing the armor once more. It was anger with his father that he channeled as he moved around the platform.

Riker dodged a thrust from Vale's stick and then changed direction and moved away. Once again Vale thrust, but this time she swept the stick to Riker's right and clipped him on the hip. He ducked low, swung his stick toward where he assumed her legs were, and missed. Riker controlled his momentum and quickly regained his balance, listening for Vale. She came directly at him, but he blocked her path with his stick, going across her shorter body and knocking her backward. Quickly, he moved the stick to entangle her legs, forcing her to the mat. He then placed the red tip on her abdomen. A beep signaled a completed strike.

Both flipped up their visors, and she grinned at the commander. "Nice move," she said, reaching out for a hand getting up.

"This feels good," he said. "Been years."

"Did you ever compete?"

"No, I always played strictly for myself," he replied. Had he entered competition while he and his father were both in San Francisco, it might have brought the two together, and at the time, Riker had no interest in seeing his father.

"Another round?"

"Sure," he replied.

They exchanged the ritual greeting, closed their visors, and bowed. Better prepared this time, Vale went directly at Riker, her stick held low. She swung it so the blunt end caught him in the back, forcing him forward. She then raised the stick, clipping him on the helmet. Before he could react, she upended him by sweeping the red-tipped end between his legs and throwing him off balance.

Another beep. This round went to the security chief.

"Well, that was fast," Riker said with a grin.

"Didn't even work up a sweat," she replied. "Moving around in circles and parrying could get boring."

Riker scrambled to his feet.

"Spoken like a true security officer. You'd have liked serving with Worf, although he was more disciplined."

"I can be disciplined when I want to be, but it just felt like the right time to do this."

"Well, you certainly caught me off guard. I think we need one more round to see who buys drinks later."

"Done."

Once more they began their competition and as the two went around and around the platform, this time Vale was showing patience. Riker approved, since it made her unpredictable. In the time they had served together, he had found her a competent chief. She ran her section well and came through again and again, earning his and Picard's trust. Ever since Worf had left for Deep

Space 9, the *Enterprise* had gone through a few chiefs before Vale came on board after the end of the war.

A soft sound alerted Riker, and he ducked just before Vale's stick came swinging at him. He moved toward the center of the platform and then spun around, straining his hearing to detect her location. Instead, he banged into her back as she herself was moving into the center. He chuckled at that and used his butt to shove her toward the edge as he swung to his left and used his weapon's padded end to get her in the rib cage. He turned to face her, he thought, and listened for her heightened breathing.

Vale tumbled forward and kept her stick low, clipping him across the ankles. This staggered Riker just enough for her to regain her footing, and they turned to face one another. Their sticks made contact again and again until Riker thought he would fool her, using his height to strike high. As if she sensed his intention, she ducked low and avoided being hit. They separated and moved around the platform again.

Riker this time lunged toward her and with three rapid strikes knocked her to the ground. He lifted his visor and smiled at her prone form. "See? I can learn to strike fast, too. Drinks are on you."

Riker bowed to his adversary, who bowed back, signaling the game's completion.

It was only then that Riker noticed Deanna standing off in a corner, arms folded across her chest. She was off duty, and her pale green dress was one he did not recognize. He did, though, approve, given the way it hugged her curves. Will grinned at her and she returned the smile, approaching the combatants.

"He used to ask me to try this, and not once did I have the nerve," Deanna admitted, handing Vale a towel.

"I can still teach you," he said. "Any time."

"If not with him, then come spar with me. I could use the practice," Vale added.

"Thank you, no," Troi replied. "I prefer my exercise to be a little less strenuous. My yoga with Dr. Crusher suits me just fine."

"Well, I for one can't complain about the results," Riker said.

Rather than reply, Troi just tossed his towel in his face. Vale laughed and moved away, heading for the locker room and a shower.

"You haven't done this in a long time," Troi said when they were alone.

"No," was all he would say.

They stood in silence for a few moments, and Riker suddenly felt uncomfortable around Troi. He wasn't used to the feeling and didn't like it. Something else to hold against his father.

"Will—"

"Don't say it, Deanna," he interrupted. "I know this is all about me and my unresolved feelings toward Dad. I thought we began a thaw when I last saw him, and then . . . nothing. I told him I was glad he came to the ship, but then he vanished."

"And how often did you try and reach him?"

Riker paused, considering. He honestly couldn't put a number on it. Certainly fewer than a dozen, so maybe it was once a year on average. Not a great effort, he realized.

"There are two ends to a communication signal," he said.

"Yes, but, Will, these feelings will cloud your judgment if you can't come to terms with them by the time we reach orbit. You need to channel the feelings or tuck them away. Right now an entire planet has been destabilized, and you have to help repair the damage. Then we can find out exactly what your father's involvement was. And if you can't do that, then perhaps you'd better stay aboard the ship."

He narrowed his eyes as he looked directly at her. "Did the captain send you?"

"No, he knows us well enough, so he knew I would come talk to you with or without orders."

He finished toweling himself off and unsnapped the helmet. As brilliant as she was gorgeous, Deanna was right. But then, when wasn't she? He, on the other hand, had a ways to go before he would get things right, personally and professionally. So much of his life was in limbo, and it was his own damned fault.

"I hate unfinished business," Riker said.

"Is that why you're back here, in that armor?"

"At least Vale doesn't cheat."

"No, she doesn't," Troi agreed. "But you've left more than a few things unfinished."

"Have I?"

"You haven't accepted command, you haven't resolved things with your father, and . . ."

He reached out and took her somewhat awkwardly in his arms, trying not to crush her against the unyielding polymer armor. "And I haven't finished with you, have I? You're also unfinished business."

He leaned down and kissed her with passion. This felt real, it felt good, and he savored it. She returned the kiss, adjusting her arms around him and pressing him close.

When they broke the embrace, she looked deep into his eyes and said, "I hate unfinished business, too."

And with that, she left the gym, with Riker holding just the towel and the weapon.

Chapter Four

THE *ENTERPRISE* SMOOTHLY slid into orbit only a minute off its projected schedule. Picard nodded approvingly toward conn officer Kell Perim, the Trill who had served on the alpha shift for the last few years. He turned his attention to Data, who worked at the operations console next to Perim.

"Mr. Data, planetary specifics, please."

"Delta Sigma IV is a class-M world with four large continents and several strings of islands. It is unusually stable, with little tectonic activity recorded since the Vulcans first charted it some four hundred years ago. When the Bader first surveyed the world, only animal and fish life were found. No avian life developed here, which is anomalous. The continents are fairly even in size, as are the polar ice caps. Mean temperature in the capital is currently eighteen degrees Celsius."

As Data spoke, Riker and Troi entered the bridge and took their accustomed seats, flanking the captain. Troi crossed her legs and wrapped her hands around her left knee, while Riker checked a screen at his station and then looked at the android. Picard tried to get a sense of what, if anything was going on in his first officer's mind. Having Kyle Riker, a man of great accomplishment, in the mix normally would bode well for a mission. However, he recognized there had been little softening in the hard line the son took toward the father. It was a complication Picard hoped would not become an impediment.

"Counselor, current status on the planet?"

"The Bader, who inhabit the two northern continents, have filled the airwaves with a lot of political commentary, all of it critical of the Federation."

"Number One, any word on your father?"

"None, sir," came the clipped reply.

"How goes the search for the murderer?"

"From what I can gather, they have a police force that's on a manhunt," Vale added.

"Counselor, is the Federation ambassador still on the planet?"

"Yes, sir, a Colton Morrow was here heading up the delegation Kyle Riker was a part of," she replied.

"Let me speak with him first," he ordered.

Moments later, Morrow, a fairly young man, appeared on the viewscreen. He seemed haggard, as if he had not slept much. The man was standing in a darkened office, the details of which Picard could not discern. The captain rose and addressed the screen.

"Ambassador, I'm Jean-Luc Picard of the *Enterprise*."

"*Colton Morrow.*"

"What's happening down there?"

"Chaos and confusion sums it up best," he replied. The man seemed young for the diplomatic corps. Delta Sigma IV could well have been one of his first assignments. While the planet was a cultural curiosity, it was not strategically vital, so a newly minted ambassador was about all that the Federation could spare for a centennial party, the captain surmised. At least he hadn't had time to develop the know-it-all crust Picard found so grating in many senior diplomats.

"And the cause?"

"Well, the people down here believe the Federation did something, somehow, to their people, and given the timing I can't say I blame them, even if they are jumping to conclusions. Kyle Riker's disappearance hasn't helped matters, either. That said, no one has hard evidence that the Federation bears any responsibility for this mess."

"Have they found the murderer?"

"A ground vehicle was stolen nearby, and it has been traced to an airfield. It's suspected he stowed away aboard one of dozens of flights leaving the city. He could be anywhere."

"Is it safe for us to beam down?"

"I would be happy to have you. The leaders are also anxious for some guidance."

Picard recalled from Troi's earlier briefing that each of the two races elected four councillors to their High Council. From the eight councillors, one was chosen to act as Speaker, a system patterned after many democracies. Based on her description, the planet remained tranquil for so long, the government seemed more like a town council than anything else. He could only imagine how they were faring under these circumstances.

"So be it," he said. "We'll be down shortly. Should we use these coordinates?"

"These will be fine," Morrow said, a hand brushing back the slightly unkempt sandy hair.

"Picard out. Lieutenant Vale, I want an escort, and alert transporter room two we'll be on our way. Counselor, notify Dr. Crusher, and have everyone assemble in fifteen minutes. Local time, Mr. Data?"

"At the ambassador's location, it is 1624, sir," he said.

"You'll have the bridge, Mr. Data. Maintain yellow alert. We'll stay in touch at thirty-minute intervals."

"Understood." Data rose and stepped toward the command chair, while another bridge officer replaced him at operations. The captain watched the routine with satisfaction as the turbolift doors silently closed before him.

Below, in engineering, La Forge sat at a terminal, looking at a viewscreen that showed the image of an Andorian. The Andorian's face had aged a bit since Geordi had last seen him, when they were attending a symposium on Tellar.

"Whis, how have you been?"

"Well, Geordi. And you? I've been hearing things."

La Forge answered with a frown. "Yeah, well, you know not to believe all the scuttlebutt you hear."

"A shapechanging ship sounds pretty amazing."

"Not after everything else we've experienced. Now

that you have your own ship, you must know what I mean." Whis had been recently named chief engineer aboard the *Nautilus* after serving with distinction on several other vessels. He was younger than La Forge and deemed an engineering wunderkind.

"So, why the call? Looking to commiserate?"

"Not quite, Whis. How many RCS quads do you have?"

"Four in our cargo bay."

"That's amazing. We just replaced one on the port nacelle and we're fresh out. If we wait until the quartermaster finds another one this far out, we might have a problem."

"We're due for a refit in six months," the Andorian said. *"I sincerely doubt we'll need all four between now and then."*

La Forge laughed. "I doubt you'll need even one. These things are built to last."

"What happened to your supply?"

"We needed to replace one in a burned-out system after an encounter with a comet that caught us by surprise. And it turns out the backup was damaged. Can you lend us one?"

"Geordi, we're five parsecs apart and our courses don't overlap," his colleague replied.

"Tell you what," La Forge replied, "if I can figure out the logistics, will you lend me a quad?"

"Absolutely," Whis said.

As they cut the signal, La Forge sat back, happy to have found one of the items on his list, but now he had to get it to Delta Sigma IV. He gave it some thought and then contacted the bridge.

"Data, can you spare me a minute to help with a logistics issue?"

"I am in temporary command, Geordi, so if you can come to the bridge I will be happy to oblige," the android said. *Happy?* La Forge thought. *Not by a long shot.*

As the transporter effect ended, Picard was already on the move, eyes surveying the office. It remained dark, as it had appeared on the viewscreen, and also eerily quiet. Morrow waited near a desk, reading something on a padd. In person, the ambassador seemed even younger, with a clear, unlined, somewhat handsome face. The diplomat strode over and shook Picard's hand, his grip firm.

"Ambassador, how bad is it down here?"

"Not as bad as it will be, Captain," Morrow replied. "Without a real understanding of what's happening, people are letting fear and suspicion get the best of them."

"And the leadership?"

Morrow frowned. "In over their heads, if you ask me."

"I should think so," Crusher said. She walked over, and Picard realized he needed to make a round of introductions. When he said Will's name, Morrow looked shocked but covered it quickly. Picard was pleased to note that his security officer, George Carmona, was alert and assessing their situation. Carmona was an olive-skinned, burly man, recently assigned to the ship. Picard had met him for the first time in the transporter room.

"When was the last time Riker was seen?" the first officer asked. Picard started at hearing him refer to his father so impersonally.

"Not for three days," Morrow replied. "We were at the quarantine facility, meeting with the local doctors and the test subjects when the attack occurred. Riker ran out after the man and vanished from sight. I've been staying with the Council, doing damage control. I have to admit, it's good to have some backup."

"Well, hopefully we can do this the easy way." Picard stepped away from the group, tapped his combadge, and called to Data.

"Mr. Data, scan for all human bio-signs on the planet. Screen out the away team and Ambassador Morrow. Logic suggests the remaining signal should be Kyle Riker. We can then beam him aboard."

"Just one moment, Captain," Data replied.

The captain and Riker exchanged glances as they waited patiently. After a minute, Data's voice once more filled the air.

"I am sorry, Captain, but there are no other bio-signs."

"The hard way it is, then," Picard sighed. "A man like him knows a hundred ways to avoid detection."

"I would assume so," Data replied. *"Kyle Riker's work as a strategist would give him access to highly sophisticated equipment for his field work."*

"Thank you, Data. Picard out."

"Terrific. I guess I'll start there and see if I can pick up the trail," Riker said.

"The planetary protocol officer is ready to act as your guide," Morrow explained. "He's waiting for us in the

Council chamber." He led the away team from the dim office into a broad, low-ceilinged hallway.

They stopped before an unimpressive doorway with yellow block lettering above it. In Federation Standard it read COUNCIL CHAMBER. To Picard's mind, there was a distinctive lack of pomp and circumstance here—even the most modest of governments usually treated their leaders with a higher level of respect than they did common shopkeepers. He filed the notion away, straightened his jacket, and prepared for the worst.

Inside the square chamber was a semicircular raised platform with a metal table where the councillors sat. At a smaller table directly before the platform, there were five seats, which appeared to be set aside for administrative staff. Opposite were rows of low benches for representatives, and a roped-off area that Picard assumed was a visitors gallery. Not surprisingly, the chamber was filled with viewscreens and computer terminals, most of which depicted images of the planet.

On the other hand, the room was also filled with an almost oppressive silence. Although he couldn't say he missed the screaming matches he had witnessed on other planets in crisis, the low level of activity here was unnerving in its own way. Of course, an atmosphere of calm, if that's what it was, would prove helpful. On the other hand, Picard thought, the councillors might simply be in shock, paralyzed at the mere thought of violence on a planet that had been peaceful for so long. And paralysis didn't bode well for the mission.

On the right side of the metal table sat tall, thin people with elegant three-fingered hands. These were the Dorset, known as the artisans of the planet, but clearly they had not practiced their craft here in this Spartan chamber. There were four people on the dais, two men and two women, all with elaborate braids in their long, silky-looking hair. The men were lithe and were known as fast runners, while the women were said to be skilled at metallurgy. A handsome people, the captain concluded.

The next four, on the left, were the Bader. They were stockier, similar to Tellarites, and had tremendous strength. A blunt-spoken people, they were not known for high cultural achievement. Rather, their fierce work ethic was what distinguished them. They were the builders and armorers on this planet. There were three men and one woman, all with blunter features than their Dorset neighbors, and shorter, coppery hair.

"Councillors, I present to you Captain Jean-Luc Picard of the *Starship Enterprise*," Morrow said, when all eight sets of eyes were on him.

Carefully, Morrow then introduced all eight councillors from memory, an impressive feat given the stress of the day. Jus Renks Jus of the Dorset spoke for the group and welcomed Picard and his people.

"I am sorry you cannot partake in the celebration," Renks said in soft tones. "We've canceled everything."

"It would have been a wonder," another man said.

"No doubt," Picard said. "However, we will do what we can to restore order and help correct whatever has happened. What is the current status?"

Jus Renks Jus stood and gestured toward the left-hand wall. A larger screen showed the planet, with lights winking and changing color. "Our security forces have not managed to find the vehicle the murderer stole, so the trail is, I think you say, cold."

"And Kyle Riker?"

"We do not know where he might be. But we'd like to find him."

"Do you truly believe he has something to do with this?"

Renks paused, steepling his hands and considering the response. After a moment he said, "Riker himself, no. He was not close enough to actually contribute to the death."

"However," another Dorset said, "he represents the Federation and was glorying in the success of your cure."

"A cure we must now call into question," Renks said bluntly.

"I will need to meet with your medical staff and see what I can determine," Crusher said. "The sooner the better, I would think."

Picard saw that the other members of the Council were murmuring distractedly among themselves. Morrow was right: these people were out of their element.

Renks continued, "Logically, he and your government must play some part. The Federation, after all, is filled with violent races. You must be accustomed to such heinous acts. We, however, are not. The fact that the murder occurred at this time and in this place confirms my suspicion of the Federation's core mind-set—everything it touches becomes violent."

"A brutal culture overall," sniffed a Bader woman.

Picard tried to see things from their point of view and tried to reconcile that with the Kyle Riker he briefly knew. Riker's reputation was far from spotless, true, but he had a long list of accomplishments and had earned the Federation's trust.

"Clearly, there is more we must all learn about his role in these affairs. But first, we need to chart a course of action," Picard said.

"Yes, *you* must," declared a Bader. He stood, his bulk almost dwarfing Renks. If Picard remembered correctly, this was Chkarad, Speaker for the People. "Your government caused this problem, and now you must repair the damage."

Picard raised an eyebrow in response to the Speaker's phrasing. If even the leader of this society held the Federation solely responsible for the problem and its solution, then Picard had a long road ahead of him indeed.

"If necessary, we can bring down trained security personnel from the *Enterprise* to support your people." Picard parried, deflecting Chkarad's demand that the Federation take all the blame and expend all the effort. It was never too early to lay the groundwork for cooperation. "But first, we need information. Can Dr. Crusher speak with the medical staff?"

"Of course," Renks said. "I'll have one of my staff bring her to the appropriate people. They're across the campus." With a gesture, a fellow Dorset rose and led Crusher away.

"And I believe you have someone to help Commander Riker begin the search for his father," Picard continued.

"Father! I had no idea," one of the female Dorset said.

"Is this a problem?" Morrow interjected a moment before Picard could speak.

Everyone at the Council table seemed surprised, but no
one raised an objection. Finally, Chkarad gestured to another of the staff. "Of course not, Captain. We'll have our
protocol officer escort him to the city where it happened."

"Thank you," Picard replied. He knew the away team
had just dodged a large problem. As he watched Riker
leave the room, he felt Carmona's presence behind him.
Oddly, it gave him comfort.

Chapter Five

RIKER WAS INTRODUCED to Seer of Anann, a man almost as tall as he was but broader and sturdier, and Riker considered himself fairly sturdy. He wore a layered coverall mixing primary colors with muted patterns, only adding to his imposing form. Riker noted he had no visible sidearm, which was appropriate for a protocol man. Seer seemed to be appraising him as well.

"Riker, eh? Any relation?"

"My father," he replied, inwardly sighing, knowing he'd repeat that phrase a lot in the coming days.

"We'll take my flyer," Seer said, leading Riker to an elevator that took them to the roof, which turned out to be a broad parking area for several varieties of aircraft. Before boarding the sleek, bright red-and-gold craft, Riker looked out at the city, taking in the squat buildings. Unimpressive, like the interiors he had seen so far, emphasizing function over design. The city seemed fairly large and was located near the coast, where a number of boats were tied to docking facilities. The placid blue water was empty of vessels. The skies were clear, too.

Inside the flyer were four seats and several storage compartments. Clearly it was built for transportation and not much else. The two men strapped themselves in, and Riker sat back, watching Seer quickly go through his prelaunch sequence and then speak into a mike strapped around his neck.

A series of lights winked on between the two men, and Seer nodded to himself and placed his hands inside the front panel. Whatever flight controls existed were within the panel, and Riker couldn't tell what Seer was doing. Within seconds, though, he felt the familiar thrum of engines coming to life, and within half a minute they had built up enough power to lift off the ground. Once they were a dozen feet off the roof, Seer swiveled the flyer to the east and activated a thruster. And they were on their way through a cloudless sky.

The two sat in silence for several minutes while Riker took in the countryside. They were skimming over the coast, now headed south, their speed well under mach one, he estimated.

"Fathers can be difficult, can't they?"

That was an understatement. "Yes, they can," Riker said, trying his best to maintain a neutral tone.

"Anann isn't much of a place to live," Seer went on. "Its a mineral-poor island, so you can't mine or farm, but there's plenty of space. We owned a lot of it and couldn't do much with it. Father had no idea what to do with me, so he sent me off to school and then complained when I went into the diplomatic trade. Haven't talked to him in five years."

"I can beat that. It's been ten for me."

That earned Riker an appraising look. "Disappointment to him?"

"He said he was proud of me, the last time we really talked," Riker said, recalling the one time Kyle was on the *Enterprise*-D.

"Think he meant it?"

"I do," Riker said, and realized it was true. Kyle had actually been trying to make amends, and Will was being stubborn. Still, it hurt when his father didn't keep in touch. "At least he did at the moment."

"Had to work hard to get away from his shadow, Kresla of Anann," Seer said.

"That how your names work?"

"Sure. For our people, the land of our birth carries great distinction . . . or not."

"And the name Seer of Anann?"

"I have risen above my origins," the protocol officer said quietly. He banked the flyer and started descending. Riker looked out his window and saw a lush green land, ripe for farming, with a small town nearby. Overall, things looked prosperous, and he could see why the planet must have looked promising for colonization.

"Where are we?"

"This continent is Fith, largely populated by the Dorset," Seer answered, controlling their rate of descent. "They have the best-equipped medical laboratories, so it was easy to adapt a building for the quarantine."

Riker noted that Seer was an experienced and smooth

pilot. In many ways, the man reminded him of Worf, now the Federation ambassador to the Klingon Empire. Poor Worf; Riker had respected the man, but he knew that even he had father issues. For that matter, Data was an android, and even he couldn't escape conflict with Noonien Soong.

The small flyer landed without much impact. After shutting down the engines and engaging a security device, Seer opened the hatch and let fresh air flood the compartment. Riker breathed deeply, noting the strong scent of the trees that ringed the town.

Stepping outside, he saw that the landing pad also housed four other vehicles, one of which had the insignia of the planetary peace officers, while another had a red symbol that marked it as a medical vehicle. On the opposite side was a gleaming boxlike structure. From its widely spaced windows, he could see that it was three stories tall. The walls were a dull yellow, with no signage or markings. Beyond this building were three others, exactly the same except that each was painted a different but equally bland color.

"The pink one is the quarantine building," Seer explained, gesturing to the building at the extreme left. "I escorted Ambassador Morrow and Mr. Riker there to see the test subjects. It was a day later when the event occurred."

"Where were you?"

"I wasn't really needed, so I returned to the Council chamber. Truth to tell, I don't really like being away from home if I can avoid it," Seer said.

"Nice when you can just hop aboard and fly away," Riker admitted.

They had progressed to the pink building's entrance. Seer withdrew a round, silver-colored disc about the size of his palm and waved it casually near the side of the doors. Some hidden sensor recorded his arrival, and with a loud click, the doors unlocked and swung open.

A tall, broad security officer met them, left hand outstretched. "Identification disc, please," he said. Riker surmised that like so many others in his field, this man was going to be all business, and that suited him just fine, given the circumstances.

Seer handed over the disc, which the guard slipped inside a handheld device. He then checked a readout, glanced at Seer, and grunted. Returning the disc, he spun on his heel and said, "Follow me."

They did as instructed and began following him through the halls, which were narrow and uniformly white. Every so often there were doors painted an off-white that left them almost indistinguishable from the walls. The flooring was a royal blue utility tile, worn in the middle, deeper in color along the edges. The hallways were empty and eerily silent.

Riker looked quizzically at his host, but Seer just shrugged. Clearly, they were both unimpressed by the esthetics of the medical facility.

Finally, the guard stopped at a door, the only one with a marking on it. A bright orange circular sticker bearing the peace officer insignia was affixed to it. The guard pushed the door open with his palm and ushered the men inside. He didn't follow them in.

The lab inside was cluttered. The usual assortment of equipment was present, set in walls, atop tables, and even on the floor. Paper charts were haphazardly tacked to two of the walls, while a third wall held a bank of monitor screens of various sizes. The fourth wall was taken up by a huge picture window that looked out over a field of overgrown grass. A set of portable force-field generators blocked off a huge section of the floor space near a diagnostic bed. Red pins with yellow flags delineated an area near the center of the space. Riker presumed that this was where the deceased was found.

Footsteps approached from the hallway. Both men gave a start and swung around. The door opened and a Bader doctor walked into the room.

"Smada of Tregor, director of this facility," he said.

The men introduced themselves, and then Seer asked about the murder.

The man, somewhat older than Seer, judging by his lined face, sighed and took a seat by one of the tables. He gestured for the others to sit, but only Riker accepted the offer.

"We had turned five offices into living quarters, filled with monitoring equipment as well as recreational devices," he began in a raspy voice. "The plan was to keep the subjects under observation at least a year, taking height, weight, and blood measurements daily. We let them slowly resume an unrestricted eating routine and gave them freedom to roam the building. Because of safety protocols, everyone else here remained in clean suits, and we ourselves were checked weekly.

"After eight months, we saw absolutely nothing in the subjects' vital statistics to make us believe anything was wrong. Their blood was checked at the microcellular level, we analyzed their breathing, even checked eggs and sperm. Nothing led us to believe they were ill. In fact, they remained statistically healthier than average for Bader and Dorset from this world.

"We agreed to release them a little early, making them available to appear at centennial functions as a symbol of our progress—with the help of the great Federation. Or so the Council announced." With that, Smada looked sharply at Seer, who calmly met the gaze.

"Members of the Federation wanted to come and meet with the five prior to their reintroduction to the world. You brought them here and left. We hosted an elaborate dinner for the visitors, and it was the first time any of us dealt with the subjects without our clean suits. After all, they were to be released the next day. What harm could there be?

"The following morning, we had everything together for a final review of the itinerary—in this room as a matter of fact—including the first event, which was to be a press conference. Suddenly there was an argument between two of the subjects, and before we knew it, one killed the other and ran out the door."

"Was there any security present?" Riker asked.

Smada shook his head sadly. "We never imagined needing any."

"How was the woman killed?"

"I can show you," Smada said. He turned to a thin strip of multicolored buttons and began pressing a sequence. The largest monitor on the opposite wall flared to life.

"We may have been ready to reintroduce everyone to the world, but we were still taking scans. We were looking for any changes now that we were in direct contact with them."

The screen filled with an image of the room, crowded with people. There were five in dark brown jumpsuits, the test subjects. Smada was visible, holding some form of oversized padd while a few others crowded around.

And there, off in a corner, was Kyle Riker. Will hadn't seen an image of his father in some time—years, most likely. The skin around the firm jaw seemed to sag a bit, the hair was now a steel gray with no hint of black, and his proud physique showed the beginnings of a paunch. *He's looking older, more tired,* Will thought. But the firm body language remained. This was a man in control of himself.

A time code indicated that the scene took place mid-morning, three days earlier. The sound was off, but Smada was clearly speaking to the group, followed by Kyle Riker. Will watched the five subjects. They were leaning toward other to whisper comments. Clearly, after all this time together, solid bonds of friendship had formed.

As it appeared his father was wrapping up, the conversation among the subjects seemed to get more intense. Suddenly El Bison El's meaty hand clenched into a fist. He turned on Unoo of Huni, who looked a decade older than he, and shouted something.

Kyle Riker turned, his comments interrupted. He took a step toward the two, who were now shouting back and forth. And there it was: the glint of light off the steel of a blade. It must have been in a pocket and came out at an oblique angle to the camera. He could see drips of bright magenta blood hit the lab floor and then form a puddle. Unoo's body sagged and then hit the ground.

Several things happened next. Riker knelt by the body, the knife now lying in a puddle. Bison had rushed through the crowd and was off camera and out the door in a flash. Smada was pointing in Bison's general direction and signaling right toward the camera, for help.

The screen went dark.

"I'm so sorry," Riker said, feeling somewhat at a loss to understand what he saw. It was without provocation and senseless.

"Not as sorry as we are," Smada answered in a quiet tone. "All that time and effort, all those tests, the isolation they went through, wasted."

"What do you think caused the reaction?"

The doctor shook his head, letting a stray lock of hair shake loose. He seemed tired, and Riker didn't blame him at all.

"Every medical test on Earth matched the results we recorded here. There was a year in which nothing went wrong, but on the day we released the subjects, something changed. I have no idea what."

"Where are the surviving subjects?" Seer asked.

"In total isolation upstairs. We don't dare let them back into the general population now. They're scared, and I don't blame them one bit."

"What about the vehicle Bison stole?"

"It belonged to a member of the media and has yet to be recovered, I'm told."

"And no one has seen El Bison El or my father?"

Smada looked up at mention of the connection, studied Riker's face, and then shook his head.

This was ground zero, the starting point, Riker knew,

but figuring out where to look next, that was going to be a challenge.

"How many crystals do you need?"

"Two would be sufficient."

"One now and one upon delivery."

"Agreed."

"And you can be here when?"

"In seventeen hours if I alter course now."

"And then how long before you return with the part?"

"Three days is my best guess."

"Get moving, we're not getting any younger."

"Agreed. See you soon."

The Ferengi's image disappeared from the screen and La Forge leaned against his bridge station, situated behind and to the left of the command chair, currently occupied by Data.

"The transaction seems to be proceeding without any unanticipated problems," the android offered.

"Piece of cake," La Forge replied. "With you tracking down the necessary ship, I've got my part coming well ahead of the quartermaster."

"Will they not frown upon your giving Starfleet property to a Ferengi?"

"The way I see it, I'm paying for a necessary service that keeps us on active duty during a tough time," La Forge explained. "I need the quad, the Ferengi needs to get paid. Everyone wins."

"I see," Data said. He got up and walked to the upper section of the bridge, stopping at the tactical station where Vale was reviewing incoming data.

"Status?"

Vale looked up, pressed more buttons, and then smiled. Her smile didn't happen often when the pressure was on, La Forge knew, but it looked good on her.

"We've drilled on sniper fire and outright brawls, all with good marks," she replied.

"How many more drills will be required?"

"Building evacuation, guerrilla tactics of a few nasty varieties, thermonuclear detonation, wildfire . . ."

"There are no nuclear weapons on Delta Sigma IV," Data corrected.

"Great, one less thing to worry about," she said with a grin. Quickly, she altered the schedule. "I guess we need about another day for all shifts to be well rehearsed."

"Very good. I will apprise the captain," Data said.

"Think I'll be needed?" she asked.

"Yes," Data replied. "There is a high probability that the outbreaks will increase beyond the planet's ability to police itself and before we can effect a resolution."

"Take you long to figure that out?"

"No, I had reached that conclusion before we entered orbit."

"Wish I knew. We could have trained a little faster."

"No one asked me," he said, and walked over to La Forge's station. The engineer completed checking the relays between the starship and the planet, and everything seemed fine. Looking at the planet, he found it hard to picture all that strife brewing on the surface.

"How do you think the captain is doing?"

"He has checked in with punctuality, so I would assume he is still in a fact-finding mode. Were he actively engaged in resolving the problem, the check-ins would be handled by Counselor Troi or Ensign Carmona."

"Gotcha," La Forge said. "Wish everything were so easy to analyze."

"Humans seem to dislike easy analysis," Data offered.

"True, but we also seem to wish a lot for those things we cannot have," he said.

"The grass is greener syndrome is the term," Data said.

"That's the one. These seem like a nice people, so you don't want them to suffer," La Forge said.

"Of course not. Wishing suffering on anyone does not make sense."

"Amen to that," Vale called out.

While Riker was away with Seer, Picard and Troi were left with the Council, which was clearly paralyzed by indecision. Picard refused polite offers of refreshments and asked if they could work together with a free exchange of ideas.

"Of course, Captain," Chkarad said. The Council seemed willing to defer to him in their dealings with Starfleet, and as long as the Bader was reasonable, Picard preferred having just one man to deal with. After all, convincing one on a course of action was easier than convincing eight.

The various councillors left their table and clustered around the status board, murmuring to themselves over new reports of anti-Federation protest. Picard shot Troi a look and saw she was busily studying the people, sensing their emotions.

Picard gestured to Carmona, and the security guard approached. "I think we're going to be here awhile."

Renks was talking to Troi, explaining that the protests had started soon after the media covering the celebration broke the news of the murder. Picard joined them at the refreshment table, but once again refused a drink.

"And with Riker also missing, people added two and two," Renks said. "We're not a stupid society."

"What are you implying?"

"Captain, until I am proven wrong, I can only conclude that the Federation's treatment of our aging problem went awry. You are to blame for this."

"This could just as easily have been a lover's quarrel," Troi countered. "Or some long-simmering personal problem. After all, the other three people have not acted like killers."

"That's because we haven't let them," Chkarad explained. "We put them right back into guarded isolation."

"You're presuming they will commit murder, too," Morrow said.

"What else are we to think?" a Dorset woman asked.

"Your history is full of examples of random violence," Renks added. "The Romulan War before there was a Federation, countless skirmishes with the Klingons, the Tholians, the Cardassians, your Tomed Incident, and the recent Dominion War. Need I go on?"

How little these people understood the government they were a part of. Picard looked directly at Chkarad, meeting his eyes with a focused stare.

"The Bader, the Dorset, the Andorians, the Vulcans, the Slyggians, the humans, we've all bloodied history," he began. "But, we've all found ways to rise above the violent natures that exist as a primordial survival skill. One by one, our races have matured, evolved, and found ways to coexist with one another and then with others. And when we were all ready, we formed the United Federation of Planets. One of the requirements is that a world be united, and you people have certainly done a far better job of that than either of your homeworlds. Your Council signed a charter that spells out our vision. It's not one of violence. It's one of peace, exploration, and mutual discovery.

"What have you fought about in the past?"

The room was silent for a moment. Picard studied them all, faces scrunched in concentration. Were things that peaceful for that long?

"I guess no one can recall," the Speaker finally said. It was one thing, Picard mused, to triumph over violence. It was another thing entirely to forget how to make war.

"While the doctor is studying the present circumstances, let's go back to the colony's beginnings," Picard suggested, his curiosity tinged with just a bit of envy.

"How so?" one of the Bader councillors asked.

"You arrived here first?"

"Yes," she answered. "We used rocket-powered telescopes to help us map the region, and one of them spotted this world. It fit all our criteria. This was going to be our showcase planet, the one we could proudly point to and show our people what we could do for them. The colonization business was a growing concern in this part of the galaxy."

"Was this the first Dorset colony world?"

"First successful one," Renks said proudly. "We had established toeholds here and there, but none of that meant anything in the galactic community."

"What do you mean?" Troi asked.

"We had tried to colonize a few worlds previously, but we were not ready. Problems developed, mainly in dealing with faraway worlds with just sublight velocity ships. When we finally managed warp ships, we were ready to try again."

"And what did you find here?"

"Paradise. It was almost like our homeworld," another councillor said. "Look at the original logs and you'll see poetry in the descriptions. The founders fell in love with this world at first sight."

Morrow interrupted to elaborate. "This world is just slightly warmer than Bader itself, slightly larger, with a heavier gravity. Beyond that, it was an almost ideal match for them. It really was a wonderful find."

Picard nodded and looked at Renks. "And what did you find here?"

"Me?"

"The Dorset. How did you find this world?"

Renks got the question and explained, "Survey ships. We developed warp sooner than the Bader. In fact, we checked their system as a possible colony site but abandoned it when we found it inhabited."

"Is that the source of your conflict?" Troi asked.

"Actually, my ancestors found them distasteful, but the genuine conflicts began when they developed warp and we sparred over trading routes and then potential colony worlds. We had lost out on two in a row to the Bader when we found this world."

"Lost out how?"

"As I understand it, Captain, my people wanted to colonize to expand our reach, to spread our culture. We're a proud people and feel we have much to offer the universe. The way to do that was by owning a piece of the stars. Anyway, we tried to establish ourselves in solar systems near Bader space, but they were able to establish their presence with larger numbers."

"And superior claims," Chkarad added.

"As you say," the councillor added, a dark look crossing his features. "Anyway, when we found this world, we were determined not to give it up."

Morrow once more filled in the pertinent details. "Similarly warmer than the Dorset home planet, but the gravity is virtually the same. A rare instance when the colony world is an almost perfect match for the people."

Picard thought back to the first worlds Earth colonized, starting with the moon and Mars, and thought how far from the lush, green planet they were. He could see why both coveted this place, so far from their home stars.

"Tell me what changed when you both arrived here."

The councillors looked at one another, not sure how to explain. Picard waited, feeling time slipping by as more lights winked into existence on the world map. He glanced over at Troi, who had a neutral expression on her face. The confusion didn't seem to be troubling her.

Finally, they all looked to Chkarad and he nodded. "We nearly fought for this world, too," he began. "It was ideal for both of us, and the Dorset were not ready to give up again. We settled on different continents, keeping to ourselves at first, but the survey parties kept crossing paths.

"Finally, months later, delegations from both sides met on an island and talked. It is said that that was where the union was forged and the new era began. That's what we were about to celebrate today."

Picard frowned slightly. How could Chkarad be so vague about the root of his ancestors' monumental accomplishment? Had these people no sense of history, no curiosity? Why even bother celebrating an event about which they were so complacent? "Speaker, after Dr. Crusher has looked at your medical records and Counselor Troi has spoken to the surviving test subjects, perhaps our fresh perspective will help us find answers to this problem."

His words carried more conviction than he felt. He reflected back to what Admiral Upton said and was beginning to understand the depth of the problem he had been handed.

The sea breeze was brisk, the smell of salt in the air was bracing, and Riker allowed himself a moment to enjoy it all. He was suddenly ten again, going fishing with friends before school, the Alaska sky still dark. They rarely caught anything, but the tranquillity of the morning made for a sharp contrast to the tensions at home.

He had missed that smell and the sensation of water lapping along the sides of a boat. For some reason, when he took leave, it never involved water sports, and he now realized how much a part of his childhood the sea was. And maybe that's why he avoided it, avoided being reminded about those early years and the unhappy home he shared with his quarry, Kyle Riker.

"I don't understand why you think the craft might be here," Seer said, interrupting the first officer's reverie.

Riker climbed out and inhaled deeply before replying.

"I have absolutely no idea if it's here or not, but I do know we need to start hunting."

So here they were, in the small fishing village where the flyer originated. Seer had explained that the media personality had been here just before, covering a different centennial story. Riker withdrew his tricorder, which had been programmed with the vehicle's specs, including transponder frequency, and began scanning.

"We've scanned the entire planet for that transponder," Seer complained, watching over Riker's shoulder.

"And I'm just being thorough," Will replied. The native gave a muffled laugh when the tricorder couldn't pick up the signal. Riker snapped it closed without comment and began walking toward the village. Seer took three large steps and then kept pace.

The walk allowed Riker a chance to look at the village, its one- and two-story homes, the pubs, supply ships, and assayer's office for those who made their living from the sea. The streets were filled with both Dorset and Bader, although it took a few minutes before he noticed they kept to themselves. There was no evidence of the vaunted cooperation that Delta Sigma IV prided itself on. He and Seer exchanged glances, both noting the oddity.

A Bader in some form of uniform was sauntering toward them, a tired look to his blunt features. People of both races steered clear of him, and he seemed to play no favorites, walking straight down the middle. Will was reminded of the old-fashioned western movies he saw while growing up. Although the movies featured tumble-weeds and dust, not the tang of sea air and fish skele-tons.

"Help you?" He even sounded like the old dramas. Will had to suppress a smile.

"I am Seer of Anann, protocol officer to the Council," his companion said, arms spread wide in a gesture of greeting. The other man's arms matched the gesture, but he didn't smile.

"Mokarad of Huni. What brings you here? The party's canceled."

"I'm here with Commander William Riker of the *Starship Enterprise*," Seer said quickly. "We're looking for his father, Kyle Riker."

He paused, and Riker studied Mokarad's expression. It didn't change. *He must practice looking stern in the mirror each morning*, Riker thought. *On the other hand, it's a perfect poker face.*

"Haven't seen him."

"Well, I didn't imagine you would have, but we're try-ing to track the flyer he stole. It came from here, so we're just going to look around. That is, if you don't mind."

"Why would I mind? Nothing to see."

Riker scanned the streets and had to agree. The trio walked a block or two, the first officer swiveling his head from right to left, carefully noting the subdued ar-chitecture and distinct lack of adornment. It may have been a peaceful planet, but it was also a uniformly dull one from what he had seen so far.

As he walked, Riker mused about his father's actions. Why did he chase after Bison? Guilt? Sense of justice? Lover's rage? He immediately dismissed the notion, knowing that despite his gregariousness, Kyle Riker was very selective about the women he let enter his life. One was his mother, Ann, another was Dr. Katherine Pulaski, who briefly served with Will on the *Enterprise,* and the third was a woman he had never met but who had loved his father very much on a distant world. She had died, and Kyle never mentioned her to him, but he had heard about it from Admiral Owen Paris when he was about to graduate from the Academy.

Periodically, Paris, a close friend of his father's, checked in on Riker and worked to bring the two men together. Each attempt failed, but that never stopped Paris. Shortly after graduation, Will Riker was posted to the *Pegasus* but within a year, the ship was back at Earth for repairs. While in Spacedock, Riker had taken time to visit the Academy, saying hello to teachers whom he liked. He also took time to enjoy the lush grounds that looked brand-new in the spring weather.

"They're lovely this time of year," Owen Paris had said, stepping from behind a blooming bush.

"Hello, Admiral," Riker had replied. "Yes, they are."

"Too few students take the time to enjoy the grounds, much to Boothby's regret. For them, the grounds are just something to cross between classes or a place to meet for a rendezvous." He laughed when he saw the startled look on Riker's face.

"You think we didn't do the same thing? And no

doubt my son Tom will follow in our footsteps in a few years," Paris added.

"Is he really applying to the Academy?"

"Crossing my fingers," Paris said. "Have you heard from your father?"

Riker shook his head and grinned. "You really didn't expect him to drop me a note, did you?"

"No, I guess not. He's had it rough these last few years," Paris added. "I'm glad we were finally able to put that Starbase 312 business behind us for good." Kyle Riker had been the sole survivor of a Tholian attack on the starbase and was pulled back from near death by Pulaski, with whom he began a relationship. Years later, Riker was being framed for events related to the attack, and he fled Earth. Starfleet Security even suspected complicity on Will's part, until he was cleared. Finally, Kyle returned to Earth and the matter was settled, only a year earlier.

"I knew he was never involved," Will admitted.

"It took its toll on your old man, you know," Admiral Paris said as they continued to walk side by side.

Will shot the older man a look, and Paris's expression changed to one of concern. "He didn't tell you about Michelle, did he?"

"Sir, my father hasn't told me much of anything in years, and you know that," Riker said with a little heat.

"When your father was on the run, he wound up on a world called Cyre. He stayed there for quite some time and, well, he fell in love with a woman named Michelle."

"There was some sort of revolution on that world, wasn't there?"

"I'm impressed," Paris admitted. "Few would be able

call up the details. Keep that up, and you'll be a captain one of these days. Yes, there was a revolution. It failed, but your father was one of the chief architects, which is why it almost succeeded. Michelle was one of the leaders and died in the fighting. Took your dad months after he returned to tell me the details."

Riker recalled being stunned at the notion of his father in love. The boy in him resented his father for loving anyone but his mother, but the man also recognized that life goes on after a loved one passes away. The conflicting feelings roiled within him as he pondered this woman, Michelle. A freedom fighter, he figured, would appeal to his father.

"I'm glad he had you to talk to," Will said weakly.

"And it should have been you," Paris shot back. "Some day you boys will put this all behind you."

Now Riker stood on Delta Sigma IV, wondering if Paris would ever be proven right.

They had strolled through the main street and many of the smaller streets and had seen nothing out of the ordinary. What few flyers and ground vehicles there were had been identified by Mokarad. He knew his community, and as far as he was concerned everything was in place.

"Now what?" Seer asked.

Will paused and wondered that himself.

As Picard's discussion with the Council continued, Carmona returned to the chamber, and since he couldn't disturb the captain, he approached Troi and asked for a moment alone. He seemed concerned and uncomfortable, so she imagined the report wasn't a positive one.

"They clearly didn't build this place with protection in mind. There are too many entrances, exits, and service tunnels, and no native security guards."

"What about force fields or shielding of some sort?"

"The best they have are heavy window covers for bad weather," he said unhappily. "Ma'am, I can't do my job like this on my own."

"Well, the captain asked you to look around, and you've done that," Troi said reassuringly. "Don't worry about what you found. That's no reflection on you, Ensign. Stay here and I'll speak with the captain in a moment."

Carmona assumed a ready position near the doorway, and Troi made a mental note to commend his selection to Vale when she returned to the ship. She walked over to the captain, who continued trying to maintain a peaceful dialogue. As she approached, waves of anger and confusion washed over her, coming from both races. There was something to the strong emotions, and she would need to explore the feelings to get a better sense of their tone and origin.

Picard noticed her trying to get his attention. He excused himself and walked over to her, letting Morrow continue to try and formulate a plan with the baffled councillors. Deanna quickly filled the captain in, and he frowned at learning how vulnerable the planet's leaders were.

"I'm trying to avoid a Starfleet presence that might be seen as provocative," he admitted after a moment.

"A wise move, but right now, securing the leadership seems paramount."

"What do you make of all this?"

Troi paused, considering her experience to date. She interlaced her fingers and held them before her before she began. "They're both fighting their feelings, struggling with the blow to their society, and something feels 'off' but I can't quite define it. The aggression and threat to life is quite real."

"Agreed. Ask Lieutenant Vale to send down two more guards, and let's see if we can't at least get the leaders safe. From there, we can finalize our plans."

"Captain, while waiting to speak with the test subjects, I would like to walk among the people and get a stronger sense of what's happening. Lights on a map and bickering government officials present only part of the story."

He considered the request and replied, "Have her send down a third guard."

"Thank you, sir," she said with a smile.

"I certainly don't want to be the one to explain to Commander Riker I let you get lost in the capital city."

"I'll have you know, I have an excellent sense of direction," she said with a grin.

"Much like the commander's excellent culinary skills," he said teasingly. With that, he returned to the bickering group and joined in with Morrow. She heard him turn the discussion to seeking a more secure location for the government.

Meanwhile, Troi signaled the ship and made the request for additional security guards. Vale quickly agreed to the plan and offered to come down herself. Troi refused, suggesting she stay aboard the ship and monitor things from orbit.

"How are things around the planet?" Troi asked

"Commander Riker's flyer is safely on Tregor."

Troi felt herself blush at the reply, which was not what she asked. Still, it was nice to have the crew look out for her feelings and personal concerns. "Well, not that I asked, but it's certainly nice to know."

Vale added that all was well aboard the ship, and they ended the conversation. As they did, three figures materialized near Carmona's position. Troi watched him quickly fill in the newcomers, gesturing to the doors and windows first, then the cluster of councillors. Finally, he looked her way and she held up one finger. Carmona tapped one of the men and directed him her way.

"Ensign Lateef Ade Williams, ma'am." He was tall and lanky, with dark brown skin and an easy demeanor. She'd seen him around the ship, usually performing percussion with one of the musical groups.

"You can skip the ma'am, but thanks for the consideration," Troi began. "We're going for a stroll."

"Are we looking for something specific?" His voice was soft, a trace of an African accent inflecting his words.

"No, just to get a feel for the populace."

"Sounds potentially dangerous."

"Well, then you won't be bored," she said and headed for the doors.

The medical center was a state-of-the-art facility, much to Crusher's pleasure. It boasted equipment she had only read about in journals, and she was impressed by how much space was devoted to pure research. Everything seemed well cared for, and the place was positively buzzing with activity as both Bader and Dorset scrambled back and forth. Everyone seemed to carry both a padd and a cup of something to drink, and no one walked slowly.

She loved it.

Crusher was escorted through the bustling corridor to the office of Chum Wasdin Chum, the Dorset head of medical research. She was an older woman, with as much gray as gold in her hair, and lines around her eyes that showed fatigue as well as age.

In a voice that cracked with age—or was it just stress?—Wasdin offered Crusher a seat and a drink. "Humans have their coffee, as I understand it, and we use coolar for our stimulant," she explained. "It's brewed from a native root found on every continent."

"I'll try that, then," Crusher said.

Once they had fresh cups of the hot liquid, they sat in Wasdin's small, cramped office. Two terminals, with a pile of isolinear chips next to each one, took up most of the desk space. Her lab coat was half off the plush chair behind her desk, and a picture of the Dorset homeworld hung on the one wall not obscured by equipment. Wasdin lowered herself into the chair, blew on her drink, and looked at Crusher with tired eyes.

"What happened to the counteragent?" Crusher began. The liquid was hot and soothing, as full-bodied as coffee and as aromatic as tea. She could learn to like it.

"No, the counteragent seems fine," Wasdin said sharply. "The other three test subjects check out fine. In fact, at first glance, the murderer also seemed fine, but clearly was not."

"What about the victim?"

"Her blood chemistry also was in normal ranges."

"Did you perform an autopsy?"

"Yes, I have the results right here," Wasdin said, tapping a set of printouts.

"May I examine the three remaining subjects?"

"I can summon them from their protective isolation, but first they're scheduled to meet with your Counselor Troi. The Council thought it best to keep them away from the populace at large."

"Could you talk me through the test?" Crusher asked.

"When the studies showed that we were going to die early, something had to be done or we might have to abandon our home," Wasdin began. "Oh gods, you can't imagine what it was like to learn that."

Crusher regarded the older woman with sympathy. "Die how?" She asked in a soft voice.

"Neither the Dorset nor the Bader have long lives like you humans," Wasdin explained. "We Dorset live forty, maybe fifty of your years. The Bader live maybe a decade longer."

"Go on," Crusher said.

"After two generations, it seemed we were both dying even faster. Life expectancies were down a few months to a year, and suddenly that decline escalated."

"Your projections show that within several generations your people will start dying before puberty."

"Before my great-grandchildren can even marry," Wasdin said sadly.

"In three generations? That fast?"

"Possibly. Certainly not more than five or six generations, I would guess," the older woman said. "Our people completed their studies and met with Kyle Riker on behalf of the Federation. There's a naturally occurring gas on the planet that we both react badly to. It affects our reproductive cycles and our glands, triggering the premature aging. He read the studies and worked with your medical personnel, who came up with a serum, naturally produced from other plant life found here. It was tested on five volunteers, who were kept in quarantine for at least a year."

"From what I read, the subjects' chromosomes returned to their natural configurations, in both races," Crusher added. "Can I also speak with these researchers?"

Wasdin seemed to be enjoying the break from talking, sipping repeatedly from her cup. Crusher let her be, knowing this was a difficult time for the woman. Finally, Wasdin put the cup down on a corner of the desk and continued.

"I suppose so, if you think it will help, Doctor."

"I think so, yes. Now, tell me how the counteragent was to be introduced into the population."

Wasdin took a sip of her drink, frowned at it, and set it down on the table, pushing it away. "Inoculations were deemed too time-consuming. The Council discussed spraying the air and letting people breathe it in."

"Did you start mass production?"

"No, we wanted the celebrations first. It's a relatively simple chemical compound that wouldn't have taken longer than a few weeks to produce."

"And what does Kyle Riker have to do with all this?"

"That's a good question, Doctor. Riker was here at the beginning of our study, and he came back to join our centennial celebration. He was going to help us celebrate not only our planet's unique unity but also the, ha, success of the counteragent."

People were walking with purpose, Troi noted, as she and her security escort walked down the main street on which the Council building was located. The sun had set nearly an hour ago, and the street lamps blazed with harsh white light. The light-colored buildings were no more than four or five stories tall, but they were very wide, with no more than two on a block. Shops seemed to be tucked between the buildings, and there were no street vendors of any kind in sight.

Williams was also alert, walking just ahead of her, looking into windows, checking between buildings, and straining to make out sounds. Most away team assignments didn't require this level of personal protection. In fact, she wasn't convinced of the need for Williams' presence at all, but it was the captain's call, not hers.

The immediate vicinity was quiet, despite the noise blocks away. People seemed to be avoiding congregating on the streets and hurried along. Occasionally, she heard doors open and slam. She had no baseline reference and couldn't be sure if this was normal behavior or not. Some tension filled the air and assaulted her senses, so she concluded people were avoiding the outdoors if possible. The few grocers she saw had nearly empty shelves, leading her to believe people had stocked up on goods and locked themselves away. Atypical panic reaction based on one isolated incident.

Before she could walk farther, Picard's grim voice

came from her combadge, summoning her back to the Council room.

Crusher's tricorder displayed the Federation's reference file for a typical adult Bader male. She overlaid the file with the scan Wasdin did for the murder victim. Body temperature, brain size, heartbeats per minute, all the usual readings were matches. She adjusted the scan to go deeper and show blood flow and respiration. Again, things seemed to match. It was beginning to look as if she might have to perform her own autopsies on bodies in order to study Bader physiology at a more detailed level.

"Sorry for the delay, Doctor," Wasdin said, entering the room.

"Not at all," Crusher said.

"Here are two of the researchers who worked with Riker," Wasdin said, ushering in two Dorset people. Both seemed old, over a hundred human years, with their sunken cheeks, hollowed eyes, and age spots that covered their hands. Neither seemed happy to be in her presence, so she smiled, trying to allay their fears. She needed them to feel comfortable with her so she could find out the most information in the shortest time.

"This is Man Dolog Man and his wife, Wal Cander Wal. They've agreed to review their report with you," she said. Both waved their hands in a gesture of greeting unique to the Dorset.

"What do you need to know that's not already written down?" Dolog challenged her before even taking his seat.

"Reports don't include every thought and observation," Crusher began. "And when you combined your notes with those of your Bader counterparts in order to issue a joint study, I suspect things may have been altered out of compromise. I need to learn what may not be obvious so I can help."

Dolog made a rude noise and sat down, withdrawing a cylinder from a pocket on his sleeve. He inserted it into a computer, where it began to chime and function rapidly. After a few seconds, he seemed satisfied that the report had loaded properly. He flipped two toggles, and a pop-up screen emerged before Crusher and another before his partner. The information loaded and flipped rapidly past Crusher, who tried to catch words here and there. After a minute, the text seemed to be ready and Dolog began lecturing in a phlegmy voice.

"Whatever happened to us also happened to the Bader in a similar time frame. As a result, we began looking at what it was on the planet that could change us. We began with the water supply as the most obvious place. From there we examined the atmosphere and so on. After months and months, we had looked at everything from how we cooked food to how we interacted with the plant life and whether or not we were being affected by solar radiation."

"And how did you figure out the cause?"

"We stopped being idiots," Cander said, speaking for the first time. Her voice was stronger than Dolog's, and she ignored the nasty look he gave her.

"At first, the Bader scientists did their work and we did ours seperately. It wasn't until we combined notes that we recognized the problem. We then realized neither of us had studied the atmosphere carefully enough.

"There was the usual mixture of nitrogen, oxygen, and

trace elements. But it took a while to discover just how much liscom gas there was, something we both seemed susceptible to."

"Liscom gas?"

"A by-product released into the atmosphere during photosynthesis by one of the native plants," she patiently explained.

"We identified it as we studied the atmosphere, as did the Bader, but it took us a while to figure out how prevalent it was around the planet. The Bader saw that it was building up in trace in their bloodstream. They thought nothing of it since it didn't appear to have any adverse affects. So they never said a word. My wife found it when looking over their notes months later."

"Exactly what happened?" Crusher asked.

"The gas becomes a part of our bloodstream. The buildup is gradual and has no day-to-day effects, but it alters our chromosomal structure. The genetic changes are passed on to the next generation. The buildup continues in the blood, the chromosomes are altered a little bit more, and before we knew it, people are dying at younger ages."

Crusher called up additional blood work readings on her tricorder. "It affects everyone?"

"It's in everyone's blood, yes," Cander answered. "We've been correlating cause of death statistics and are trying to create a proper mathematical model to track the spread. From what we can tell, it was just a few percent dying prematurely in the first generation and then twice that in the second generation. The third generation is just now starting to die out, and it may be twice that again."

"How soon before your model is finished?"

Both researchers looked to Wasdin, the question also in their eyes. The administrator gazed back at them without expression and held the look for several moments.

"We never finished the model," she began, "Once your government said they found a cure, we figured it was no longer necessary."

Crusher's jaw dropped. What kind of scientists just stopped their research, not because of political pressure or lack of funding, but simply because they "figured it was no longer necessary"? If anything, they should have shifted into high gear the minute they heard about the murder. After all, if they were so sure the Federation cure was behind the recent violence, they damned well better be able to back up the accusation with some numbers. Crusher was offended to the core. If even the scientists on this world lacked natural curiosity, what hope was there for the rest of the society?

"You told me before that according to your estimates, thirty-five to forty percent of the people were infected. These scientists tell me it's one hundred percent. Which is it?" Not the question she really wanted to ask, by a long shot. But it was more likely to yield helpful answers than *what the hell is wrong with you people!*

"One hundred percent," Cander and Wasdin answered together, while Dolog coughed some more. The woman reached over to comfort her ailing husband, and Crusher could hear the fluid in his lungs. If they couldn't cure this, he'd be dead within a week. In light of their blasé attitude toward their own work, Crusher couldn't help wondering if their treatment protocols were similarly unaggressive.

"Where did the thirty-five percent figure come from?"

"An early estimate some of my staff still persist in believing," Wasdin replied.

"I need you to be more forthcoming with your answers, Wasdin, if I'm expected to help," Crusher snapped in a tone that made the older administrator's eyes go wide. "I want all the reports in this room, now. I also want the Bader researchers. And while I'm waiting for that, I'll examine Dolog and see if I can do anything to help him." *Because no one else around here will,* she added silently.

Chapter Six

IT HAD BEEN LESS than four hours since they beamed down to the planet, and yet Picard felt he had been trapped in the Council chamber on Delta Sigma IV for days.

"Tell me, Ambassador Morrow, should it be proven the Federation did do something to the natives of this world, what would they do?"

"Seek a cause and a cure, Speaker," Morrow began. *Good answer,* Picard thought. As ambassadors went this one was downright . . . diplomatic.

"And how do you compensate Unoo's family for their loss, eh?"

Morrow was silenced by the question and glanced over to Picard, who felt for the earnest young man but did not want to overstep his bounds. The Federation had chosen Morrow for this negotiation. It was his show. There would be opportunities for Picard to lend his diplomatic skills to the exchange if it became necessary.

"Well, I would imagine we'd have to discuss that," Morrow said, clearly trying to buy time for thought.

"Your government either talks or fights," Renks said in a harsh tone of voice.

Nonsense! Picard frowned. The need to intervene had arrived earlier than he expected.

"It's your government, too," the captain said. "It's time for you to own up to the fact that while this situation is tragic, there's nothing to suggest that the Federation knowingly caused harm to one of its members."

The captain was about to continue when an aide burst into the room.

"There's been another murder!"

Everyone stopped talking and froze at the words. All eyes went from the aide to Chkarad, who bowed his head, lost in thought.

A moment later he looked up and said, "What happened?"

"One of the members of the media, the ones who covered the quarantine, killed a farmer on Fith."

"How?"

"He used some implement, not a weapon from the reports."

"And where is he?"

"Being held by the local officers. But, sir . . ."

Chkarad looked at the aide warily, worried about what was to be added.

"Riker was seen at the farm as well."

Picard, already trying to process the information

quickly, was alarmed to hear that Will's father was now present at the only murders to occur on the planet in a century.

"Where is Riker now?" Picard asked.

"He ran off before the officers could detain him," the aide replied, refusing to meet Picard's gaze.

The chamber was suddenly filled with the noise of excited voices. Picard turned his back to the group and tapped his badge. After summoning Troi and Williams back, he contacted Will Riker. He passed on the news and suggested they head to the farm in question.

With that, Picard turned his attention back to the Speaker, who seemed overwhelmed by the opinions of those around him and his own emotions. Morrow caught the captain's eye, and the two exchanged concerned looks. The murder at the medical center was no longer an isolated incident, and the situation now seemed more dangerous. Kyle Riker's presence remained a concern to both men.

"What have you visited upon us?"

The Speaker sounded broken and lost, a leader unsure of how to lead.

Picard gestured to the side of the large room, and the Speaker nodded and followed him. Once they were alone, Picard looked deep into the man's eyes. He saw emotional exhaustion and resignation.

"Remember the office you hold," Picard said gently, but in a firm tone. "You are the Speaker of the People. The people and the other councillors look to you for leadership. Especially during a growing crisis, the people want someone to tell them what needs to be done. To assure them the problem is being handled."

"I'm not sure . . ." Chkarad began.

"*Be* sure," Picard insisted. "If you falter before any of these people, if you let them see any hint of weakness, then your every move will be suspect. At times like this, you need to act. Do not take too long to make a decision. Right or wrong, the decision keeps things in motion. If you let inertia take over, the government will effectively collapse. And if you cannot be a leader, then defer to another of the Council."

"You'll stay to help?"

"That's my mission."

The research reports Crusher had demanded arrived shortly after she gave Dolog something for his suffering. Crusher immediately began poring over the information, focusing on the plant life on Delta Sigma IV. She also called the *Enterprise* for the data from the initial surveys taken of the planet when it applied for Federation membership. Then she read—and read and read more until her eyes hurt and several hours had slipped by. The same nurse who had brought her the reports returned with a bowl of steaming soup, deposited it on the table, and left without a word. Crusher looked up, planning to call after the woman and thank her, when she saw Wasdin, accompanied by tall Bader men, standing before her. So these were the other researchers.

Both appeared a decade younger than their Dorset counterparts, and they seemed filled with genuine curiosity and concern. Wasdin introduced them as Jama of Osedah and Nassef of Tirnannorot.

"I don't recognize your place of birth," Crusher said to Nassef.

"It's on our homeworld. I am a first-generation citizen of this new world," he explained. "I arrived here as a child but carry my name proudly."

"Of course you do," Jama said angrily. "Tirnannorot is a desirable place to be born. Not like that hellhole I come from."

Crusher studied Jama's features and couldn't discern where the anger was coming from. She gestured for them to sit and shoved her bowl away, indicating she was here to work.

"How did you find the liscom gas to be the agent of change?"

"By being careful," Jama said. "By doing our jobs."

"Of course," she said calmly. She needed his help, not his invective, but recognized that matching his tone would get her nowhere. "But how did you focus on the liscom gas?"

"We screened out the elements in our atmosphere that were found on our homeworld, and then eliminated the elements that were also found on the Dorset planet," Nassef explained, his tone becoming that of a lecturer. "It took some time, given the number of trace gases one can find in the air. We needed to filter out the pollutants from our own industrial efforts and then eliminate the common elements. That left us with four gases."

"All four are native only to this world?"

"Of course," snapped Jama.

"I see," she said, stalling and trying to find a way to get information without further annoying the scientist.

"We then studied each of the four," Nassef continued. "Two were immediately found to be neutral, leaving us with liscom and knapp, the second being a gas coming from elements within the sea."

"Look, we studied for months and it came down to two possibilities," Jama exclaimed. "If either was the culprit, it would be found in our blood. We took samples from men, women, and children, Bader and Dorset. We discovered a buildup of liscom in the blood, but no such build up of knapp. After that it became simple."

"Not so simple, since you didn't share the information at first," Wasdin said, showing less patience for Jama than Crusher did. She shot him a look, and the medic backed up a step.

"We didn't know what we had at first," Jama said, sarcastically imitating Wasdin's voice.

"Did you match these blood types against samples from home?"

"That took a while since we don't get many ships this way," Nassef said. "And that slowed things up further."

"And how many lives were lost because of the delay?" Wasdin asked. Crusher was alarmed at the growing intensity in the woman's voice.

"Never mind that," Crusher said, cutting off a reply. "Tell me what happened when Kyle Riker arrived."

Jama made a face and spoke first. "He seemed to think it would take no time at all to find a counteragent to the liscom. Idiot never realized how widespread the plant life was or how long it might take to rewire our DNA."

"There's little gained in name calling," warned Wasdin.

Nassef's hand clamped on Jama's arm, keeping the scientist in his place. Face flushed with anger, he nearly shouted when he spoke. "He thought it was going to be easy, but seemed to lose interest when it took time."

"Well, we were at war at the time," Crusher noted. From what she could tell, the liscom gas problem was discovered toward the mid-point of the Dominion War, and the research on the counteragent occurred just as the conflict wound down. Riker would have been on constant call at the time. Crusher paused, a stray thought in her mind: why was a strategist like Riker sent to Delta Sigma IV instead of someone from Starfleet Medical? She resolved to figure that out later.

"Our best biogeneticists tried to alter the plant itself," Nassef began.

"And failed," Jama finished.

"The ecosystem is as complex here as anywhere else," Wasdin said. "And unlike the colonizers on so many other worlds, we all tried to preserve life here without alterations. This planet's beauty was one reason we were both drawn here. And it seems to bring out the best in us, so no one wanted to tamper."

"Well, we tampered all right. Look around us!"

With that, the scientists slumped into silence. Wasdin seemed as frustrated as Crusher felt. She was disconcerted to see that the much-discussed peaceful coexistence between Bader and Dorset had its limits. While the chief medic was walking the scientists out, the doctor gathered her thoughts and decided it was time to check in.

"Crusher to Picard."

"Yes, Doctor?" He sounded worn out, she thought. No doubt trying to fathom the political fallout of the murders

was taking its toll. At least he wasn't entirely on his own and had an ambassador to help shoulder the burden.

She brought him up to speed on her conversations with various Dorset and Bader medical personnel. It was hard to tell whether he was more frustrated or relieved to hear that she had no evidence of a causal relationship between the liscom and the outbreak of violence.

"How go your talks?" she asked after she finished reporting to him.

"They are . . . out of the ordinary. We can catch up later. Picard out."

Out of the ordinary? To Crusher, that seemed to sum up the entire situation on Delta Sigma IV.

"Are we getting anywhere?"

Morrow shook his head, running a hand through his thick brown hair. He seemed to be staring into space, and Picard waited patiently. "I don't understand it. They say they want peace, but they're letting pettiness take hold. They also are inexperienced in dealing with anything resembling a crisis."

"And they won't let you help?"

"I don't think they even know what questions to ask. There's something else, and I'm not sure what it is."

"They're embarrassed."

Picard turned to see Troi walk in from a wing with her arms wrapped around several tall, thin bottles. She was beaming with triumph, and he liked the way it brightened her features and his own mood.

"None of the civil servants seemed intent on the most immediate needs, so I went foraging," she said by way of explanation. She handed each man a bottle, popped off the top of another, and took a long gulp. Picard followed suit and was rewarded with a thick, cool drink clearly flavored with some local nectar. It was mostly tart, but quite refreshing.

"The first order . . . survival," Picard muttered to himself. He took another long pull from the bottle and then replaced the top. "Embarrassed by what?"

"This was a centennial celebrating cooperation, and all you've seen is the death and the bickering."

"Actually, they seem more like their homeworld counterparts than anyone here will admit," Morrow observed.

"You've had contact with the Bader or Dorset?"

"I've personally mediated with the Bader," Morrow said, still sipping from his bottle. "If you think Tellarites or Klingons are aggressive, these people make them seem like tribbles."

"Is there a root cause to the belligerence?"

"Nothing I know of, Captain," Morrow admitted. "They feel superior to the rest of the universe and act accordingly."

"Many races act superior to their peers," Troi said. "The bellicosity usually is deeply ingrained from some act in their past. The Klingons trace their warrior code to Kahless, while Surak of Vulcan turned his people away from violence and changed them forever."

"What about the Dorset?"

"I've spoken to an ambassador on Earth, but I'm not going to evaluate an entire race based on one conversation."

"Thank you, Ambassador."

"Colt, please, Captain," Morrow said with a sly smile. "If we're going to be stuck here, we may as well be comfortable."

Picard gave him a mildly disapproving look, but since he liked the ambassador, he didn't begin a lecture about the need to maintain order and protocol, especially during these trying times.

"Any food, Counselor?"

"No, Ambassador, nothing I could find," Troi answered. "I'm sure it's on someone's list."

Picard turned away from the counselor's conversation with the ambassador and watched the councillors. They continued to mill about, talking in ever-changing clusters, and nothing was being accomplished. A planet full of people were being turned against one another, and no one seemed able to act.

"Do you have any plans yet?" Picard asked the Speaker, hoping his direct question would crystallize the man's thinking.

Chkarad sadly shook his head. Picard felt for the man, who was clearly not cut out to be a leader.

"When can the counselor visit the three remaining subjects? It's imperative we explore every avenue."

"Now is as good a time as any," Chkarad said.

"Counselor, have yourself and Mr. Williams beamed over to the facility. Do not have any physical contact, is that understood?"

Troi's eyes glittered, and she gave him a tight smile. "Absolutely. We'll be fine." She gestured to Williams, who had been leaning his lanky frame against a wall, one boot up and flat against the surface. He nodded and walked over to her. She contacted the starship and within seconds the two vanished from sight. Picard envied them, to a degree.

"How can the Federation stop this?"

"My doctor is working to determine the cause, you know that," Picard said.

"What can we do, Speaker?" an older Bader asked.

"That, Cholan of Huni, is something we need to settle, and quickly, I would imagine," Chkarad said solemnly.

"Fine sentiments," Picard said. "But you need actions to back them up."

Picard found it odd that even some of the most basic steps seemed beyond the government. The reports indicated these were highly advanced people, but the reality seemed far from that.

"Our medics have found nothing."

"Do they even know what to look for?" Picard asked.

"They're trained, aren't they?"

The conversation was deteriorating as wounded pride clouded better judgment, and Picard once more felt stymied because the people preferred talk to action. What he had not noticed was that other clusters of people spoke among themselves, ignoring the Speaker's group, and suddenly the discussions began to get louder.

"Martial law should be ordered," a female Dorset said.

"Absolutely not," countered a Bader male.

"We need to contain this, and sending people home is the only way," called another.

"And that would close the stores, stop the shipping of supplies, and incite more fear than is necessary," a woman countered.

"An economy can be rebuilt. We can't animate the dead!"

"Dead! You expect more murders?"

"If you cannot contain this, more people will die," Morrow interjected.

Chkarad turned to Picard, a pained look in his eyes. The captain felt pity for him, a man out of his element, but shoved that aside and concentrated on the need to govern the planet. Once more he beckoned the Speaker aside and stepped close so no one else could hear him. Morrow and Troi had picked up on the action and positioned themselves to block the other councillors from coming closer.

"A starship captain is used to adversity," Picard said softly, but with firm conviction. "I am trained to react quickly when circumstances demand. I recognize that's different from running a planet. There are towns, cities, states, regions, and even two races trying to coexist here. Until recently, you have never been asked to take drastic action to secure the planet's safety.

"I recognize the difficult time you are all having. I am sympathetic, and the *Enterprise* is committed to staying and helping as best we can. But we are not here to run the planet for you. The people elected the Council to lead, and you were elected the Speaker to lead the Council. Earn that trust and provide a vision and a voice. Lead the people away from violence and buy us the time we need to find the cause of this outbreak. Stop the fear any way you know how. It might be martial law, it might be more stringent work conditions. I don't know this planet. You do. Use that unique knowledge and put it to work.

"It's growing late, and I am returning to the *Enterprise*. I'll be back in the morning after I tend to the running of my ship."

He turned away from them and walked over to where Morrow was waiting. The ambassador pantomimed polite applause, earning another disapproving look from the captain.

"Are you really needed back on the ship?"

"No, but if I remain, they will either continue to point blame at the Federation or increasingly look to us for the leadership they need to provide themselves."

"But you yourself just said this is beyond their experience," Morrow protested.

"Yes. But as I told Chkarad a little while back, leaders act. Right now, they can't even get that far, right or wrong."

"I thought the people were successful running the planet."

"As did I," Picard admitted. "Something deeper than a murder has affected the people to the core of their being."

"Actually, two murders. If you don't mind, Captain, I'd like to stay and observe," Morrow said. "I promise not to run the planet until you return."

"I'll hold you to that, Ambassador. You will not be this generation's John Gill."

Picard turned to beckon for Carmona when the ambassador added with a grin, "Of course not. He was a professor, I'm a diplomat."

Ignoring the joke, Picard addressed the lead security officer. "Lieutenant Vale will be sending relief shortly, Ensign. Keep the building secure and keep the councillors from committing homicide. Use any means short of sitting on them."

"No, that wouldn't be dignified at all," Morrow quipped.

"*Enterprise,* this is Picard. One to beam up."

Picard headed for a safe part of the stage to beam back to the starship. As the transporter effect took hold of him, Morrow spotted the reproving look cross Picard's face.

Seer's dusty flyer landed amid towering stalks of something purplish, and Riker thought it looked wonderful. The sun was already low on the horizon, painting the clouds with golden hues. Seer had already explained that everything they could see from the landing spot belonged to one family, an inheritance dating back to one of the first Dorset settlers.

"In another few weeks, the grains will be ready for harvest and then stored for the winter," Seer explained as they climbed out of the craft.

Riker knelt and ran his hand through the loamy soil, trying to recall the last time he had a chance to actually enjoy a planet. He knew exactly how many worlds he had visited since graduating from the Academy; it was something he liked to keep track of. But the ones he actually got to know well, that was a much smaller number.

"This is one of the oldest establishments on the planet," Seer said. He led Riker toward a narrow, long, one-story building with a high-tech weather vane located on the roof. "The people here pride themselves on that. Recently they've developed some new hybrid grain from

Bader and Dorset plants. This farm is the first to try it out. The grain is called Unity, and the yield is expected to be nearly twice that of normal grains."

"Very symbolic," Riker said.

"Yes. Which is why they had journalists swarming all over the place."

They arrived at the front porch, a wooden platform that was just one step off the ground. Four chairs were arranged artfully on either side of the door, with an elaborately carved wooden table to the right of the door. A pitcher of something sat on the table, with six blue glasses carefully arranged in a semicircle around the refreshment. It was clear they were expected.

Confirming Riker's observation, the door smoothly slid open and an older woman appeared, wiping her hands on a towel and smiling a welcome. She seemed to Riker to be in fine health. A hand shot out from behind her and an excited teen emerged.

"You must be from the *Enterprise!* I'm Col Mander Col and this is our farm."

Riker broke into a happy smile and shook the hand, pleased not to be in any danger for a change. "Will Riker, first officer," he replied. The rank seemed to impress the teen.

"And I'm his mother, Col Meryn Col," the woman said in a reedy voice that indicated advancing years. "Welcome to our farm. Welcome, Seer of Anann."

"Welcome to you," he replied formally. "Is Col Hust Col about?"

"Still bedding down the animals," she replied. "After what happened today, well, we're all backed up on chores. Please, have a seat, both of you." She gestured to two of the chairs opposite the table and the men sat. The chairs were wooden, rough-hewn but worn in spots from years of use. There was a definite sense of peace here; it was an oasis compared to what Riker had witnessed elsewhere on Delta Sigma IV. With a nod, she sent the teen off for his father. As he ran off, kicking up bits of dirt, she sat and began pouring drinks for the men.

"We brew this ale right on the farm," she explained as she handed out the glasses. "In fact, it's what Mander has been specializing in, learning from his grandfather."

The liquid was thick, cool, and delicious, Riker judged after one sip. He also detected the potency of the alcohol in the ale and disappointedly concluded that he would have to nurse the one glass, given his empty stomach and his growing exhaustion. This would have to be the final stop for the day.

"He's doing his family credit," Seer said, allowing himself a healthy swallow. Riker felt jealous.

"Can you tell us what happened?" Riker asked. "We've only heard sketchy reports on our flight."

Meryn sat back and considered the question, summoning up memories of the events of a few weeks past. "Hust saw everything. I came around after things started happening." She paused and looked intently into Will's eyes.

"In all my days, never saw anything like it. My husband was repairing a fence over to the far edge of the property. He was working with three other men, chatting away with the reporter. One of the men said something in jest, but the reporter I guess didn't see it as funny."

"Wasn't that funny," Col Hust Col said as he rounded

a corner of the house. He was a husky man, his hair going from jet black to snow white in a stark fashion. His coverall was dusty but in good repair, and he clearly had stopped to wash his hands before greeting the visitors. As he approached, Meryn was already pouring him a cup of ale.

"Not worth dying over anyways," he added.

Formal introductions were made, and then Hust held up the glass, aimed it at the sky, and took a large swallow. He then allowed himself to sit, refilling the ale to the top by himself.

"As Meryn said, there were several of us around, but the man just lunged after Alin. They grappled a bit and then Alin's spanner was in the man's hand and . . . well, it happened."

They sat in an uncomfortable silence for a few moments, each absorbing the image and the information. Finally, Hust continued, "Meryn heard the commotion and called for help, but the man was long gone before the peace officers got here. We're just a little too far from town for emergency help like that.

"So anyways, Alin goes down, my other men scatter. Next thing I know, this human comes up the road, chasing after the reporter."

"That would be Kyle Riker, my father," Will said. The others looked at him askance. Each took a sip and then sat silently.

"Yes, Kyle Riker is just what the peace officer said. Remember?"

"Sure do," his wife said, sipping and letting him run the conversation.

"The guy runs off, your father chases after him, and then they're out of sight."

"And you . . . ?"

"Stayed to look after Alin. Tried to save his life, but his skull was caved in. No helping him at all."

Seer looked over at Will, a serious look on his features. "How did your father know to be here?"

"Wish I knew," Riker replied, slowly shaking his head in bewilderment.

"We heard about Unoo's death," Meryn said. "Never thought it would happen again. They were all still locked away."

"We have no idea what happened," Seer said, "and that is why Commander Riker and I are investigating. We hope to find the reporter, hopefully find Kyle Riker as well. Once we can talk to them, maybe examine them, we'll know something."

"I understand that violence is very rare on this planet," Riker said gently. "I'm very sorry you had to experience it at all."

"The war never came out this way, so we listened to the media reports," Hust explained. "In fact, the war kind of helped our world. Once the fighting stopped, people were hungry and we had plenty of food stored. We managed to sell tons of food at a good profit. Used some of the profit for planetary improvements, research and the like, and then we farmers got a bonus. Let me build some new silos. Yeah, we're doing just fine."

"How long was my father here?" Riker asked.

Hust heard a sound Riker missed, looked around, and spotted Mander running back to them. Hust took another drink and set the cup down. "Don't want to discuss this much around my boy, if it's all right with you."

Seer and Riker immediately nodded in agreement.

"Once we planted the Unity in one spot, Mander and I used the combine to plant about fourteen acres with the seed. Taking to the ground pretty well, I'll tell you that. A good use of those profits I just mentioned. We're one of the largest and most successful farms on this world. Never would have had a chance if my forefathers had stayed home."

"It's getting dark, and we don't want to keep you from your chores," Seer said, standing. He had finished his drink, refused a refill, and seemed as alert as ever to Riker.

"I think young Mander here has plenty of questions for the commander," Meryn said with a laugh.

"Walk me to the flyer," Riker offered to the teen. The youth accepted eagerly and began to ply Riker with questions before the two were even out of earshot. Seer stayed behind to more formally thank the adults, and that was fine with Riker. The youth's infectious enthusiasm would help carry him forward.

Crusher paused at her quarters to change her uniform, take a quick shower, and brush out her hair. Looking in the mirror, she saw the darkness under each eye. She was used to working long hours, used to the emotional toll she had to pay to perform her duty, but she was starting to feel tired all the time. It wasn't age or disease, just an accumulation of experiences building up in her psyche, much like the liscom gas in the Bader and Dorset blood.

She shook her hair, letting it fall naturally over her shoulders. Zipping up the front of her uniform, she appreciated the way she managed to maintain good physical conditioning. Her overall physique had been given a brief boost by exposure to the natural environment of the Bak'u homeworld. The effect faded gradually with time, but it made her and everyone else from the command team feel good. Indeed, she felt as if she had taken a long leave of absence and come back to the starship thoroughly refreshed. And that did not discount the harrowing experience of helping the Bak'u people leave their village and go into hiding when their lives were threatened. Still, it was another successful mission with an unusual dividend.

Slipping into her blue lab coat, she stole one more look in the mirror and declared herself fit for duty. She paused at her cabin's replicator, ordered up a portable meal, and took it with her to sickbay. As she strolled through the corridors, she let her mind wander over the words, tone, and body language of the Dorset and Bader researchers. She considered herself a pretty good judge of character, but she regretted not having Deanna handy to confirm her suspicions. Clearly, these were dedicated professionals, but there was an uncomfortable undercurrent of hostility that filled the conference room. It wasn't there when it was Wasdin, Dolog, and Cander, but it emerged clearly when Jama and Nassef were present. Jama was the more belligerent, but his mere presence seemed to annoy Wasdin. Additionally, he seemed annoyed with Nassef, a fellow Bader. Was it just a character trait or something more?

Once in sickbay, Crusher checked in with the duty nurse, a tall, fair-haired woman named Susan Weinstein. They reviewed the activity, since Crusher had gone down to the planet, and she was relieved to hear there were few problems: an acid burn from a research lab, a maintenance worker's deep cut and strained tendons from an overachieving ensign preparing for a triathlon competition on the holodeck. No patients were currently being kept in sickbay, which also made her feel good.

Weinstein returned to her desk, singing some aria, filling the air with music. Crusher appreciated hearing a trained voice, although opera was not necessarily her favorite type of music. The nurse was a new arrival, replacing Nurse Lomax, who was killed at Dokaal by a Satarran agent, and Crusher had taken an immediate liking to her.

Before sitting, Crusher took a moment to recycle the packaging from her meal, promised herself to have a real sit-down supper later, and activated her desktop terminal. She had downloaded the information from her tricorder to the main computer while still in her quarters and had the computer begin analyzing the new information. Now she took a close look at the blood work she personally took while on the planet. Sure enough, the amount of liscom in the blood was way beyond the baseline. From the original surveyors' records, there was no liscom at all in the Bader or Dorset blood. A close study of the blood work taken during routine examinations the first few years showed trace amounts of liscom in the blood, but a growing presence. She had the computer graph the increase and then matched it to the changes in life expectancy.

Sure enough, there was a correlation, but you had to really look for it to understand the cause and effect.

She then made a study of the chromosomal structure of the Dorset from their arrival to the first study after the problem was noted. Crusher repeated the examination with the Bader records. The chromosomes were changing, but you'd have to look to notice since it didn't affect anything overtly.

Wasdin was right, from what Crusher could tell. Every blood sample she could access showed similar amounts of the liscom in the blood. And the liscom came from a form of plant life, so it was time to look at that. She'd need the ship's resident botanist, a Bolian named Moq, for help.

Opening the com system, Crusher called to the bridge and within seconds, Data's voice filled her office.

"Data, I need some atmospheric surveying done. Will that be a problem?"

"No, I can task the lateral sensor array to the job. May I ask what you are looking for?"

"There is a plant by-product called liscom, a gas that I'm told is found around the world. I'm going to be looking for confirmation of that, and I need to know if the concentrations are greater in some places than others."

"Understood. We will need several orbits for a complete study, so the final results should be available in no more than five hours, twenty-nine minutes."

"That's fine, Data. Have everything sent to botany, and I'll work with Lieutenant Moq there."

"Very good, Doctor."

"Any news from below?"

"Nothing that would qualify as news," Data answered. *"Commander Riker has not found his father. Captain Picard returned to the ship one hour and fourteen minutes ago. Counselor Troi is currently interviewing the surviving test subjects."* He made the situation sound as dry a statistic as a pollen count. She missed his having the emotion chip.

"Too bad, it'd be nice to see some progress."

"I agree, since it would make the general mood more positive."

"Okay, thanks for the help, Data."

"Bridge out."

It was a little awkward for Troi to maneuver herself across the cluttered room in the bulky clean suit the medical staff asked her to wear. An unnecessary precaution, perhaps, but any measure that comforted their anxious hosts was worthwhile as far as Troi was concerned. She noted the hastily mounted cameras and recording equipment. Everything was going to be recorded, no doubt for later analysis.

The three subjects—two Bader one Dorset—were not in clean suits, but instead wore civilian clothing that looked a bit past its prime. Probably their own belongings, which would give them some sense of the familiar. She was impressed by the care that had gone into little touches like that.

"I'm Deanna Troi, ship's counselor on the *Enterprise*. Thank you for taking the time to meet with me."

"Not like we had anything better to do," the woman cracked, her voice harsh. She was Iraid of Anann, the oldest of the three.

"Still, I appreciate it. Let me start by saying that I am sorry for the loss of your countryman," she said.

The male Dorset, Lulh Shunks Lulh, waved his hand in the air. "She was an idiot, getting into an argument like that."

Troi frowned at that. "Can you explain what the argument was about?"

"Well, that's the interesting thing about it," the Bader male, Osani of Tregor, said. "They'd never argued over anything more serious than music. Until that damned day. We were going to get out, be free at last, in just a few more minutes."

"Her taste was awful," Shunks agreed.

"No, it wasn't," Iraid snapped.

Troi remained silent, examining their body language. She had to take into account their frustration at remaining in quarantine, mixed with the fear that one of them might be the next to go mad. Carefully, she sifted through the feelings, not sure what she was picking up on yet.

"The argument was about . . ." she prompted.

"I'm getting to that, if you can wait," Osani said. He was middle-aged and overweight and was going gray. He seemed used to being in control, so she remained silent and let him speak.

"There was a lot of yammering, everyone had to give us instructions like we were children. Then that Federation guy, Ruken . . ."

"Riker," Iraid corrected. Osani just glared at her and then went on.

"Riker, yeah. He was going on about something inane, and the two of them were just going at it back and forth.

Finally I caught a few words. The two blockheads were debating the merits of coolar versus sorki."

"Of all the things," Iraid interjected. Troi didn't bother to ask what those items were, just nodded and let them continue.

"Right. Anyway, it was getting pretty heated, which is damned funny if you think about it. They're just drinks after all."

"Well, Unoo takes her coolar very seriously. She was always carping about it never being the right temperature when we were on Earth," Osani said.

Both of the others looked at him as if to wonder who gave him permission to talk. Shunks also turned his gaze to Iraid, who seemed to ignore it.

"Before you know it, he pulls the knife and stabs her, just like that," Shunks concluded.

"Unoo was a pain, but I wouldn't have wished that on her," Iraid said, her voice dropping to a whisper. Her whole expression changed, her emotions flickering enough to catch Troi's attention. She was fluctuating from anger to despair to other feelings.

"Tell me, Iraid, what happened next?"

"Bison went nova, just flared up. Killed her and then bolted. Everyone was so stunned, no one was moving at first," she said, her voice a bit faraway as she recalled the incident.

"And you, what did you do?"

"Cried," Iraid answered. "Cried and wondered what went wrong."

"I'll tell you what went wrong," Osani said, his voice angry. "We wasted a year of our lives. The Federation screwed up and one of us is dead. Maybe there'll be more."

"Better not be," Iraid said, her tone shifting back to defiance.

"You mean to tell me, you don't think they experimented on us for their own purposes? Of course they did! They didn't want to cure us."

"Yes, they did," Shunks said, sounding conciliatory. "They showed us nothing but kindness."

"All that poking wasn't kind at all," Iraid said.

"It was necessary," Shunks added, his voice firm in its conviction. "It was all necessary. Yes, something went wrong; yes, one of us died, but it wasn't from the serum."

"And you know that how?" Osani asked. Troi watched his eyes go wide, felt the agitation radiate from him.

"It's happening again, isn't it?" Iraid asked. She now was fearful; the complete change in emotion caught Troi by surprise.

"I won't let anyone get hurt," Williams interjected in a soothing tone. Troi knew that he had a phaser ready in his hand but was wisely keeping it under the table and out of sight.

"When will we be freed?" Iraid asked Troi.

"As soon as we understand what happened and how to fix it."

"And what have you learned so far?" Osani challenged.

"We just arrived today. We need to do our own studies, and that will mean our doctor will need to examine you."

"Oh great, more poking," Iraid said, her tone shifting once more to resignation.

"Probably," Troi agreed. "But it's necessary."

There was a lull in the conversation as the three subjects took stock of the information and Troi observed. All three were shifting about nervously, but she worried the most about Iraid, who struck her as the most in danger of having a psychological problem. Was it related to the counteragent serum or the isolation?

There was little Troi felt could be learned from more time with these three, so she decided to release them to Crusher and return to the *Enterprise* for some rest. She nodded to Williams, and the two Starfleet officers rose.

The subjects exchanged confused glances back and forth, and Troi finally explained she was leaving. She wished them well and then signaled her readiness to leave the conference room.

As she changed out of the clean suit, Troi considered the people she had just met. They had endured quite a bit over the last twelve months, but there was something else at work and that, she feared, was the problem.

Picard ordered a cup of tea as he sat behind his desk in the ready room. He was mentally exhausted and a bit physically worn. But the ship needed tending to, and with Riker off the ship, there were things he could not delegate. His first order of business was reviewing the latest communiqués from Starfleet Command. Nothing of import according to the subject headings, so he had the files transferred to a padd for some reading in bed.

He quickly checked the departmental status reports, and all seemed quiet. He was thankful for the lack of distraction and turned his mind back to the planet below. Until Crusher could report something positive, everything was guesswork. The biggest puzzle piece was Kyle Riker, and much as he wanted to think like his detective hero Dixon Hill, he was resigned to let the son hunt the father.

What was it about command that had sons with troubled parental relations? He and his father had issues; even Data seemed troubled by the actions of his creator/father Noonien Soong. If he looked deeper within his crew, he would probably find other such issues. Well, except Deanna. He smiled at the thought of the overbearing, irrepressible Lwaxana Troi. The captain knew Troi loved her mother very much and had had no trouble with her while growing up. She had even endured the loss of a parent and wasn't bitter for the experience. Would that everyone could feel the same way.

Clearly Chkarad was out of his element and would need as much support as possible. While Crusher did her work, he would have to help with a holding action. And for that, he needed muscle.

"Picard to Vale."

Seconds passed and a somewhat sleepy Vale responded.

"Please come to my ready room."

"May I put my uniform on first?"

"If you insist," Picard said. While he frowned at Morrow's flippancy in front of the Delta Sigmans, he allowed himself a more relaxed attitude with his own crew. Especially when he troubled them on their own time.

"Five minutes."

"Make it so." He sat sipping his tea and checking over ship's functions until Vale arrived in his office. When she entered, Picard would have been hard-pressed to guess this was a woman he had just woken up. The uniform was crisp, her thick auburn hair perfectly combed into place.

He pointed to the couch by the far wall and joined her there, keeping the meeting less than formal.

"Would you like something to drink?"

"No, thank you, sir," she replied. "If it's all the same to you, I intend to be dead asleep three minutes after I'm dismissed."

"Of course," Picard said with a smile.

"Is this about the planet?"

"Yes. We already have two dead people on a planet that hasn't seen a homicide in a century. Since one murderer was a test subject, the Federation is being blamed. The local government has never encountered anything on this scale. In the morning, I would like you to plan out a full deployment of your people. They are to support local officials in helping maintain the peace. You will be a resource, representing the very best Starfleet can offer."

"Sir, I have one hundred fifty people ready to die if you order it, but that's nowhere near enough to protect a planet from itself."

"That's why you get a full night's sleep before you begin the deployment. It will require timing and planning without benefit of too much help below."

"We'll do what we can, sir, but this is the tallest order you've given me yet," Vale said.

"I'm well aware, Lieutenant," Picard said. "But there is little choice. I do not know how long this will go on, so I suggest two complements in twelve-hour shifts."

"I was thinking more like twelve on, six off," she said.

"They can't be worn out and slow to respond on the fourth or eighth day," Picard warned.

"Let me sleep on it," she said, grinning.

"I like your thinking," Picard allowed. "I know this is a potentially difficult assignment. Use whatever resources you need. In the morning I am ordering that no one beam down without a sidearm. Please convey that to Transporter Chief T'Bonz when you begin."

"Excellent suggestion," Vale said.

"Any questions?"

"Captain, if I may . . . why do you think Kyle Riker went off after the murderer Bison?"

"None of us have an answer for that," Picard replied. "Yet. He may know something we need to learn."

"Or he was guilty of something."

Picard looked at Vale. Her pixie-like features were disarming. She was more than competent, and could go toe-to-toe with any opponent. But what he admired about her was her sharp mind.

"Maybe."

"I'll want to be planetside, checking on my people," she said, changing the subject and stifling a yawn.

"I will be entrusting that entire operation to you," the captain said, nodding. "I will ask that a seasoned officer remain on tactical in case things escalate."

"Jim Peart's very good; I'll ask him to stay on the ship, coordinating the skeleton staff as needed."

"Mr. Peart's received good reports, as I recall."

"I've rarely served with better," she replied.

Picard nodded, a look of finality on his face. "Go back

to sleep, Lieutenant. I can't guarantee when the next un-interrupted night will be."

"Count on me," she said firmly.

"I've come to do so with complete assurance," Picard admitted sincerely.

She got up with a smile and marched from the room. He thought highly of the officer and appreciated her efforts. Christine Vale stood right up there with the best security chiefs he had commanded over the years, and he was glad to have her on hand for this mission. He collected his padd, recycled his teacup, and fed his fish before retiring for the night.

He knew enough to take his own advice.

Crusher sat in her cabin and was taking her boots off when her desktop monitor beeped at her. With one boot off, she hobbled over to the desk and activated the screen. She was greeted by the pleasant face of Yerbi Fandau, current surgeon general of Starfleet Medical. While Picard had his issues with Starfleet Command, she felt nothing but warmth toward Fandau. A pioneer in medicine, he was a highly decorated physician who served a total of twenty-five years on starships before going to work on Earth. His experience was vast, and his rapport with the doctors still in space was excellent.

"Beverly, so nice to hear from you," he began, all smiles.

"How have you been, Yerbi?"

"Getting some joints replaced next week, but that's nothing to talk about. You look tired. Are you . . ."

". . . not getting enough sleep? Not right now, I'm afraid," she said with a laugh. "Do you know where I am?"

"To be honest, no. I tell the computer to find you and return your message, it doesn't tell me where. Please say it isn't Tholian space."

"Not at all. I'm in orbit around Delta Sigma IV studying an outbreak of . . . well, violence."

Fandau looked startled by the word. He closed his eyes, a signal to her that he was summoning details on the planet from his computer bank–like memory. Seconds later, his eyes opened and he nodded slowly.

"What do you need to know?"

"Have we any idea if the test subjects might have been exposed to something on Earth during their tests? Something that might have tainted the treatment?"

"Not that we know of," the older doctor replied. *"I could forward the reports to you, but I suspect you have them already. They came here, we did the tests, made sure they didn't turn purple or grow a third eye, and then gave them a clean bill of health and sent them home."*

"What about en route?"

"Well, that's something you'll have to check. They were escorted home with personnel from the diplomatic corps."

"We have two murders, with Kyle Riker on the scene at both but at no time actually wielding a weapon."

"They think we've done something to them," Fandau finished.

"Yes. But you and I both know better."

Fandau seemed to be looking for another fragment of memory, and when it arrived his eyes showed surprise. *"You serve with his son, Will."*

"Small galaxy, isn't it?"

"Indeed it is." Fandau paused. *"Have you given any thought to my offer?"*

"Honestly, Yerbi, I can't give you an answer yet." Crusher sighed. "Between the Dokaalan and this mess, I haven't had a moment to think."

"Understandable," he said. *"Focus on Delta Sigma IV. But keep in mind, Beverly, I can't keep this offer open forever."*

"Understood," she answered. "Thank you again for this opportunity . . . and for you help. I promise that I'll be in touch with you soon."

"I look forward to it. Fandau out."

The screen went dark and Crusher sat back, her feet splayed out before her, and let out her breath. She had a lot to consider.

La Forge had no sooner lain down on his bed when the com signaled him. Wearily, he rolled over and activated the screen by his desk. The image was that of a Starfleet officer he did not recognize.

"This is Geordi La Forge, how can I help you?"

"I'm Male'finkatta of the Pegasus," the green-skinned officer replied. *"Am I disturbing you?"*

"Not at all," he replied automatically, though the opposite was true. He had been looking forward to getting a decent night's sleep.

"I understand you have some spare chambliss coils, and we need one pretty badly," the man said.

"Been talking to Whis, have you?"

"We're one sector over from his position, so we're

keeping in touch. He's sending you a quad, right? Well, I was kind of hoping you could send me a coil, otherwise we might lose short-range communications. We're a little short on supplies until we're rotated back to Starbase 312."

"I know the feeling," La Forge agreed, already tapping his desktop computer to access the inventory. Sure enough, there were two extra coils, and the *Pegasus* needed one more than he would.

"Okay, I have a Ferengi trader bringing me the quad. I can probably persuade him to bring you the coil. Of course, it'll cost something, but we'll manage. Can you hold out four or five more days?"

"I should think so, Commander," Male'finkatta said. *"I can't thank you enough. If we can ever supply you materials, I'll be more than happy to return the favor."*

"That won't be necessary," La Forge replied, stifling a yawn. "We'll make this happen, count on it."

"Will do. And thanks again. Pegasus *out."* The screen reverted to the UFP emblem and then faded to black. As the engineer returned to his bunk, he began to imagine how stretched things were on the Federation's fringes if starships needed to trade among themselves.

While en route to her quarters for some much needed rest, Troi spotted Anh Hoang getting out of a turbolift. *She must also live on this deck,* the counselor surmised. She put on her professional smile and approached the woman.

"Good evening, Anh," she said.

Hoang was startled, having been lost in her own

thoughts. She returned the greeting, but seemed uncomfortable standing there in the corridor.

"How has your day been?" Troi asked.

"Uneventful, unlike yours," the engineer replied. "I hear it's growing worse down there."

"Yes, it's bad, and it's likely to get worse before we're done. Right now we don't even know what we're dealing with."

"More death and destruction for the Federation," Hoang muttered. The bitterness in her voice was unmistakable. Troi could only imagine the memories this mission was bringing back for this poor woman.

"Actually, Anh," Troi began carefully, "these problems are internal, and I'm sure they can be resolved peacefully."

"One can hope," Anh replied.

"We intend to do more than hope," Troi said. "Look, I think it would be a good idea for us to set up another appointment. How is 0900 for you? I'll post a note to Mr. La Forge so you can report for duty late tomorrow."

"I guess so," Hoang said.

"My office, then. Have a pleasant evening," Troi said, and continued to her quarters.

She entered the cabin, keeping the lighting at half strength. She took off her uniform, placing it in the recycling bin, and then brushed her hair for several minutes, feeling the tension ebb from her body. She looked appraisingly at her eyes, saw the stress, and shook her head sadly. There would be plenty of death, stress, and tension, just as she promised Anh. And she'd be in the thick of it.

After washing up, she slipped under the sheets and lay

on her side. Outside the windowport were the stars, which she always found comforting. Some twinkled, reflecting through the window. Others seemed still and peaceful. She thought of those as her eyelids grew heavy, and in less than a minute, she slipped into sleep.

"Daddy!"

A bundle of arms and legs seemed to suddenly envelop Seer before he could even clear the doorway. Riker, standing behind him, tried to count and thought there might have been four children, all under eight, tackling their father. Seer let himself tumble to the ground, rolled onto his back, and hefted one girl over his head. He set her down and began peeling the others off him.

"Come on in, Will," Seer said between laughs. Riker entered the home and caught the whiff of something fresh cooking. It seemed pungent with ingredients he couldn't identify. He stepped around the tangle of children and took in the house. Similar to the farmhouse they had just left, it was narrow and long, but this was two stories tall, with a pitched roof. The room he stood in was a common living area, with couches of differing sizes lining the walls. Shelving bordered the room above the couches; it was filled with pottery, photographs, and small boxes. Things were somewhat haphazard, giving the room a comfortable, lived-in look. The color scheme ran to earth tones, but everything worked in harmony, so careful thought had gone into the choices of woods, paints, and fabrics.

"My one," a soft voice called.

"My only," Seer replied, finally getting to his feet. The children squealed in happiness but were finally calming down. Two, both girls, stared at Riker, clearly unused to seeing a human in their living room.

A woman Riker immediately classified as lovely walked into the room and embraced Seer. The protocol officer seemed to cast off his officious nature and gave her a bear hug. They whispered private things between them for a moment. Turning away from the sight, Riker crouched down and smiled at the children.

"Hi, I'm Will," he said.

The two girls were joined by their two brothers. They all stared at Riker, uncertainty in their eyes.

"It's okay," he assured them. "I've spent the day with your father, and he's told me a lot about you." That seemed to work a bit, as their expressions changed to questioning looks.

"One of you is a dancer," he said, studying the four with mock seriousness. He then pointed to the boy farthest from him. "You."

"Yes," the boy said in a small, high-pitched voice.

"And one of you is a painter," Riker said, considering the others.

"Me!" a girl shouted.

"They're all special," the woman said. She approached Riker and crouched down next to him. "She is a racer, fastest runner in her school, and he's my climber. And I somehow gave birth to them all. My name is Dorina of Anann."

"Will Riker. A pleasure to meet you."

Dorina quickly named the four children, all with the

formal "of Anann" at the end of each name. Then they stood up and she led Riker and Seer from the great room. Down a hallway, they went left into a dining room. Riker was surprised to see how long the table was, with chairs enough for twelve.

"We live with my parents," Dorina explained. "And of course, we need seating for guests such as yourself. Hungry, my one?"

"Very much so," Seer admitted. "We've had something little better than rations, topped off with a strong ale you'd love."

"And you let him fly?"

"Well," Riker admitted, joining in the teasing tenor of the conversation, "he knew the controls far better than I did."

"I've invited Will to spend the night so we can get an early start tomorrow," Seer said. "Our hunt for his father has been pretty fruitless."

"Tell me all about it as you eat. Both of you, go wash and be back here in three minutes. It'll be filling but not too much since it's late," she told them. With that, she left the room, crossed the hall, and entered the kitchen directly opposite.

Seer looked over at Riker and grinned. "That went well," he said. "You need rest. We both need it, the creators know. The trail is cool to begin with, so we're not losing anything by getting rest."

Riker wasn't so sure about the trail but totally agreed about the need for rest.

"And thank you for the invitation," Riker added.

The men did as they were told, and Riker could hear a

much older voice corral the children and shoo them off to the bedrooms, farther back in the house. Clearly, waiting up for Seer was a treat, and it was well past time for them to be asleep. By local time, it was nearly midnight, and that explained a lot of his exhaustion. The *Enterprise* automatically adjusted its schedules to match the local capital's time, given their extended stay, so he imagined the night shift was well under way.

Riker had taken advantage of the flight back to the capital to check in with Picard. The conversation on both sides was less than promising. He heard the disappointment in the captain's voice with regard to the lack of direction from the government. He did approve, though, of Picard's relying on Vale to help keep things from spiraling further out of control. In turn, he explained that despite their best efforts, tracking his father was fruitless. He was despondent to hear that things had grown worse, but at least the death toll remained at two. The blame directed at the Federation seemed foolish but somewhat understandable. While he enjoyed touring the planet, nothing of value had been learned regarding Kyle's whereabouts or his activities on the planet. Suspicions remained, more on Riker's part than Picard's, but that was to be expected.

Riker had then contacted Troi, missing her voice. Seeing the farm couple reminded him of how much he had come to rely on her presence. Once more, he congratulated himself on rekindling their romance. They were quite happy and content with one another, but watching the farmers and now Seer and Dorina, he saw there could be more.

Much more.

He finished washing up and stopped thinking with his heart and let his stomach be his guide. Seer was already at the table, seated at one corner, while Dorina sat at the head. A large bright orange earthenware pot stood on a trivet, steam rising. Bowls and cutlery were set out for just two, although a beaded cup was before Dorina.

"Sit, Commander," she said.

"Will, please," he insisted, preferring informality while a guest in someone's home.

Dorina stood and ladled out something thicker than a soup but not quite a stew. It contained some form of barley and plenty of colorful vegetables. She next sliced thick slabs of bread and indicated a bright violet spread.

She filled her husband in on some of the doings at home while the men ate, and then she asked about their experiences. Seer was the perfect host, letting Riker add his own commentary and observations, while merely correcting the occasional mispronunciation. Each slip of Riker's tongue earned him a grin from the woman.

The brief meal over, Riker nodded his head toward Dorina. "It has been a long time since I enjoyed something so much. I cannot thank you enough for your hospitality—especially on short notice."

"Being the wife of a protocol officer, you get used to these things," she admitted. When Riker insisted on clearing the table, she let him, and he was glad, since it gave him a chance to check out the kitchen setup. He asked about certain tools and the herbs used to season the soup. They chatted amiably while Seer went to check on the children. Riker was enjoying the respite after a long, ultimately frustrating day.

However, it had been a long day, and he began stifling yawns. Dorina took him by the hand and led him toward the back of the house, where a staircase led them to the second floor. At the top of the stairs, she opened the first door on the left and let Riker cross the threshold.

"You should find everything you need here," Dorina said.

"I'm sure I will," Riker said. "Thank you again."

"Get your sleep. Seer says you want an early start, but first, breakfast."

He grinned. "Absolutely."

Moq was somewhat overweight by human standards, but for a Bolian he was considered in excellent shape. He had served aboard the *Enterprise*-E ever since the ship was commissioned, and he'd performed his job well. There hadn't been many calls for a botanist during the Dominion War, but he had used his time well, conducting research on several worlds ravaged by the Jem'Hadar. His results had proven useful during the rebuilding.

The botany lab was normally bright, but when Moq was on duty, he preferred to keep the lighting dim, letting the display screens appear that much brighter. More alive, he told Crusher when she had asked. The lab was filled with chambers for experiments, microscopes at long tables, and other equipment. Crusher herself rarely needed to visit the lab, but thought Moq would appreciate using his own equipment to help study the situation.

"Right on time, Doctor," he said by way of greeting. They agreed to meet six hours after the study began, allowing Moq at least half an hour to look at the compiled results. She noticed that a long, slender green leaf was laid out under the microscope, and she made a note to herself to take a look at the culprit.

"What do you have, Moq?"

"This plant is tenacious, growing wild on all four continents and eighty-seven percent of the islands," the Bolian explained. He activated a screen near Crusher and the planet appeared with a bright green overlay indicating the presence of the liscom plant. Both studied it in silence for several moments, the doctor thinking that under normal circumstances, they'd never think twice about a plant this ubiquitous. Of course, this situation was anything but normal.

"Tell me about the plant," she said, breaking the silence.

"It's wild, not used for food by the people, but seems to be liked well enough by several species of insect. From what I can tell, it's generally ignored by the people."

"But it does emit a gas that's hurting the population," Crusher said gravely. She tucked her hands deep in her lab coat and paused to think. There was no point in upsetting the ecosystem to remove the plant. And it was probably an impossible task to eradicate only one form of plant life.

She walked over to the microscope, her touch activating the viewer. Peering into it, she looked at an unremarkable plant, so much like the ones she had seen on countless other planets. And yet, it was a silent harbinger of death.

"Anything further to add?"

"Not really, Doctor," Moq replied. "I ran it through the normal planet survey tests, and they matched the results from the original Bader survey ship. It's just a plant."

"Nothing 'just' about it, Moq. Nothing at all," Crusher said sadly.

Chapter Seven

POURING OUT TEA into his cup, Jean-Luc seemed to savor the aroma, using his vintner's nose to check the bouquet of his beloved Earl Grey. As he sipped, Beverly reached for the fruit platter, appreciating the rainbow presentation. Not for the first time, she marveled at his thoughtfulness. Jean-Luc always put his whole heart into preparing the breakfast they shared each morning in his cabin.

"Let me guess, you were up by six hundred, reading reports from the watch command," she said, teasing him for his predictability.

"Oh, more than that," he said casually. "I also checked the latest reports from Starfleet Command and the other sector ships in the area. Spoke with two other captains and checked in with Commander Riker." He reached for a muffin and a creamy spread, a smile on his face.

"Any luck finding his father?"

"None yet," he said quietly.

Time for a change of subject, Beverly thought. But what could they discuss that would lighten the mood?

Certainly not the lack of progress in her liscom gas research.

So they ate in companiable silence for a minute until Picard began talking about some of the galactic scuttlebutt he heard from his fellow captains: promotions and reassignments and the like. Good. Some harmless gossip would cheer them both. The change in topic worked its magic until Picard raised another troubling matter.

"The brass seems to think we need a looking over," Picard said, referring to an upcoming inspection tour.

"You think this is related to the demon ship?"

"No. All the ships this far out are on the schedule," he explained. "It just strikes me as a waste. From everything I read, the rebuilding has been hampered by supply issues, so the schedule for putting ships on line has slipped. Those are problems they should be focusing on, not whether or not there's dust in a crewman's quarters."

"Well, dust can be a virulent breeding ground," Crusher said.

He smiled at her, the mood changed. "Thank you, Beverly."

"It's what any good CMO does," she replied. She hadn't yet mentioned Yerbi's job offer to Jean-Luc, and she had no intention of doing so today either.

"So, what's your plan this morning?"

"I need time to review everything. There's an awful lot of information to absorb and process. Medical mysteries take more time than most other problems."

"Indeed. Well, stay here if you think that's the right thing to do. I'll be beaming back down to see Morrow within the hour."

"How's he handling this?"

"Actually, he's one of the more impressive ambassadors I've encountered," Picard said as he patted his lips with a cloth napkin and rose. "Rather refreshing."

"And cause for hope," Crusher finished.

"May it stay that way," he replied with a smile. Gesturing, he led her out into the corridor as they went their separate ways.

Riker woke up, his senses alert. Someone else was in the room. He looked up quickly, hands balled into fists, ready in case the violence had invaded Seer's home.

It was one of the girls. The racer, he thought, blinking at her. She just stared at him.

"Good morning," he managed, smiling but confused.

"Hi," she replied, her voice high and soft, not scared.

"Can I help you?"

"No."

"What are you doing in my room?"

"Watching you. Ma sent me to wake you for breakfast."

"I see. Well, you were up late last night. Shouldn't you still be in bed?"

"No. We don't get a lot of visitors. Ma said this was special."

Riker considered that and continued to smile at the notion of children, of home life, and of options he had let slip by. But rather than fall back into reverie or, worse, fall asleep, he sat up. The girl just continued to watch, and he was now feeling conspicuous. Unsure of social customs, he decided to stay in bed until he was alone.

"Well, then, if I'm to get up, you need to step out and let me get ready. Why don't you go help your mother with breakfast?"

"Will you wear your uniform again?"

"Yes," he said. "I'm here on official business and need to look the part."

"Good," she said and turned to leave. As she opened the door, cooking aromas entered the small room, and he sniffed a few times. Then he inhaled deeply, trying to sort through the smells. There was that bread again and . . . coffee?

Swinging his feet to the floor, Riker rose and looked over at the small metallic case decorated with the *Enterprise* insignia. Troi was thoughtful enough to send down toiletries and a fresh uniform. He snapped open the case and sorted through the contents, pleased she knew him so well. Then something caught his eye and he chuckled to himself. Hefting the razor and small canister of shaving gel, he looked at the rare handwritten note from his lover. "In case you change your mind, *Imzadi*," she had written.

A few minutes later, a freshly washed but still bearded Riker strolled downstairs and went directly to the kitchen. Dorina was busying herself over a stovetop while two of the children, including his morning visitor, carried things from kitchen to dining room. There were heaping platters of food, some of which he could only guess at, while others were obviously cooked vegetables and fresh fruits. And a pot of coffee.

"Good morning," he said, announcing his presence.

Dorina turned and smiled at him, her face looking pretty in the soft light coming through the window. He estimated the local time to be just after six in the morning, and he liked the notion of the sun coming up and being there to watch it. Before he knew it, one of the carved ceramic mugs was placed in his hand, steaming, and the smell of coffee caught his attention. Taking a sip, he recognized a fine brew, similar to one he preferred on the *Enterprise,* and with that he gave his hostess a quizzical look.

"My husband *is* the protocol officer," she said with mock seriousness. "He checked with your duty officer when you first entered orbit. He knew you would be on the surface for a while and wanted to make you feel welcome and comfortable. It wasn't hard to bring those details home."

"Still, I appreciate the effort," Riker replied. "Let me help. What're you making?"

She gestured to a large pink bowl filled with a batter-like substance and explained, "It's a spiced bread, filled with fruit called *cacheen.* If you want to help, hand me that jar."

The first officer turned to his right and saw an open jar filled with a yellow powder. He lifted it, took a whiff, and handed it over quickly. "That'd clear out your sinuses."

She laughed as she took no more than a pinch and then sprinkled it around the bowl. While he sipped the delicious coffee, he watched as she tossed in some dried herbs and then something that looked like dark brown berries. He grabbed a whisk and insisted he be allowed to whip it all together while she finished with whatever was still bubbling on the stove.

The children ran in and out of the room, all sneaking peeks at their guest, and he could hear older voices as well—the grandparents. The house was full of life and it sounded like a happy one. More than ever, he wanted to end the violence, today if possible, and preserve this feeling.

"You seem comfortable here," Dorina noted as she lifted the pot off the stove and set it aside to cool. "I thought you starship types lived off replicated food."

"Most of us do," he admitted. "But I find cooking a soothing hobby. I consider myself pretty experienced and not too bad. If time permits, I'll repay your kindness with a meal of my own."

"You do me honor," she said. "But first, stop stirring and put the bowl in that kiln." The woman pointed to a square metallic box with a variety of controls lined up and down one side. He did as instructed, and then she reached across him and hit one oval blue button. The kiln hummed to life. "Fine, we'll be able to eat in about five minutes. Time to go chase my husband out of his room." With that, she gracefully moved past him and out of the kitchen.

Riker finished his coffee but held on to the mug, hoping for more with the meal, and wandered toward the sounds of laughter. The children were trying to build a human pyramid with just four bodies and not a lot of co-ordination. Each attempt left them sprawled on the floor in a tangle, which may have been the intended result. Two older people sat at their places at the table and watched benignly. They each wore something akin to caftans with embroidery around the shoulders. Neither seemed perturbed by his presence.

They introduced themselves and started asking Riker questions about life on a starship. Neither had ever left their continent, let alone their planet, which reminded the first officer just how different every society was. And they were one of the first generations doomed to die off prematurely. His heart went out to these people.

As he answered their questions, Seer hurried into the room, quickly putting up his hands to indicate now was not a good time to try and tackle him. He looked rested, but his eyes kept moving and he clearly had some information. Riker gave him a look, but Seer shook his head with a small smile. Nothing urgent, then, Riker concluded. Damn. It meant his father was still loose.

Dorina had returned to the kitchen and was taking the *cacheen* out of the kiln, which seemed to be some sort of rapid baking device. It was something he was unfamiliar with, but then again, he wasn't much on baking of any sort. As she entered, holding the bowl in gloved hands, the children shrieked in unison and scrambled for their seats. There was a space between the youngest son and Dorina, which Seer indicated was for Will. He took his place, putting his mug down and scanning hopefully for a carafe, and watched everyone else to follow their lead. All raised their hands and then clasped them, forming a ring around the long table. No one spoke, but each seemed to be in silent meditation, so Riker paused a moment to reflect on how lucky these people were and how dedicated he was to preserving this way of life.

When the small hand slipped out of his grip, he let go of Dorina's hand and suddenly everyone was chatting, grabbing platters and bowls, filling their plates and passing everything with practiced ease to their left. Riker followed suit, making sure to sample a little of everything. When he wasn't looking, his mug was magically refilled, bringing a smile to his face.

"Where are you going today, Pa?" the youngest boy asked.

"Today, Will and I will fly over to Fith," Seer said as he sprinkled some powdery substance on the *cacheen*. "We've been looking for someone, and I understand he might be there."

"Is he lost?"

"A very good question," Riker answered. "I don't think so."

"Then he's hiding," one of the girls said.

"Maybe," Seer said, looking carefully over at his guest. Riker gave him a neutral look and shrugged his shoulders.

"What will you do when you find him?" another child asked.

"That's an even better question, one I don't have an answer for yet," Riker said.

The conversation drifted onto other subjects, with the children telling their father about accomplishments at school. Clearly, the planet's problems had kept Seer from home for stretches of time, and now Riker felt a bit like an intruder, taking the children's father away on a wild-goose chase. But it was necessary, to ensure there'd be more time for the family to live in peace.

He ate, keeping silent for the moment and letting the family carry on. The food was hearty and flavorful. Not all of it was to his liking, some of the fruit being too tart for him, but overall an excellent meal. Probably better than the last five state dinners he enjoyed on other worlds. Dorina beamed at his effusive compliments as the meal ended and the children began clearing plates. Riker wanted to help, but Dorina insisted he and Seer take a few moments to organize themselves before running off again.

The grandparents remained in their seats, staying out of the way, but were looking less than happy. No doubt they knew what was really happening around the world and maybe even that Riker's father was the quarry. He couldn't tell from the way they acted, but clearly something was troubling them.

"Why Fith?" Will asked when they were finally alone in the front room of the house.

"Because there was another murder. A farmer near where we were yesterday."

"Was it Bison?"

"No, nor the journalist," Seer said. "A man turned on his wife."

"And my father?"

"Not seen at all."

Riker looked at him in confusion. "Three murders in almost as many days? What's going on?"

Seer shook his head sadly. He clearly had no further knowledge.

"How is the Council holding up?"

"Not well," Seer admitted. "From what I gather, they're at a total loss how to stem this thing."

This thing, to Riker, sounded like an outbreak. Something that spread like a disease. But murder wasn't contagious.

"The captain will be back down soon and that should help. With luck, things will stay calm for the day."

"For all of us, Will," Seer said. "For all of us."

Dorina came into the room, holding a large box that she thrust at Riker. "Some leftovers of the *cacheen* and some of the other food. You seemed to like it, so better this than rations in the flyer."

"And coffee, my only," Seer said.

"I was getting to that," she said, laughing. "With two hands I can only handle so much."

The girl who woke Riker came out from behind her, it seemed, with a thermos nearly half her size. Riker reached down, took it from her, and with his free hand tousled her hair. She grinned up at him.

"They all like you," Dorina said proudly.

"They don't know me too well, then," Riker said with a grin. "You have a terrific family, Dorina. I can't thank you enough for letting me visit."

"And you'll come back," she insisted. "I want to try your cooking next."

"Absolutely," he said, and with that, the men were out the door, headed for the flyer. Dorina followed them and let Seer finish loading it and do a preflight check. Finally, she came over and took him into her arms. They embraced for several seconds, and Riker turned his attention to a check-in call with Data aboard the *Enterprise*. When Seer finally got into the pilot's chair, he seemed happy and wistful at the same time.

The flyer's engines whined to full power and without a word, it lifted up into the air and pivoted around. Aimed directly at the rising sun, it took off, letting the house and its precious contents fade from sight.

Feeling refreshed by an uninterrupted night's sleep, Troi kept her promise to herself and enjoyed a large breakfast. She ate in her quarters, reviewing the command staff news summary as prepared by the communications staff. The rest of the Federation seemed to be at peace for a change, which pleased her. A part of her wished they were still on patrol rather than in the quadrant's sole maelstrom, but then there was the problem of boredom.

As she ate her eggs, Troi considered that the ship's morale remained fragile. She had devised a series of booster programs, aimed at improving self-image and keeping the crew sharp. There would still be those wishing to transfer off, trying to get out from under the cloud of suspicion that trailed the *Enterprise*. Those, like the ones she discussed with Riker only days ago, would put themselves first. Picard preferred crew that put the ship and the Federation first, so it might be an addition via subtraction. However, Riker was right, the numbers showed a discouraging trend. Much like the growing violence on the planet below.

Where she could make a great difference with a Starfleet crew, she doubted she could personally make as big a difference with a population hell-bent on fighting. She put those thoughts aside and called up Hoang's profile. Sipping her tea, Troi read once more about the life and career of Anh Hoang. It was an unremarkable life, filled with accomplishments and good reports from supervisors. At this point in her career, she was on track for a typical rise through the ranks, finishing somewhere around the commander level, maybe getting to be second-in-command of engineering, but that would be it. And for most, that seemed to be fine. Nothing in Anh's profile indicated she aspired to command or even a chief engineer's position. Prior to the Breen attack on San Francisco, she had preferred planetary assignments in order to put family first. Again, not unusual.

Finished with her meal, Troi tidied up, checked her appearance in the mirror, and headed for her office. When she arrived, Anh was already standing by the door.

"Good morning, Counselor," she said.

"Good morning, Anh. Come on in. Do you want a drink?"

"I just had my breakfast, thanks," Anh said.

"Well, take a seat. Will you be late for your shift? I forgot to notify Mr. La Forge."

"I've got the swing shift for the next month," she said. Anh took the same chair as before, but wasn't as tense. She still seemed less than thrilled to be spending time with the ship's counselor, but that was fairly normal.

"You're in uniform early," Troi observed.

Anh looked at herself, shrugged. "I guess I don't like changing often."

"How will you spend your mornings?"

"I guess I'll read, work out, the usual," Anh said.

"No other activities? There are different interest groups that might be good for you, give you a chance to make some real friends."

"I don't need real friends," Anh said. "When I do, I know there are plenty of people here."

"Have people tried to befriend you?"

"I guess. I haven't paid attention. The first few months I spent making sure I knew everything I needed to about how this ship performs."

"But you haven't learned about its crew, have you?"

"What do you mean?"

"Well, how many singing groups are there? Or musical groups?"

Troi's questions were met with silence.

"What about the winner of last month's chess tournament?"

More silence.

"You're a smart woman with a lot to offer this crew. We work one-third of our day, sleep another third, and have a third for whatever we want," Troi said patiently. "With so many people aboard, there are plenty of activities going on, and you seem not to partake in any of them."

"Well, I have seen some performances," Anh admitted. "I guess I'm not much of a joiner."

"On Earth, you danced," Troi said quietly.

Anh was startled by the counselor's words. Troi sensed the change in emotions and sat silently, waiting out the engineer.

"I gave it up when I got married," she said. "I gave up the troupe for my Sean."

"Were you good?"

"Pretty much. It was a fusion dance, mixing Andorian with old-fashioned line dancing. Terrific exercise, actually."

"Couldn't you be married and still dance?"

"I wanted to devote myself to building the marriage and maintaining my career."

"You compartmentalize things, I see," Troi observed. "You know you can dance here."

"I suppose," Anh admitted. "I just haven't given it much thought."

"Perhaps you should. One thing I've learned is that picking up where you left off is not always a bad thing."

"Counselor Troi, report to my ready room." Picard's voice sounded serious.

"Something must have happened," Troi said to her visitor.

Anh looked at her with an unreadable expression. Troi stood and Anh followed suit. "Think about it. We'll talk again when I'm back."

"Be careful, Counselor," Anh said, a sense of urgency in her voice.

"I always try," she said. "Don't worry about me."

In her security office, Christine Vale ran a hand through her short, dark hair, looking over duty rosters. When Picard told her of the third murder, it became even more imperative to have experienced personnel on the planet. She wanted to go directly to the crime scene and only relented when the captain told her Riker was on his way. He was one of the few people aboard she would have trusted to study the fresh scene, other than herself. Her people were going to have to work twelve hours on, twelve hours off if possible—just like Picard suggested. She figured there'd be little need for a full squad on the ship, but she refused to take everyone off. Stroking her chin, she scanned the active list and selected a squad of three to remain on duty aboard ship plus one at tactical. She then looked over a link to the Council computers and the continuous updating of violent hot spots. There were too many for the peace officers to handle, but even if she brought down everyone at once, they'd be stretched way too thin. There was little choice but to respond to the areas where her people would make the most difference.

She and Picard had already discussed the ordnance to be used. He disliked the notion of phaser rifles, seeing them as provocative in an already tense situation. She would have preferred if each team had one, just in case, but deferred to the captain's wishes. They would all, though, carry phaser pistols and an emergency medical kit.

The *Enterprise* had inherited an important legacy, and she wanted fiercely to protect it. Picard lost Tasha Yar during his first year of command, and the sting remained with him for quite some time, despite the valiant work done by Worf, her successor. He then lost Worf to a transfer to Deep Space 9, following the destruction of the *Enterprise*-D. Vale was the latest of several security chiefs on the *Enterprise*-E, and Picard expected much of her. He deserved it, and she was ready to die for the man who had earned her respect and, more importantly, her trust, time and time again.

If he wanted her to keep a planet at bay, so be it.

"Vale to Peart," she said, tapping her combadge.

"Peart here."

"Have the first squad leaders report to the conference room on deck seven, Jim."

"Aye, Lieutenant."

Ten minutes later, Christine Vale sat at the head of the table in the largest conference room aboard the starship, matching faces with names on the duty roster.

"You'll beam down in five teams of four for a twelve-hour shift," she began without any preamble. "I'm sending you to places without peace officers present. Each squad leader will use discretion in handling any problem that may arise. Our mission is to keep the peace, protect lives and property."

"What's causing this?" asked Clemons, a dark-skinned man who was a twenty-year Starfleet vet.

"Dr. Crusher is working on that very question," Vale replied. "What we do know is you're immune to whatever is happening to both the Bader and the Dorset. Neither side is at fault, and all are worried. Never forget that. They need us to keep things together until the doctors can solve this. Never forget that either. I'm a transporter beam away. Good luck and be careful."

With that, the people filed out in four-person squads, Studdard, Clemons, Seo, Gracin, and Van Zandt leading them. The teams would go to assigned transporter rooms and await a signal for beam-down. Vale watched them, wanting to go down there beside them and wishing they didn't have to go into battle at all.

Peart turned to her with an expectant look on his face. "I don't get to beam down?"

"Sorry, Jim, but I'm going to keep myself on call to assess problems in the field. The captain wants someone he can count on at tactical . . . just in case."

"I think I could do better for the captain on the planet than a rookie like Aiken."

"Maybe," she admitted, "but if the captain needs immediate support from us, I need someone up here who knows that board perfectly. Aiken hasn't logged a single hour on the bridge."

"I know," he said. "I'm just a little disappointed."

She grinned at him. "With this ship and captain, there's always going to be something. If it's not Delta Sigma IV it'll be something else next month. Have faith. You'll see some action."

"And now I have to be careful of what I wish for, right?"

"Could be. I'm going up for the rest of alpha shift. You get some rest and take beta."

"Aye, Lieutenant."

Vale took a deep breath, walked out of the room with Peart, and watched as he veered left down the corridor. She then headed for the nearest turbolift and within seconds was on the bridge, walking to the tactical station. Almonte, who was on duty, started to move away, but she gestured for him to stay. She wasn't planning to be there long.

The continent of Fith, Dorset-founded, seemed to be the one with the most problems. It was there the first murder occurred, and then on another part of the continent the second attack occurred, and now a third murder had occurred. She scanned the most recent reports from the Council, selected four areas that required help, and sent the coordinates to Juj. Without taking her eyes off the board, she watched as the transporters all worked at once, the power levels on the ship compensating for the sudden drain, and then saw the Starfleet insignia pop up in four places.

The hard work was about to begin.

* * *

Picard and Troi materialized in the Council chamber, taking a moment to let their eyes adjust to the dimmer lighting. The Council seemed not to have moved, sitting at their table with adjutants and sycophants scurrying around. The noise was subdued, but the chattering continued unabated, like a swarm of insects circling a swamp. An apt image, considering the mess things had devolved into. The captain looked over at the screens behind the Council table and noted the various newsfeeds, all talking about the latest murder, no doubt.

And still, the Council talked.

From what he could tell, they had not acted with any universal policy, deploying peace officers only as dictated. Entirely reactive at a time when leadership was required. Chkarad, pleasant as he was, was clearly not the right man in the right position. How often had history tested a leader, and how often had the leader failed? Countless billions had died on Earth alone through inadequate leadership, dating back to the first conquerors.

Morrow, who had been leaning over the table and whispering with a councillor, looked up and spotted the captain. He gave a short wave, excused himself, and walked over at a brisk pace. His clothes were less than crisp, a golden fuzz was evident around his chin, and his face was haggard. He seemed to be running on adrenaline.

"What progress have you made?" Picard inquired.

"Little, I'm afraid," Morrow said glumly. "They seemed most interested in securing this building and then contacting their families to make sure they were safe. There's been a great deal of idle speculation that has derailed substantive work. Then they slept wherever they could. I managed to grab two chairs and got some rest myself."

"Clearly not enough, from the looks of it," Troi offered.

"Good morning to you, Counselor," Morrow said brightly, ignoring the observation.

"Is our security holding up?"

"Carmona's been wonderful," Morrow said. "He's done a lot to make sure they feel safe here. If only the Council felt safe enough to get something accomplished."

"Then that is what is on today's agenda," Picard said with a decisive tone in his voice. He detested having to do the work of others, but the Council of Delta Sigma IV had been given protection and support and still they chose to do nothing. The captain's talk with Speaker Chkarad had clearly failed, so he had to act on the other part of the threat—he had to step in. As the captain strode toward the Council, he fully expected his actions to be welcomed by those who continued to want to serve their people.

"Good morning, Councillors," Picard called out as he approached. He felt it necessary to project a stern voice, letting the Council chamber's acoustics work to his advantage. No stranger to the stage, he was going to put on a one-time performance that he hoped would inspire these people. They didn't have time for an extended run.

"We expected you sooner," was all Renks said by way of greeting.

"I do have my own ship to tend to," Picard answered curtly. He saw Troi and Morrow exchange surprised glances in the back of the room. Just as well they weren't sitting closer to the dais, for they would urge him to speak gently, to proceed diplomatically. Ship's counselors and ambassadors were both professional advocates of tact, which was normally a useful tool. But at this point in this case, the time for tact had long since passed. Protests had sprung up on every continent, most of them peaceful, but there had already been a few minor scuffles. It was only a matter of time before they escalated to brawls.

"I want to strongly recommend you order curfews around the planet, lock down all the transportation hubs, and urge people to stay home. I know this will affect your economy, but so will all this senseless violence. If people let quarrels turn to fights or fights turn into riots, then the damage to your economy will be much, much worse."

Picard paused, letting his words sink in and studying Chkarad to gauge a reaction. The Speaker didn't meet the captain's eyes.

"He's right, Speaker," one of the men said from behind them.

"Act," another said.

"They won't listen," Chkarad said to no one in particular.

"You need to sell it to them as the best course of action," Picard said firmly.

"And if they reject my orders?"

"We'll take this a step at a time. Give the orders, set the curfew time, and see what happens. Once we see if they listen, then we can redeploy your peace officers to any hot spots. My people can help enforce the curfew." He disliked the notion of involving his crew further, but felt he had little choice.

"I will try. Let me compose something for broadcast."

"Of course," Picard agreed, sensing an overdue victory. "But keep it brief. And be quick, please."

The Speaker seemed to shuffle out of the room, seeking some solitude in which to prepare his message. Picard turned and got positive reactions from not only Morrow but several of the Council. One had even summoned an aide, and he could hear the orders to prepare for a global broadcast. *Good, finally some activity.*

Troi looked over her shoulder, then at Picard, and then motioned toward one of the monitors. The captain walked over, keeping his distance, and listened to the murmurs.

"It broke up on its own?"

"No, someone dropped the spokesman and everyone scattered."

"Not like them at all, usually a hardier bunch."

"May I inquire as to the activity?" Picard asked, keeping his voice even.

A Dorset man looked over his shoulder, stiffened a bit at the captain's presence, and then gestured to the screen. "Here on Tregor, there was a protest rally."

"What were they protesting?"

"You, actually."

"I see. Go on."

"Well, the speaker was whipping them up into a frenzy and suddenly he fell over. Not dead or anything, but knocked out. People just scattered, ending the event."

"What caused his collapse?"

"Seems to be a concussion from a stone."

Picard blinked at that. So they were throwing rocks now? He watched the media feed on the monitor and saw the replay. The stone hitting the man at the base of the skull, the man falling forward, off the podium and into the crowd.

"Captain!"

Carmona entered the chamber at a run. His uniform was dirty and his face streaked with what Picard hoped was mud. The lieutenant jogged to the dais and Picard met him at the edge.

"A riot has broken out. It's like it's alive—growing by the second."

"Is the Council in danger?"

"The building is secure at the moment, but if the mob grows any larger, I can't guarantee the situation won't change."

"How many can you spare to quell things?"

"Two, maybe three," the officer replied.

"You stay here, the Council knows you," Picard ordered. "Deploy your people and stop the fighting. The Speaker is about to order something short of martial law. That should help."

With a nod, he headed back outside and Picard watched him, concern now overwhelming any sense of momentum he may have felt minutes earlier.

Three murders sparking a protest was understandable, but a riot was something else entirely.

"Testani's on fire!"

Picard turned and saw Morrow and a Bader councillor running to a screen to the right of the dais. He and Troi exchanged glances and approached the monitor, which showed tongues of flame rising above a cluster of buildings.

Testani was a city.

"We have a Ferengi ship approaching," Peart called from tactical. "He says he is here by Commander La Forge's invitation."

"That is true, Lieutenant," Data replied. "Allow him docking access if he requires it. But, given the circumstances below, please make sure his stay is brief."

"I'm on it," Peart replied. "I don't recall us inviting Ferengi traders to visit."

"Normally we don't, but I have business with him," La Forge said from his station.

"You lose a bet?"

"No, actually, he's bringing me a part I need from the *Nautilus*."

"I'm assigning a detail, for when he steps on board."

"Is that necessary?" Data asked.

"He's a Ferengi trader, and I don't want him 'sampling' the equipment," Peart said with a wicked grin.

Date nodded in comprehension and returned his gaze to the forward viewscreen.

La Forge tapped in a few final commands at his post and looked over to Peart. "He won't cause trouble, and I need a favor from him."

"I'd make it quick if I were you," Perim chided from her post.

"I didn't invite him for high tea," La Forge said, heading for the turbolift.

"That is wise, since we do not normally serve high tea," Data said.

La Forge chuckled to himself, remembering how unintentionally amusing Data could be without his emotion chip. As the lift brought him to engineering, he thought once again about the chip and its absence in Data's life. They had been convinced his neural pathways were sufficiently evolved for the chip to be used on a full-time basis eight years earlier. He wondered if the pathways would continue to evolve or would regress with the chip's absence.

Once in engineering, he walked to a small supply room and tapped in the command codes granting him access to the dilithium crystals that were the lifeblood of a warp engine. Without the crystals' properties helping to regulate the flow of anti-matter and matter, the balance would never be stabilized. The Federation had managed, over the years, to learn how to recrystalize used crystals and even synthesize dilithium, but it was a protected technology most other races had yet to develop on their own. So, for nonaligned people such as the Ferengi, the real crystals were still highly valued.

Rubbing his thumb over the smooth surface, La Forge could easily see why these were valued prior to warp technology. They were brilliant when polished, flawless and tough to crack.

Leaving a thumbprint to acknowledge the withdrawal of the crystal, La Forge left the store room and proceeded to the main engineering section. He strode over to Lieutenant Taurik, who was in command when La Forge was on the bridge.

"Taurik, please have someone grab an extra chambliss coil and meet me at docking bay two."

"Of course, Commander," the Vulcan replied.

"Then, have someone run a full scan of the Ferengi ship that just arrived. I'll need the report at the docking port."

Taurik nodded, cocking his eyebrow in a questioning manner.

"What's the matter?"

"I am trying to determine the use of a chambliss coil and a dilithium crystal, and I can see no practical use for these two items in concert."

La Forge smiled, hefting the crystal in his right hand. "No connection other than some old-fashioned bartering."

"Indeed," the younger engineer replied.

"When you run an engine room, Taurik, you'll learn that improvisation is almost as important as knowing why things work."

He was met with a stony silence. La Forge thought about prolonging the conversation since the Vulcan showed a lot of promise but clearly needed some practical lessons. "Tell you what, let's have a drink after the shift and I can explain it all to you."

"Agreed."

"Great, now get that part to the docking port," La Forge called, hurrying to the nearest lift.

Once he arrived at the docking port, La Forge realized he was late. An unpleasant Ferengi named Dex was already waiting for him on the deck, surrounded by two of Vale's people. They towered over the slight, older Ferengi, who seemed ready to bolt back to his ship.

"Is this how you greet guests?"

"Sorry about that," La Forge said by way of greeting. "However, things are a little volatile down below, so we have to be extra careful."

Dex seemed to cower further away from the guards. "Volatile as in shooting?"

"Nothing aimed this way," La Forge said in as friendly a manner as possible. "Now, do you have the quad?"

"Of course I do," the Ferengi snapped, finally eyeing the glittering dilithium crystal in La Forge's hand. He licked his lips, finally putting his fears behind him. "And that's my pay."

"Where's the part?"

"Inside my vessel. You'll get it after we discuss the final price."

Folding his arms and trying to look unamused, La Forge waited.

"Entering hazardous space, putting my ship at risk is worth a twenty-five percent premium. Ten percent for a rush delivery, another five percent for general sector tariffs. That should amount to at least a third crystal."

"I see," La Forge said, trying to avoid tapping his foot in impatience. "Is that all?"

"I think so," Dex answered.

Just then, an ensign arrived, carrying a box with the chambliss coil and a padd. She put the box down by La Forge's feet and handed over the padd and stood at attention. Geordi almost immediately began scanning the padd's report, ignoring Dex. After thirty seconds, he finally noticed the ensign remaining ramrod straight.

"Anything else, Ensign?"

"No, sir," she snapped back.

"Dismissed, then," La Forge said with a sigh. You could always spot the newbies. Finally, he closed the report and exhaled loudly, slowly shaking his head.

"Well, Mr. La Forge," Dex prompted.

"Here's the thing, Dex," La Forge began. "Because this is such a volatile part of space at the moment, we took the liberty of scanning your ship to make sure it could escape under fire if necessary . . ."

". . . but you said no one was firing this way," Dex interrupted.

"Well, you can't be too careful. It seems your reactor is not up to specs and you have faltering shield generators. Looks like your landing gear is also fused, so you're spacebound. All in all, I should have this vessel impounded, at least until things calm down."

"You can't!"

"I can," La Forge continued. "And these friends of mine will see to it that you remain aboard, under our protection."

Dex stole a look at the larger of the two guards and stepped closer to the engineer.

"Unless . . ." La Forge began.

"I'll do it! Whatever it is, I'll do it!"

"We need this item transported to the *Pegasus,* back in the direction you came. In exchange, we'll do repairs to your reactor and generators. Won't take more than a few hours, and then you can be under way."

Dex eyed the gray box on the deck. He looked back at La Forge's face and studied it.

"I don't know," he stammered. "I can usually read a man by looking into his eyes. You, er, make that a bit difficult."

"This is the best deal you'll get," La Forge said, fighting

off exasperation. "You get an improved ship and I get to help another Starfleet ship."

"I see, well then. I guess we have a deal." He held out his hand, attempting to shake the way humans did. Instead, La Forge handed him the crystal.

"There, payment for services rendered," La Forge said. "These fine people will take you to a lounge where you can have something to eat and wait while we fix your ship." He nodded to the officers, who returned the gesture and stepped toward the Ferengi. La Forge turned and started back to the bridge, but stopped when Dex called out.

"How do you know you can trust me?"

La Forge turned and smiled coldly at him. "Because, Dex, you wouldn't dream of double-crossing Starfleet. We'll get your transponder code, and we'll hunt you down if the *Pegasus* doesn't receive that part on schedule."

"Point taken."

The flight from the capital to Tregor took several hours, during which Riker grew more anxious. A part of him wanted to use the transporter and move around Delta Sigma IV quickly, but he also wanted to be a respectful guest and do things in a manner the locals were comfortable with. Fortunately, he liked Seer and liked him even more after seeing him with his family. As they traveled, Riker used the time to speak with Picard, Crusher, Troi, and Data, letting them know he was fine and getting their perspectives on the mission. It sounded like a lot of time and effort was being expended but not a lot was being learned.

"Do you mind having Vale and her people on the planet?" Riker asked Seer after Picard had informed him of the unusual step.

"I recognize the need for help, but I must admit I'm not happy we need to ask for it."

"Do you blame the Federation for the murders?"

"Of course not, Will. But something happened and the people feel the need to blame someone. The Federation is an easy target, and blaming the Federation allows the people to avoid pointing fingers at each other. Still, this was bound to happen and catch us unprepared."

"What do you mean?"

"I was on the Council for a time," Seer explained. "And I advocated for a larger and better trained security staff. The Council had grown complacent, feeling we were off the usual pathway of Romulans or Cardassians and didn't have anything to be worried about."

"Aggressive races usually turn up sooner or later," Riker said.

"Exactly right," Seer said emphatically. "*Exactly* right. I wanted us ready should someone turn up in orbit. Instead, I was told the treasury couldn't handle such expenditures for at least another generation. Trade was growing, but slowly, and my fears were unfounded."

"What happened?"

"I was seen as a one-topic candidate and was not reelected," Seer said with some bitterness. "Instead, when Chkarad was named Speaker, he asked me to stay on. Since I was thinking of the stars, it made sense to him that I be trained to represent the planet to visitors."

"What if they came with weapons, not open hands?"

Riker heard the sigh before looking over to see the strained look on Seer's face. Seer said, "Then I'm the first to be shot. Or eaten, I suppose."

"Not a cheery thought," Riker said.

"Not at all. Once the war ended and we were contacted to sell food, I was suddenly a man in demand. It was nice meeting with delegations from the Federation and specific member worlds. The first thing we did was send seventy metric tons of grain as part of the Cardassian relief effort. Chkarad wanted to make sure we were counted among the more enlightened worlds."

"So, you've been a busy man," Riker said.

"Rather too busy at times," Seer admitted, banking the craft as it neared the shores of Tregor. It was a rocky coast, barren of the lush vegetation just a few miles inland and slick with the residue from waves that crashed every few seconds. Further inland, things got drier and greener, and they flew low as Seer pointed out some of the trees that were unique to the continent.

"The only good to come from the sales has been increased revenues, so I've begun speaking again about planetary defenses."

"Makes sense. Are you winning the argument this time?"

"No," Seer said bitterly. "Now we're an important supplier, so Chkarad feels Starfleet will respond more quickly should the need arise."

"The man's a fool," Riker replied. "Member worlds do not receive response based on importance at a given time. It's strictly based on need."

"But don't your ships patrol sectors with more strategically important worlds?"

"Our borders obviously receive a bit more attention," Riker agreed. "But elsewhere, we travel each sector fairly evenly. I will admit a few of the sectors may not see ships very often, but that's only because we took heavy losses during the war. You can't replace hundreds of vessels overnight."

"No, you can't," Seer had said. "Another point I raised. And besides, I wasn't speaking only about extraterrestrial problems but internal ones as well. I never could have imagined our two races suddenly having a falling out, but rebellions of different kinds were certainly possible. All our people are primarily trained to handle, out of the usual crimes, are natural disasters, and there hasn't been one of those for five years."

"You're lucky," Riker said. "On many worlds, these things happen all year round. But if your disasters are that infrequent, I can see where the Council may grow complacent."

"So I stand as the lone voice," Seer said. Once again, the flyer adjusted course and this time they were headed deep into an interior valley. Nestled at the bottom of the valley was a town. Riker noted it seemed well-established, probably among the first in the area. It was fed by two different rivers nearby and protected by the rising slopes of hills and mountains.

The flyer was now over more familiar terrain, and Riker actually recognized landmarks from the day before. He thought about Hust and his family, seeing a murder and his father in hot pursuit of the killer. But what of his father's hunt for Bison? Were Bison and the journalist somehow connected?

Once again, Seer smoothly landed the craft and quickly they clambered out. Riker didn't bother to enjoy the fresh air or the terrain, but pulled out his tricorder and did a quick scan for bodies. No one was within a kilometer of them, so the farmhouse was empty. He nodded the all-clear to Seer, who dipped his head once in understanding. Grimly, they set out for the murder scene.

It was a few minutes' walk from the landing field to the house, and the silence bothered the first officer. Normally, a farm should have been filled with animal sounds, even insects. Instead, there was the barest hint of a breeze and that was all. The sun was bright in the cloudless sky, making everything pastoral to the naked eye. The house was another nondescript affair, two-story and wide, painted a pale violet. Behind it was a huge barn, flanked by tall silos, all painted an uninspired white.

"An Haslam An," the stocky male peace officer said by way of greeting. Seer introduced himself and Riker, and then the trio went to the house.

"I understand the murder took place around midnight," Seer said.

"Yeah. Col Hust Col heard screams all the way over to his place and notified us. My night man rushed right out here, but by then it was too late. Probably too late by the time he got the call."

"What did he find?"

"Fox Denks Fox, the owner of the farm, was kneeling beside his wife's body. Blood was everywhere, and he was crying uncontrollably."

"He in custody?"

"Yeah, but he hasn't said a word since the attack.

Sleeps and cries and stares. I've got people watching him just in case he tries to send himself after her."

"Good," Seer said.

"May I go in and look around?" Riker asked.

Haslam shrugged and gestured to the house. Riker nodded and pulled out his tricorder while Seer stood by.

The tricorder provided a new sound as it was activated and Riker bent low, scanning the steps leading to the wraparound porch. Seer stayed behind him, scanning the horizon, a hand providing shade for his eyes. The day was warm and pleasant, perfect for working the land.

Slowly, Will went from the porch to the doorway and finally into the house. Adjusting the settings, he waved it from room to room until they reached the bedroom, set upstairs in the farthest corner of the house. Inside the bedroom, the huge canopy bed was a mess, the sheets soaked with blood. More blood had spilled from the bed to the hardwood floor. There were scratch marks on part of the floor, and a similar mark on a post at the foot of the bed. Everything else was immaculate.

Will shut off the tricorder, pocketed it, and just stood, looking. He imagined the fight, the knife flailing until it found its target, and then the death. The blood hadn't splattered but pooled. From the smudges in it, Riker suspected that was where the farmer knelt over the body of his wife and remained until he was arrested.

"Let's go see him," Riker said, and turned on his heel.

"Won't say much of anything, but sure, why not," Haslam said.

Within minutes, they had reached the edge of the

town. It was small, squat, and uniformly dull, much like the rest of the planet.

They had gone past several blocks, and Riker took in the peaceful life of a town. Assayers' offices mixed with mining suppliers indicated the mountains nearby were still ripe for the picking. These establishments gave way to a variety of small jewelry stores, with holographic projections showing off the individual designs. Riker found himself slowing down to look at some of the creations. When time permitted, he knew he'd be back to select something for Deanna.

Seer noticed that Riker had slowed his pace and walked over to him. That, in turn, caught the attention of the others and within moments, five people were clustered around a holographic display.

"That an emerald?"

"Sure is, Will," Seer said.

"The cut is pretty nice," Haslam said admiringly.

"Do you think the setting is too ornate?" Riker asked.

"Depends on the woman. Is she the ornate type?"

Before Riker could reply, the sound of breaking glass caught their attention. They turned to see a man hanging halfway out a broken shop window, his back sliced up by the remaining shards still in the frame. At the man's neck were two black-clad arms. Then a red-gloved fist emerged and struck him as he dangled.

An Haslam An broke into a run, but Riker and Seer were only a step behind him. When they got to the storefront, the victim had been hauled back inside, but someone else had been tossed through the door. Literally through the door, which splintered into many wooden pieces. Tripping over him on their way out the door were two other men. The sounds of a full-scale brawl were clear in the morning air.

Alerted by the noise, two peace officers, a Bader and a Dorset, came running toward the store. Haslam hefted one man off the street and roughly tossed him to his counterpart, who more gently placed him out of harm's way. The officers then rushed into the store. Riker had already withdrawn his phaser and was ready to stun the entire crowd. Haslam shook his head violently, indicating he'd prefer that weapons not be used. Respecting the local authority, Riker holstered the weapon and waited to see if he was needed at all. The question was quickly answered as the Bader officer came tumbling out of the store, a piece of clothing clenched in one fist.

"Enough of this!" roared the peace officer.

He waded into the store, manhandling one brawler after another, tossing them aside or out the door. As they emerged, Riker and Haslam lined them up against a wall. Seer was tending to various bloody lips or cuts. The man who had torn up his back on the glass was lying on his stomach at one end of the line. Within a minute, the final man was shown the door and then slammed up against the wall with a whoof of expelled air.

"Now, what started all this?" Haslam demanded.

Not one of the brawlers looked him in the eye. The street seemed to be receiving most of their attention. A few were flexing their hands, either massaging bruised knuckles or getting ready for round two. Haslam walked up and down the line, studying the men, recognizing none of them. He was flanked by the two officers, neither of whom were looking their best.

"We'll lock the lot of you up until I get some answers. Call for a medic and for a wagon. Let's get them out of here."

"I don't know if we have enough cells to keep them isolated," the Dorset officer said.

"If they know what's good for them, they'll behave themselves no matter where they get locked up," his counterpart added with a growl.

"If you don't mind," warned the Dorset, "I'll take care of my own people as I see fit."

"I do mind, since we're in this together," the other replied. "If more violence occurs, it'll make us both look bad, and I'd rather not look any worse."

"Gentlemen, please," insisted Haslam.

"You'll mind what I tell you," the Dorset officer said, and turned his attention to the men against the wall.

The Bader officer leapt across the space and tackled his counterpart. Haslam reached out to grab them both. He couldn't get his hands on either of them long enough to maintain a grip. Finally, he looked at Riker, who needed no prodding. The phaser was out and fired in a second, and the two men lay still. Immediately, the phaser was aimed at the men against the wall.

"Thank you, Commander," Haslam said, catching his breath.

"Don't mention it."

"I never thought I'd see something like this," the peace officer said with obvious disgust. "It's here, too, isn't it?"

"An Haslam An, you have my apologies for this incident," Riker said gravely. He was more disturbed by the suddenness of the attack than anything else.

Riker stepped back and let his mind process everything he had seen and heard over the last hour. He knew there were pieces that connected but hadn't allowed himself the opportunity to concentrate. He wandered away from Seer and the others, enjoying the sun's warmth and the quiet.

There was a pattern to the contagion. Was there a pattern to the odd eruptions of violence? Riker tapped his combadge and asked Data to filter Picard's incident reports and chart their progression.

"Data to Riker," came the expected call several minutes after additional peace officers had arrived to clear the scene. A medic was still tending wounds before moving people. Seer was acting as nurse while Haslam was coordinating events with people back at his office.

"Go ahead, Data."

"You were correct. There has been a pattern to the protests and violent incidents. In fact, the origin point is your current location."

"Send the information to my tricorder. Can you tell where the next occurrence will be?"

"I can only hypothesize a westerly direction based on the available data, sir."

Seer walked over, getting close enough to overhear the conversation. He received a welcoming expression from Will.

"There may not be a specific destination, Data."

"Do you know what the significance of this pattern is?"

"If I'm right, my father is behind each of these events."

"On what do you base that assumption?"

"We haven't seen him and in each case, a horrible

situation has been defused. By extension, he might be continuing to help out. Deanna said earlier he might have chased El Bison El out of some sense of obligation."

"Interesting."

"What's happening with the other test subjects?"

"They are in sickbay, currently being examined by Dr. Crusher."

"And the biofilters didn't pick up anything?"

"No."

"Then we're to assume the ship's crew will be unaffected by this," Riker said hopefully.

"So it would appear."

"Thank you, Data. Riker out."

Will turned toward Seer and jerked his thumb west. "What's out that way?"

"Next big city over that way is Keslik," Seer replied.

Keslik here we come, Riker thought.

As she patrolled the streets of Testani, Vale could hear people calling out to one another, seeking help. No one was laying blame, for which she was thankful. Retardant foam was being sprayed several blocks away, and it seemed to be slowing the fires down.

Shouts caught her attention, and she jogged down a dirty block and rounded a corner in time to see a small mob forming around a Dorset woman. They were shouting angrily.

"What did you do?"

"Why is the city burning?"

"This is all your fault!"

The woman, on her hands and knees, certainly didn't look like a troublemaker of any kind.

One of the men in the crowd turned and picked up a ceramic planter. Vale gripped her phaser tightly, readying herself to protect the woman's life. The man hefted it over his head and screamed obscenities at the woman, who began to wail in fear and confusion.

The others began egging the man on, wanting him to cause pain. However, he didn't seem as eager, just angry. Whatever common sense he had left must have been fighting with his feelings, and he hesitated.

Then he reared back, ready to throw.

The woman shrieked.

Vale calmly raised her phaser and fired at the planter, shattering it in the man's hands. Ceramic bits and pieces rained down around him. Several turned to face Vale, their faces twisted into confused looks. The Dorset woman sobbed loudly.

"That's enough," Vale said as calmly as she knew how. "She's done nothing wrong. Now, go home. All of you."

"What's Starfleet going to do about this?" one of the men yelled.

"Our doctors are working with your doctors trying to find out what's happening to the planet," she said.

At the word "doctor," some of the people stepped back and away from each other. Others looked around in confusion, none offering to help the woman off the street. Vale stood her ground, phaser at the ready.

Within two minutes, the area was clear except for the woman, who remained prone on the street.

"You're not gonna shoot me, are you?"

"Have you done anything wrong?"

She shook her head, tears once more running down her cheeks.

"Then I have no reason to shoot you, do I?" Vale reached down and offered a hand, making certain the phaser was still in plain sight. The woman looked at the phaser and then scanned the area. Finally deciding things were safe for the moment, she accepted the proffered hand and struggled to her feet. Her face was smeared with grime and streaked with tears.

"You go home, too," Vale said gently.

"Will I be safe there?"

"Safer than out here."

"This won't hurt a bit," Crusher said as she laid the Dorset woman on the diagnostic bed.

"That's what Dolog said, and he was rough," the woman replied. She struck Crusher as being nervous and it was perfectly understandable. She and the other two test subjects had been brought to the *Enterprise* in the last few minutes, with little notice, and it was just another jarring moment for them.

After it became clear their presence had something to do with sudden violence, the next logical step was a direct examination. Crusher prided herself on her diagnostic skills and was hoping they would stand her in good stead. They had to, since an entire planet was counting on success.

The question remained, as always, success against what?

While Nurse Weinstein and the others on her staff settled the other test subjects on beds, Crusher checked the basic readings now coming on screen. She immediately matched them against the baseline readings she had taken from members of the Council and from Wasdin's own files at the Medical Center. The autopsy results remained on a side screen, and Crusher consulted it regularly.

The woman remained fidgety, so Crusher tried to calm her with the good news that at first look, everything was fine.

"How do you feel?"

"Just fine," the woman replied.

"Have you felt fine since you returned to the planet?"

"Yeah."

"And you felt fine on Earth?"

"Yeah, even if the food was horrible."

Crusher was surprised at the comment, but from the woman's perspective, the food was foreign to her and just not to her taste. *Her loss.* Taking a medical scanner, Crusher set it for a deep cellular scan, waved it over the woman's right hand and right leg, and paused.

"I'm going to need to take some cell samples and blood samples. May I?"

"If you must."

"I must. Something's happening. . . ."

"I know, I know, and it's ever since we came back. I got that."

Crusher ran her hands around the Dorset woman's jaw, neck, abdomen, knees, and elbows. The woman squirmed a bit, which made her difficult to examine, but not half as difficult as she had been when the poor nurse did some initial scans an hour earlier. All of sickbay had gotten a

Dorset vocabulary lesson. Too bad none of the newly learned terms were repeatable in polite company.

"I'll be back in a moment," Crusher said, moving toward an instrument tray in the corner.

Now, where had she put that gauge to measure the patients, . . .

"How long do I have to stay here?"

"Just a little while longer."

"Well, that doctor said the same thing and I was there for two days! Tell me now if it's going to be two days, because I have plans." *With whom?* Crusher wondered. She couldn't imagine a person with this disposition having a very full social schedule.

"It will be a lot less than two days," Crusher said as soothingly as possible.

The woman settled herself on the diagnostic bed and sneered. "See to it."

Crusher gritted her teeth and moved on to the next patient, another Dorset, who was, thank heavens, asleep. The test samples had already been taken, so she did her physical exam and found nothing wrong. The next patient looked fine as well. Good news for them in the short run, but in the long run somebody had to find something, or a whole world faced destruction.

Walking her cell samples to the microscope set against a far wall, she sat down and placed the first one under the lens.

At first glance, she saw nothing. Maybe the computers would have better luck comparing these samples with the samples that had been taken earlier. As she checked the data she saw an anomaly that gave her some hope.

Deep in one of the chromosome packs, she found the original discovery that started this entire event.

Sure enough, the liscom gas had mutated the chromosomes, advancing the metabolism and shortening life spans. This was shown in the first scan taken on Earth. And the second through eighth scans. The ninth scan on Earth, though, showed a different change. The chromosome was mutating again, or rather, reverting. The tenth scan matched the scan she was looking at now, which showed the chromosome restored to what was considered Dorset norm.

That was all to be expected. The life span was being restored to normal. Starfleet Medical had done its job.

So what was going wrong?

"The Ferengi ship is departing," Perim said from the helm.

La Forge looked up and watched the coppery ship streak across the screen. "And he didn't even say goodbye."

"Did you expect him to?" Data asked.

"No, Data," La Forge answered.

"But you do trust him to deliver the chambliss coil to the *Pegasus*."

"Yes, because I made him a good and fair offer. He's a trader and recognizes that he now has an improved ship and the gratitude of two Starfleet ships. That's something you can't deposit, but it can make a difference somewhere down the road."

"I did not know you had this much experience with Ferengi," the android said, joining La Forge at the engineering console.

"I've had my dealings with them over the years, including this one time I was vacationing on Rigel II. There were these two Ferengi who were trying to sell Spican flame gems as aphrodisiacs and . . ."

"We're being hailed by your friend on the *Nautilus*," Vale announced.

La Forge looked up in surprise and indicated for the signal to be put through to his station. Whis's face appeared, looking tired.

"What's wrong, Whis?"

"Been trying to get ready for the inspection tour. The brass has decided they need to look over every ship this far out. Long hours."

"Well, the Ferengi is on his way to you, so look for him in a few days."

"Great. With luck he'll be here and gone before Starfleet Command arrives."

"He should, since I've got him running a spare part to the *Pegasus*."

"Oh good," Whis said. *"I was hoping you could help Mal out. Listen, that's why I'm calling. Turns out, the* Prometheus *needs a deuterium supply tank. Know of any in the area?"*

La Forge let out a breath. "I'm not the quartermaster, Whis. I haven't got a clue who can spare one near them."

"You've been great helping us out, so I just figured it couldn't hurt to ask."

"Never hurts to ask," La Forge agreed, trying desperately to figure out how to help. The shortages were not limited to Starfleet ships. Entire worlds were going through rationing programs until their industries and infrastructure could be rebuilt. The postwar Federation was hurting from one end to the other.

As the engineers talked, La Forge did not notice Data standing still, his eyes darting from right to left and back again. When La Forge finally noticed his friend, he cocked an eyebrow in Data's direction. It took the android a moment or two to respond but when he did, a faint smile crossed his face.

"I have an idea," Data said.

Speaker Chkarad had spent the two hours since the fighting began in the capital city hunched over a table, writing his speech. An important speech, to be sure, Picard reminded himself as he stood in a corner of the Council chamber, clenching and unclenching his hands. The people of this planet desperately needed some firm and reassuring direction from their leader. Still, while rocks flew through the air, while the injured stumbled out of damaged buildings onto crowded, chaotic streets, while Testani burned, Chkarad sat scratching his head and fussing over a padd.

Finally, the speaker walked toward the computer displays, his address in his right hand. He moved slowly, without any sense of purpose, but as he approached, the others snapped to action. Several councillors rose from the table and walked over to him, hands outstretched. Clearly, they wanted to see the address before it was made, but he waved them away. Sulkily, they hung back out of camera range so all the people would see was their elected Speaker.

Picard joined Morrow and Troi at one side of the

room where they could watch the address as well as the reaction of the other members of the Council.

An aide pushed a final set of buttons, checked a panel, and then, with both forefingers, pointed at Chkarad.

The man took a deep breath, clutched the padd tighter, and began speaking without looking at it once.

Picard nodded in silent approval as Chkarad spoke eloquently of commitment, tolerance, and most importantly, peace. It was a good speech, one worthy of the careful attention paid to it by everyone in the chamber and, Picard hoped, everyone on the planet. Perhaps he had misjudged the Speaker, the captain reflected. Perhaps Chkarad would prove a more effective leader than anyone had imagined.

"Alas, it is my lack of action that has caused this problem to escalate. I have let you down, and therefore, effective immediately, I resign both as Speaker and as a member of the Council. When this is all over, you may select my replacement.

"Go home, stay inside, and if you want, pray to the creators for salvation."

Then again, Picard thought, *perhaps I judged him correctly in the first place.*

Chkarad put the padd down and walked away from the camera, continuing past the stunned aides, councillors, and Federation personnel. He continued at the same slow speed until he reached a side door and left the building.

"Damn," Picard muttered. Morrow nodded solemnly beside him.

"Maybe it was his time," Renks called out. That seemed to shock the others out of their stunned silence. The Dorset councillor rushed forward, gesturing with both hands for the aides to keep the signal running across the planet.

"This is Jus Renks Jus of the Council. The Speaker's decision has come to us all as a surprise. We are going to be in touch once again after we reconvene the Council, but for now, be advised that there is a curfew at dusk. Be in your homes or you will be arrested. This is for your own safety."

With a gesture, he indicated he was done, and an aide punched several buttons, closing the signal.

Renks turned to the others with an expectant look, and they quickly huddled, whispering excitedly among themselves. Picard, Morrow, and Troi wandered away to give them some privacy.

"Did you see this coming?" Morrow asked Picard.

"Not in the slightest," the captain replied, slowly shaking his head. "If anything, this adds fuel to the fire threatening to engulf this world."

"He was in deep pain, Captain," Troi added. "A deep emotional pain. He knew he failed in his task and he let his people down."

Morrow turned his head, looking at the doorway Chkarad used. "I'd better arrange an escort home for him."

"Make it so," Picard said softly.

Three peace officers—two men and a woman, all Bader—greeted Seer and Riker as they disembarked from the craft just outside the city of Keslik. None seemed too happy to see the duo, and one man in particular was looking harshly in Riker's direction.

"I am Caledon of Osedah," one of the men, obviously the leader, said in a no-nonsense voice. "How may we help?"

"Seer of Anann, Protocol Officer to the Council. This is Commander William Riker of the *Enterprise*. I believe you were told to expect us."

"Are you still in power?"

"Excuse me?" Seer said.

"The government. It seems to be in a state of flux."

"Explain," Riker's newfound friend demanded.

"The Speaker has resigned and Jus Renks Jus has seemingly assumed control of the Council. I was just asking if you still represent them."

Riker was taken aback by the news. No news had come over their communications channel during their travel, and he would have thought someone in the government—or even Picard—would have been in touch.

"I have not been notified of any change," Seer said coldly. "I am performing my duties with this representative from Starfleet."

"You seek this man's father," Caledon said.

"Yes, and we have reason to believe he is coming here or is here now."

"We have flashed his image to all of our officers, and it's currently posted to all the news screens, but we have had no reports of Kyle Riker being seen."

"Now we can't even predict his movements," Riker said in frustration.

"This was our first time," Seer said sympathetically. "We were as likely to be right as wrong."

"Well, I'm getting tired of being wrong," Riker said.

"Have you any further business with us?" Caledon asked.

"In a rush for us to leave?"

"No, Protocol Officer. However, whatever has happened to this planet has barely affected this city. We wish to keep it that way, and if Riker is responsible, we'd rather be vigilant than idle."

"We'll be off in a few minutes," Seer said. "Thank you for your service." Seer looked anything but happy with the officers, who stiffly marched off. Riker had to agree.

"We'll be off to where in a few minutes?"

Seer shook his head, clearly wondering the same thing. He returned to the flyer and immediately checked for messages from the Council. None were awaiting him, and at that he cursed rather loudly. As he began looking over maps of Tregor, including ones with the overlays they had recently obtained, Riker contacted Picard. The captain sounded as frustrated as Riker.

"I wish I had happier news to report, Number One," Picard said from the capital.

"Well, I'm getting the grand tour of the planet, but that's about it," Riker grimly admitted. "It's a nice place, with people working hard and trying to live in peace. No one's even bothered to notify Seer about Chkarad."

"Things are less than tidy here, I'm afraid. These people seem thoroughly inexperienced in a crisis."

"It's almost like they've never been challenged before," Riker noted.

"Indeed, Number One. I know you've been trying to guess your father's next move."

"If he knows I'm looking for him, he's making a game of it to prove something."

"By now he must know we're the ship in orbit . . ." Picard began.

". . . and that I'd be the one personally hunting him down."

"More than likely."

"Then I need to think like him, thinking about leading me on a wild goose chase," Riker speculated aloud.

"Quite likely."

"Are you sure you're not a counselor in disguise?"

"Last time I checked, Number One. Happy hunting. Picard out."

Seer was clearly lost in the conversation and patiently waited while Riker gathered his thoughts. It made perfect sense that his father would access the planet's data sources and learn the *Enterprise* was in orbit. That meant he would sooner or later go to ground, trying to outsmart his son. And now Riker had to think like the father he barely knew.

But Kyle knew that.

So it had to be Kyle outthinking the son he thought he knew.

"Can I check your maps?"

"Sure." He moved out of the way and let Riker sit at the main controls, as the first officer began plugging in information to be sorted.

"I'll need your help identifying likely locations for celebrations," Riker said as he busied himself. A feeling of anticipation had returned, and he tried not to let it govern his actions.

"Sure. Do you know where we're going next?"

Riker smiled.

"North."

Studdard wiped the sweat from his brow and cursed out loud. The communications center for Tregor had taken severe damage, and he wondered if it could be repaired while his team protected it. The mob that rioted and attacked the building had been dispersed an hour earlier, and he had seen to it those who had been injured were treated. The facilities staff had fled for the most part, but the security officer was also told that some had joined in.

"Studdard to Commander La Forge."

"La Forge."

"Can you spare someone to help assess the damage at the com center on Tregor?"

"Sure. Expect Lieutenant Taurik. La Forge out."

While Studdard waited for the engineer, he continued to look at the damage, shaking his head in bewilderment. "You mean to say they thought the media was hiding the truth?"

"Yes, sir," Caldwell, a young, blonde woman replied. "They said the broadcasts were skewed, that the Council had to know the truth, otherwise we wouldn't have been called in."

"Do you think that makes us targets, Lieutenant?" asked DeMato.

"Doubt it," he replied in his deep voice. He wiped at more sweat, this time cursing under his breath. Studdard disliked the heat most of all, followed by the sense of danger and the lack of concrete information. The confusion and anger and fear among the people made things way too unstable for his liking. One reason he signed on with Starfleet was for the structure and order it provided. Chaos was anathema to him, and this planet stank of it.

Taurik's lean form materialized moments later, and Studdard saw he carried the all-purpose tool kit. With a gesture, he had Caldwell escort the engineer into the building while indicating DeMato and Grigsby were to protect the entrance. He'd walk the perimeter and make certain things remained calm.

The building was an almost perfect circle, squat like much of the rest of the planet's architecture, and was made from a dark gray stone, perhaps a type of slate. It was built to last, he observed, with underground cables and microwave antennas positioned to work with satellites that orbited the planet. Some graffiti had been scrawled near a doorway, calling the Council liars, and Studdard made a disapproving noise as he passed.

Wherever the mob had gone, they were out of earshot, so Studdard appreciated the quiet as the day wore on. It was going to be better when the sun finished setting and the planet cooled off. He strongly disliked the heat and humidity, preferring cooler climes, and for that he envied Gracin's team on Osedah, farther north than his present location.

Everything seemed peaceful, a fact that caused Studdard concern. A mob had just been here. They were gone now, but the damage had been done and the paranoia that fueled it had not dissipated. The security officer quickened his pace, wanting to complete his circuit of the graffiti-covered communications center and hook up with Grigsby and DeMato by the main entrance. He figured it would take him another minute, maybe two, and along the way he scanned the nearby streets. The unnatural silence had his internal senses screaming a warning.

He continued to look at the concrete and brick buildings, now falling into shadow, and saw nothing in the doorways or windows. Studdard stopped short, straining his hearing. Voices. More than one, the words indistinguishable. He let out his breath and smiled. It was De-Mato laughing at a joke, so they were fine.

Then Studdard heard something else, a scrabbling sound against brick, and he whipped his head around, scanning every building, his hand tightening its grip on his phaser. Another sound, a scratching of some sort. Twisting his large form, he thought he saw a shadow atop a building behind him. He focused his gaze and was rewarded with a silhouette, its arm raised.

The concussive sound of a bomb went off a moment later, its shockwave carrying with it part of the building's wall. Studdard was still twisted around. He lost his footing and as he fell to the ground, he covered his head with his arms. Heavy pieces of slate fell on him. He knew there'd be bruising later.

Studdard lifted his head and saw the heavy figure rear back, ready to throw another explosive. He raised his phaser, took aim, and fired, hoping he was not too far away.

The crimson beam crossed the street at an upward angle and hit its target. The figure staggered, dropping the device. A moment later, an explosion rocked the roof of the building. Studdard knew that whoever was up there was most likely dead. He uttered a loud curse, not wanting anyone's death on his hands.

Grigsby rounded the corner, phaser at the ready. He gazed up at the smoking remains of the nearby rooftop, at the smoldering hole in the communications center's wall, and then at his lieutenant.

"These people are crazy," Grigsby said.

"No kidding," Studdard replied. "And we have to protect them from themselves."

As La Forge left engineering for an appointment, the shift change was beginning. Among the first to arrive was Anh Hoang; after all, she had nothing else pressing. Despite her session with Counselor Troi earlier, she hadn't given any thought to picking up her dancing or other hobbies. Normally, she used her free time to read and correspond with family, most of whom were still on Earth. Taurik, just back from effecting repairs to the media center on Tregor, waited patiently for the beta shift to arrive and take their positions before handing over command. While Yellow Alert had long since been canceled, it was prudent to follow protocol at shift turnover.

"Lieutenant, this engineering section is yours," Taurik said gravely. Actually, he always sounded grave, but Hoang knew that was endemic to his people.

"What do I need to know?"

"All systems are nominal. We remain at station keeping orbit."

"Heard we had a visitor," she said. While she didn't interact with her crewmates much, she did pay attention to the talk in the corridors or commissary.

"Yes, a Ferengi trader. It appears Commander La Forge is engaging his services to acquire the parts we lack."

"Sounds odd, doesn't it?"

"The commander seems to have a plan, and we will just have to trust him."

"If you say so," she said, and fell silent. Taurik nodded to her and left the section. She idly wondered what he did during his free time. Vulcans, she heard, preferred to keep to themselves. Meditation was popular, Anh knew. None danced, and no one questioned their motives.

She checked the status board and the tabletop schematic of the *Enterprise,* making sure every system was fine. With the warp engines not in use, she figured now would be a good time to make some modifications to the intermix chamber that might create a faster warp field. La Forge had approved the plan a few days earlier, much to her pleasure.

Grabbing a tool kit, she headed for the warp core, positioned in the middle of the section. It thrummed with energy, even in a passive mode, and acted as the ship's heartbeat. As she busied herself with tools and a tricorder, Hoang allowed her thoughts to turn to her conversation with Troi. Until the counselor raised the issue, she hadn't given any thought to dancing once again. Could she really have been closing off her entire life on Earth by joining the *Enterprise?* Was she betraying her family's memory by moving on? It took her months after the war ended before she could even make a decision as momentous as leaving Earth. One of the many grief counselors she spoke with had made the casual suggestion to put it all behind her, and Anh did so, literally, by requesting a ship assignment. Her commanding officer on Earth thought it would be a good idea to get some starship experience. Be good for her career, he said. What went unsaid was it would also be good for her to get away from the memories, let time heal the wounds.

She didn't feel wounded. She didn't feel much of anything. Her time in engineering seemed to be the only time she felt it was worth continuing. And she knew deep down that was not any way to live and she truly appreciated Troi's trying to help, but she had had enough of that kind of help on Earth.

Anh wanted to make a new life for herself on her own terms. If only she knew what kind of life she wanted.

"Can I go home now?"

Crusher looked over from the microscope, noticing she had remained in the same position for way too long and her back ached. The first Dorset woman was calling across the room, disturbing everyone's efforts. Using this as an excuse to get up and stretch, Crusher strolled over to the woman, who seemed uncomfortable on the bed. Crusher decided it was simply irritation that was making her squirm, because her biobed readings remained normal.

Despite the time invested, the doctor had little to show for her efforts, so she could sympathize with the woman's frustration.

"Soon," she told the woman.

"Now."

"I will be the judge of that, not you," Crusher said, adding steel to her voice. If the woman was going to cause trouble, she would be ready for it.

"What more do you want from me? You have my blood! Want my soul?"

"No thanks, I have one of my own," Crusher replied. She glanced at the other beds and noticed they were being watched. Nurses and technicians were also surreptitiously keeping an eye on things. Weinstein gave her a questioning look, asking about summoning security. Crusher shook her head no with as little movement as possible. She would handle this.

"We have a problem, and you are as much the solution as anyone else. Do you want to help your people?"

"Give me a gun or a pike and I'll help them! There's work to be done, to preserve our way of life. No more contamination from *them*."

"Us?" shouted a Bader woman from the other side of the room. She sat up, resting on her elbows, a look of disgust on her face. "You give us dung for music and boxes to live in and call it architecture. We've been as contaminated as you claim and I for one am sick of it!"

"And what will you do?"

"You will both settle down or I will have you restrained," Crusher shouted above the noise. "And if you continue to hurl insults, I will put you both to sleep. This is my domain and you will both abide by my rules of conduct." Turning to the Dorset woman who had started the argument, she said, "We show patience and manners. We use pleases and thank yous, and we show gratitude when someone helps us."

To the room in general, she added, "You're celebrating a century of unity, and that extends to sickbay. We are all working for a common goal, and don't forget that."

She stalked into her office, heard the door close, and, out of sight of the patients, allowed the tension to flow from her body. Her back still ached so she stretched it a little, hearing vertebrae make satisfying popping sounds. Regaining her composure was a quick process.

She toggled a control and within seconds, Weinstein came into her office. The nurse looked relieved to see Crusher calm.

"Well, that was certainly entertaining," Crusher said ruefully.

"You do have a convincing bedside manner," the nurse admitted.

"Took extra courses for it and everything. Give them an hour to cool off and then have them taken to different transporter rooms for beam-down to their original coordinates. Have each one escorted by whatever spare crewman you can find, the bigger and more intimidating the better."

"Excellent prescription," Weinstein said with a grin, and left.

Crusher sat back in frustration. There was nothing else to learn from the test subjects themselves, but their blood and cell samples would hold clues. She just needed to keep looking because that's what doctors did. No matter how maddening the people, no matter how long it was destined to take, a solution would be found. The violence didn't just arrive as a by-product of the celebration.

She just needed to keep focused, ignoring the belligerence and the increasing violence below her.

* * *

Morrow, carrying a borrowed phaser, insisted on escorting Chkarad back to his home. The former Speaker seemed no less relieved than when he was in office. When the ambassador attempted to converse with him, he gave monosyllabic replies. As they walked through the debris-strewn streets, they encountered no inhabitants. People remained behind closed doors, a fearful face occasionally appearing in an upper-story window. Smoke rose in thin columns from farther away, a stark reminder of the violence that continued to threaten the planet.

In his short career, Morrow had been to three riot-torn worlds, helped mediate two civil wars, and once got caught up in an embassy raid. A lot had happened to him and the rest of the diplomatic corps over the last few years. The Dominion War had stretched them beyond their limits, and like Starfleet, they had taken deep losses, usually at the hands of the Breen, the Founders' lapdogs. He could count at least a dozen friends who died when San Francisco was attacked. Since then, his promotions came through attrition, and his assignments grew more challenging. He actually thought coming to the celebrations on Delta Sigma IV would be a nice break, a change of pace from the tense negotiations that were usually required.

Colt Morrow smiled wryly to himself at the grim reality he faced, instead of the parties and fireworks.

By now, Morrow and Chkarad had turned several corners and were entering a residential section of the city. Brightly painted townhouses flanked only slightly less decorative office buildings and retail centers. There were certainly more plants and trees in evidence, making the area seem tranquil, almost an oasis from the madness. Not quite, though. Litter marred the streets, and two of the homes had been marked with racist graffiti.

Another turn, and Chkarad's pace quickened perceptibly. Morrow assumed this was the street he lived on with his wife and three children. The heavy Bader took five steps and then stopped dead in his tracks. The street was a cul-de-sac with a ring of four homes and a tall, leafy tree in the center. Windows had been shattered and three of the doors had been pried off their hinges or kicked in. Furniture had been splintered, the pieces hanging out of windows or marring the gardens. Clothing had been ripped, fixtures taken.

Chkarad stared in silence and then, resuming his shuffling gait, headed for the house farthest to the right, which seemed no more or less damaged than the others. Morrow began hoping that the Speaker's family had managed to flee before their home was ransacked.

A man stood in the doorway of Chkarad's ruined home, a haggard look on his face, his dull red clothes torn. Recognizing the home's owner, he didn't smile but began to cry. Chkarad tried to pass and enter his house, but the man, a fellow Bader, held his arms to stop him. They struggled in silence and Morrow hung back, sensing no malice from the man.

"I don't think you should enter, Speaker," the man said.

"I'm not Speaker anymore," Chkarad said slowly.

"Still, stay out here for now. People have been called."

"What people?"

The question was left unanswered as the man seemed to debate with himself. Finally he let out a deep breath and let go of the Speaker. Chkarad looked deeply into the man's eyes and then entered his home.

Morrow hung back, waiting to see when it would be appropriate to walk in. The man finally looked his way and shook his head slowly. Then, the ambassador knew what was within.

He entered, keeping the phaser in his pocket. It wasn't going to be needed. The hallway was bright with daylight, but the walls were marked up or gouged by furniture wrestled out of the house in haste. He paused a moment, listening for Chkarad, and realized the man was further up the hall, in the kitchen.

Morrow moved slowly, giving the Speaker time, but finally reached the entranceway and saw that the man had sunk to his knees. His family sat at the table. His wife was slumped in her chair. Her throat had been cut open, and her head hung back. A boy was slumped over, facedown in a bowl. A girl had been stabbed repeatedly and hung as limp as a rag doll in her chair. Another girl looked as if she had struggled. Knives had been used to pin her hands to the tabletop while another had been used to kill her.

Chkarad sobbed in silence, ignoring the bodies, oblivious to the manner in which his home had been stripped. After a minute, summoning up his strength, the ambassador returned to the hall and used his communicator to contact Picard. He asked for local police help and perhaps Counselor Troi.

He then staggered toward a sink and splashed water on his face, struggling to keep the bile down.

* * *

La Forge walked into stellar cartography and noted that their sector was projected on the huge circular screen. Data was at the master controls, continuing to input information, and therefore did not acknowledge his friend's presence. Knowing better than to interrupt, La Forge occupied himself with studying the stars, trying to recall as many as possible without designations.

"Ah, Geordi, I am glad you are here," Data said.

"I've been curious about this idea you've had," La Forge admitted.

"Out this far from the normal support of starbases, we need to provide a level of self-sufficiency most starships are unused to," Data explained. "I had determined that there are currently two dozen different starships spread over the nearest dozen sectors, all of which are more than several light-days from support starbases."

Data manipulated the controls, and a grid pattern now overlaid the stars, breaking them into the blocks of light-years that formed the sectors recognized by most star-faring races. He noted that Starbase 214 was their nearest supply base, and that was some distance away.

"Therefore, it makes sense for all ships in these sectors to share with one another their supply manifests and potential supply needs to see how much support we can offer one another."

"I see your point," La Forge said admiringly. "You want to go galactic. I could coordinate the efforts here, since we're the only ship stationary at the moment."

"A logical point," Data admitted.

La Forge thought about it a bit and nodded, smiling. "In fact, by channeling everything through us, it'd give me a chance to chat up the other engineers. A little off-the-record gossip here and there just might help convince people we're still right in the thick of things."

"You mean, convince them through unofficial means that the speculation regarding our collective competency is incorrect."

"Just what I said," La Forge said with a laugh. "Let's get started."

Picard needed action. Or progress. Something other than standing around and offering advice to the Council. Much of it had been taken in the hours since Chkarad resigned his post. Some of it was ignored or forgotten as people struggled to learn how to run a planet in crisis. He finally asked Christine Vale and Beverly Crusher to join him at the Council chamber for an update. Both women materialized within moments of each other, and he had to admit he had seen them look better.

Crusher looked strained, her eyes bright but her jaw set. The injuries treated on the *Enterprise* had clearly taxed her and her staff. The same held true for Vale, who had been literally around the world working on tactics with her people. He imagined how much worse things would have been had the starship not been in orbit.

"I heard about the Speaker," Crusher said by way of greeting.

"Morrow says he was devastated by the circumstances," Picard said sympathetically. The memory hung over the trio for several moments, none quite knowing what to say about the most horrifying example yet of what what happening to the planet.

"Lieutenant, how goes your work?"

"Fine, Captain," she said somberly. "We're stretched, and I've left only a few on-duty people on board in case something really bad happens. Fortunately, the crew doesn't seem to be affected by the liscom gas."

Picard looked expectantly at Crusher, who shrugged.

"From what I can tell, the liscom gas or any other element on the planet seems neutral to all life-forms on the ship. No chance of infection."

"Well, that's something," Picard concluded, hanging on to this news as the first positive thing to have happened all day. "Tell me what you've seen of the disturbances."

"Nothing's organized on a global scale," Vale reported. "It's all pockets of violence, ranging from bickering over fish to full-scale riots. There's no discernible pattern."

"Just to be safe, have your information sent to Commander Data for further analysis. Let's make sure we cross-check each other to see if there's anything we missed."

"Aye, sir," Vale said. She paused, running a hand through her short hair, and finally added, "You know, it's odd. The way things have been escalating, it seems as if these people have never done anything like this before. It's all very basic—street fights, mob mentality, looting, racial in some cases, socioeconomic in others. You ask me, these people have never been violent before."

Crusher stared at the security chief and then exchanged a look with Picard. He sensed this was a missing piece, a large one by the doctor's expression.

"Do you have records of the spread of violence?" Crusher asked.

Vale gestured to the monitor boards, which contained all

the available data. Crusher led the way and the trio went to one of the larger monitors. Several of the councillors, who had been talking among themselves, wandered over to see if something new was about to happen. The aide at the screen was instructed by the doctor to project the initial reports of violence with time codes. In seconds, the screens flickered and then a fresh map of the world appeared followed by purple lights, each with the time posted.

"Good. Now give me the second twenty-four hour period."

Again, the screen flickered as more purple lights dotted the map. Picard stood back, watching with interest. Morrow, who had been keeping to himself since returning from Chkarad's home, had joined the crowd watching the doctor at work.

"Okay, good. Now just give me a moment."

Crusher studied the screen, her right hand under her chin, the elbow resting on her left wrist. Everyone remained silent, but no one took their eyes off the screen.

"Can you project the cities Kyle Riker had visited during these times?"

"Yes, but it will take a little time to correlate."

"We don't have a lot of time, but do it," she instructed.

The man worked at the board and finally, after a tense few minutes, amber lights started to pop up. Several were nowhere near the violence. Murmurs broke out among the councillors. Picard himself was intrigued.

"See, Will was right. His father appears to be seeking out crisis points along the original string of violence," Crusher said. "Show us only the path from the test facility."

Another minute or so passed and then blue lights

winked on, replacing the amber and purple. It was a straight line heading west.

"I don't understand," Councillor Cholan said in a soft voice.

"This contagion has been spreading like a virus, but Kyle Riker has been following a singular path. He's been following the first victim, Bison."

"What is the significance of this?"

"The computer models show us how the virus has been spreading around the planet. It's extremely contagious and moves quickly. But Riker clearly has information we need, and here's the path he has taken."

"You think he has a cure?"

She shook her head, her red hair swinging freely. "No, that's my job," she said with finality. "I'm going back to the ship."

"What about the test subjects?" Renks called from the gaggle of people behind her.

"Whatever's happened has spread beyond them. They may have started it, but they're not the problem now." With that, she exchanged a deeply concerned look with Picard and then ordered herself back aboard the *Enterprise*.

Vale turned to look expectantly at Picard, while the captain stood with his arms folded, deep in thought.

"Is there some way Riker has been evading detection?" she asked.

"He's a clever man, Lieutenant," Picard answered. "Could be any number of ways. What would you do?"

Vale thought a moment and then suggested, "He stole one flyer, so clearly he knows how to operate them. He steals one, he might steal more."

The security chief walked over to an aide, who stood idly by a computer board. "Can you call up peace officer reports of all stolen flyers along the Riker path?"

"I guess so," she stammered.

"Don't guess, get started," she said. Then she looked over to Picard and got an approving nod.

"Are all the ports closed?" Renks asked an aide.

"Yes, Councillor."

"Any word on the curfew?"

"It's mostly being observed," another said from across the stage. "Those ignoring it are being escorted inside buildings by peace officers."

"And the violence?"

"Still spreading," the aide at the computer answered.

"Authorize the peace officers to use every means save lethal ones to restore order," Renks said. "Have them get volunteers to handle fires and other problems that don't require expertise. Rodak, please coordinate."

El Rodak El nodded her head and then gestured for two aides to follow her to another computer terminal. Renks nodded in satisfaction and continued giving instructions. Picard watched and approved. Finally someone was rising to a leadership position.

Morrow turned to the captain and quietly said, "Finally."

Picard smiled tightly.

Gracin left Smith to watch the monitoring station and took the other squad members with him to check out the incident they had been summoned to deal with. As people fled the nearest town, there was a tremendous accident.

Several flyers collided because people had abandoned recognized flight routes. Local emergency workers had cleared the dead and extinguished the fire, but one of the flyers had crashed near one end of a dam. With no one else available, the team was dispatched to ensure the dam was safe and that any survivors were rescued.

The smashed flyer was nothing more than corrugated metal with horribly twisted wings that would never again take to the air. Holding his phaser at the ready, Gracin scanned the scene with a tricorder and saw that the vehicle was empty. Satisfied there was no danger, he signaled for Locke to investigate the craft while he and Olivarez checked out the perimeter of the dam. They had known each other at the Academy and had even shared a bunk on numerous occasions. She was a big woman, with a ready smile, dimples, and constantly changing hair color. Today it was something close to fuchsia, and he was amazed Vale let it pass inspection.

"Where are they?" she asked him.

"Nothing on the tricorder."

Olivarez was a better tracker than he was, so Gracin let her take point, staying close behind her.

"Not a damned thing," Olivarez said after ten minutes of patrolling. Gracin grunted in response and they continued in the same direction. Locke jogged up to join them. Gracin got a signal on his tricorder, held up two fingers, and motioned for the others to follow. The lieutenant closed the tricorder and pocketed it, adjusting his grip on his phaser at the same time. He could feel himself tense up, ready for anything.

After another minute or two, they finally heard sounds

ahead: feet running on the ground. All three acknowledged the sound and fanned out, forming a V shape with Gracin now taking point. Up ahead, he spotted a bright yellow shirt and knew he had found his quarry. In fact, there were two shirts—one white, one yellow—and they were moving quickly but without purpose. Their motions indicated they were unharmed by the crash of the flyer. Neither looked armed.

They grew closer and finally Gracin decided to force the issue. He called out, asking the men to stop. Both were Dorset. They seemed surprised that anyone else was around. Their eyes grew wide when they saw three phasers aimed their way.

Walking toward them, Gracin flashed a brief smile and spoke. "We're from the Federation. You have nothing to worry about."

"Then why are you here?" one Dorset asked in a high-pitched voice. His fear was evident.

"No one is experimenting on anyone," Gracin said tiredly. "Are you hurt?"

"What's it to you?"

"If you're hurt, we have a medical kit."

"Well, we're fine, so go away."

"The dam area is restricted. We'll escort you back to the operations center where we can arrange a ride for you."

"Right to your labs!"

"No, to your homes. Or wherever else you'd like to go," Gracin said, now trying to control his frustration.

"We'll not follow you to our deaths!" the second Dorset shrieked. He hefted a rock and threw it in Gracin's direction.

As he bent to avoid the clumsy throw, Olivarez and Locke fired their weapons at the two men. They slumped forward, face down on the ground, stunned.

"Swell, now we have to haul them back to ops as is," Gracin grumbled.

An ensign arrived on the bridge and brought La Forge a padd but hesitated to hand it over. The engineering station on the port side of the bridge was covered with padds, and La Forge was using one hand to read a padd and one hand to stem the tide of falling padds. The ensign stood, indecisive, not wanting to interrupt her commanding officer.

At the tactical station, Jim Peart looked over and sighed. The deputy security chief was busily tracking the different teams on the planet, watching a bright blue signal pop from group to group. He took three quick steps to his left and grabbed the ensign by her right arm. "Come on, Ensign, he's only going to lose his place if you interrupt him," Peart said. Together, they grabbed the padds and began reorganizing them into neater stacks, no more than three high. Peart pointed to where each stack should go, muttering about rookies under his breath.

Finally done reading the manifest, La Forge looked up as if just noticing the others working beside him. He shrugged and tried to help but Peart slapped his right hand. "Oh no you don't," he admonished. "That's what you have ensigns for, to keep things organized. Okay, Ensign, finish up and see what else the commander needs. I'll give you a tip: initiative gets you noticed, smart initiative gets you promoted."

The ensign's face flushed and she didn't know what to say.

"You're welcome," Peart said, returning to his station.

Data, who had been watching, finally inquired how La Forge was doing with the supply inventories and requests.

"If I were a parts salesman, I could buy a moon," La Forge noted. "Every ship's needs are so different, so no two ships have the same inventory. Everyone needs something, some needs are even critical."

"Can we be of service?"

"I think so, but the trick will be getting parts from one ship to another. Looks like we'll have to put Dex under a long-term retainer until things straighten themselves out, and who knows how long that will take."

"It is a solution that has proven it can work, at least for the short term. In the meantime, we can begin making recommendations to the quartermaster's office."

La Forge continue to mull over the possibilities and began to like the notion of a dedicated courier. Why search for someone new each time parts needed to be moved? The trick would then be to organize the routes to maximize the single ship's time. In turn, they could continue to upgrade and modify the Ferengi vessel or find other items to trade. He'd certainly be willing to give it a try.

"Well," he finally said, "it's an original approach."

"Quite true," Data said, returning his gaze to the control panel before him.

La Forge put down the padd and was ready to pick up another when he finally noticed the ensign standing before him. Her presence surprised him and his expression must have shown that. The ensign frowned.

"Have I done something wrong, sir?"

"No, not at all, Ensign," La Forge said, racking his brain to recall her name. She had transferred aboard only recently. But if he could recall the location of every ODN conduit, he could remember one name.

"Listen . . . Conners . . . can you take all these padds down to the conference room next to engineering? I'll finish my work there next shift," he said, sounding more confident by the word.

"Absolutely, sir," she said, and started gathering the padds.

"The Riker line extends back hundreds of years and we've always been soldiers," Riker explained to Seer as they flew away from Tregor. The trip north was made difficult by strong headwinds that forced the native to adjust his flight path.

"When my world was made up of competing countries, one of the largest was called the United States of America, forged by a people who declared themselves independent and fought to prove it. In every major conflict, a Riker served, so over the generations, there's been an expectation that we'd continue the tradition. And when humans made it into space, Rikers were there. After a race known as the Xindi made a preemptive attack on Earth, a Riker helped lead the defensive forces while *Enterprise* went off to confront the attacker."

"So, Rikers have been a part of Starfleet, too," Seer said.

"Yep," Will replied, leaning back in the passenger chair. "The family's thinned out with time, and I'm the only one serving." He didn't think Thomas's brief stint worthy of mention.

"Do you have children to carry on?"

An innocent question but one that Riker was never comfortable with. While he was far more at ease with children than Picard ever was, Riker never imagined himself a father. Part of that was the drive and ambition that got him through the Academy and launched a career. Another part—the largest part if he was to be honest with himself—was the fear of being as bad a parent as his own father. In fact, when Riker had looked back over the family history, more than one male Riker had proven a failure at child rearing. Yet, there were women to love those men, women willing to make lives and families with them and let the family line continue. Years ago, during his romance with Troi on Betazed, he fleetingly imagined having children with her, and the thought didn't horrify him. He later had other relationships, others he loved, and never once had he imagined children with them. Only with Deanna.

Being career officers in Starfleet presented complications, especially in these darker days when civilian families no longer lived among Starfleet crew aboard the larger starships. The Federation had been buffeted and needed to adjust and that put a priority on duty and protection at the expense of a more enlightened view of exploration.

Yet, with each passing year, and the first signs of gray in his beard—which he hadn't noticed until he allowed it to grow back recently—the notion that the family tradition was being threatened by time had begun to preoccupy his thoughts. He refused to just have children to extend the line, but his romance with Troi opened up those possibilities all over again.

Seer asked a simple question but presented him with both simple and complicated answers.

"No, not yet," he finally said, refusing to meet Seer's eyes.

The pilot must have sensed that this was an uncomfortable topic and changed the subject. "Since we live much shorter lifespans than you humans, we have many many more ancestors to recall and trace. My family is one of the unfortunate ones, only looking back twenty-three generations."

"What do you mean?"

"An internal conflict on Bader caused untold devastation across one continent, including the destruction of my family's Memorial. One way we measure status is the ability to trace the familial line, so twenty-three generations is a fairly short span compared with the more prosperous families. Some can go back hundreds of generations. They're the ones who opposed colonization. They didn't want new families starting up, beginning their own dynasties that might one day compete with them."

"And what happened? How did you manage to get free of the planet?"

"Those most highly placed in society were so few, they couldn't stop the masses, most of whom wanted to see what the heavens were hiding. We, too, consider ourselves explorers. Delta Sigma IV is hopefully only one of many colony worlds to come for my people."

Riker listened and nodded, fascinated at hearing another race's hopes and dreams. There wasn't a lot of the belligerent pride that the Bader were known for in his tone, but something more enlightened. This planet had certainly been an excellent experience for the Bader, so he continued to wonder exactly what the problem was.

The two rode along in companiable silence for several minutes until Seer began adjusting controls and Riker felt the ship begin to descend.

"Problem?"

"Port stabilizer is acting up and it needs tending. Since I have to land anyway, we'll refuel. Sorry, but this will delay us a little."

Riker smiled. "Not to worry, stretching my legs will be good. Where will we land?"

"Right below is a town with the facilities I need. Shouldn't take us more than an hour if the problem is what I think it is."

"So, you're a mechanic, too?"

"My father was. Taught me on earlier models so I have a good ear for identifying problems. The systems are too complex today for me to fix on my own." Seer fell silent, clearly thinking back to those earlier times.

"Is your father still around?"

"No, he joined the creators about four years ago. A good solid thirty-seven years and he went with no regrets," Seer said, the affection obvious in his voice.

Happy thoughts of his father were as alien to Riker as living to a hundred was to Seer.

The flyer wobbled a bit as gravity exerted its hold, but the landing went smoothly enough. People in coveralls came over to the ship and Seer explained the problem. It turned out that another ship was almost done and they could fit in the protocol officer's flyer ahead of the others. Riker appreciated the respect his companion's title finally earned them. Several of the workers were studying Riker closely, a natural reaction given his human appearance. He ignored the looks and did as promised, stretched his legs by walking around the flyer and checking out the flying field. It was a square space, lined with hangars to store or repair flyers, most of which were larger or newer than the one Seer used. Launch pads dotted the space in the middle and seven other vessels sat, either just having landed or preparing to launch.

He also used the opportunity to report in to Data, learning that nothing new was happening aboard the *Enterprise*. Picard was working with the new Council Speaker, and Riker was saddened to hear how the violence touched Chkarad's family. Out of Seer's earshot, he inquired about the protocol officer's family and was relieved to hear all were safe. He was also pleased to hear Vale had made it planetside and was personally directing her forces. She was a good, solid officer and he liked her approach, casual on the outside but steel on the inside.

And it was her detective skills that turned up a second pattern for Kyle Riker: the stolen flyers. Their locations matched the western spread of these mysterious interruptions to the violence. Will Riker had additional justification for his decision to head in this direction.

"Tell me more about where we're going," Riker suggested to Seer as he rejoined his new friend.

"From what you described, if your father has truly retreated north to environs similar to your home, there are several large islands near the ice caps that would fit the description. We'll fly up there and check them. Most are uninhabited this time of year so any bio-sign will be cause for suspicion."

"Good fishing up that way?"

"I suppose. I really don't know much about it."

Riker laughed, clapping his hands together. "We'll have to fix that. You can't imagine the feeling of tranquility you get just standing there, the sun on your back, your line in the water, and it's just you and nature. Great thoughts happen or big fish get caught. Either way, it's a terrific way to relax."

"Sounds a little boring to me," Seer said. "No offense, Will."

"None taken, because you haven't tried it for yourself yet," Riker replied with a grin. "When this is all over, if time permits, we'll get you outfitted and spend a morning."

"Why do you think your father is headed north?"

"I'm betting he's drawn to familiar environs," Riker mused.

Seer seemed less certain than Riker, but clearly Riker's enthusiasm would win over the Bader bureaucrat. The two men continued to walk and talk, sharing observations about other leisure activities as the workers repaired the flyer. Sure enough, just over an hour after landing, they were ready to take off. Seer thanked the men, signed an official chit assuring them the government would pay for their services, and they were cleared for takeoff.

The departure was far smoother and the whine in the engine seemed diminished. Even some of the dirt had been wiped off, exposing some more of the crimson paint. Seer seemed happy with the way the craft handled as he moved this way and that, checking the repair work. Riker enjoyed watching the man delight in something as simple as checking out a repair job. Seer then oriented the flyer to the north and once more they were on their way.

Flying low for a bit to stay under the winds, Seer and Riker did more sightseeing. A thick plume of smoke on the horizon caught their attention and without stopping to ask, Seer angled them toward it and increased the thrust. As they approached, he checked communications frequencies, listening through an earpiece and frowning. Riker chose to remain quiet but could read the man's expression well enough to know that what they would find was going to be bad.

Sure enough, as they circled the smoke, it turned out to be a village in flames. Riker couldn't make out the architecture through the smoke, and the people fleeing the streets were a mix of Bader and Dorset. Bodies littered the streets and were being driven into the pavement as people ran over them. What fire suppression systems there were could not possibly be enough to save the village. Riker could discern no pattern to the fire's spread and suspected there were multiple points of origin. Ground vehicles and the occasional flyer emerged from the smoke, and at one point Seer had to veer out of the way of a vessel that flew within several feet of them.

"What happened?" Riker finally asked after they had flown once around the village.

"From what I can tell, there was a fight that turned into a riot that turned into this," Seer explained. "It's horrible. Countless dead, the entire village already being considered a loss."

Riker looked once more out the window and was reminded once more that this was more than personal, more than father and son. An entire planet was at risk.

Chapter Eight

SICKBAY HADN'T BEEN so filled with the smell of burning flesh since she could hardly remember when. No. Wait. She could remember. It smelled like this, and for that matter, looked and sounded like this during the war. Crusher tried to shut out the chaos so she could concentrate on closing a wound on a Bader woman's shoulder. The seriously injured who were far from hospitals were being beamed to the *Enterprise* as part of the coordinated efforts to keep panic to an absolute minimum. Members of her staff were summoned to the surface by Vale's people when necessary.

The first serious cases started arriving only a few hours ago. Some form of ordnance struck a cabin in a wooded area and a family was caught in the resulting conflagration. Alerted by the Council, the *Enterprise* transporter crew had beamed the survivors right to sickbay, where they were being treated with a gel that would reduce the chance of infection.

Since then, Crusher had dealt with broken bones, a cracked skull, a gouged eye, one ear ripped off, a piece of metal spike imbedded in a leg, and numerous other problems. Her staff was being rapidly depleted as more and more cases required attention. From what she could tell, Wasdin and her people were stretched to their limits, their ability to travel impeded by the fighting. Meanwhile, Dorset and Bader doctors had stopped communicating with one another, which did nothing to help the situation.

On top of it all, she was kept from her research, and she felt that every second saving a life was another second the mystery disease had a chance to spread and cause more destruction. She hoped her subconscious mind was sifting through the data and would help provide her with a solution. It was at moments like this that she envied Data's ability to apportion parts of his amazing positronic brain to work on different tasks simultaneously.

When she finished suturing a wound caused by debris falling on an elderly man, Crusher forced herself back to her office and slumped into her desk chair. Calling up her staff roster on the desktop, she checked where everyone had been sent and who was left. Reluctantly, she put every member of the medical and science staff on full alert and started scheduling rotations so those on the surface could come back for food and rest or simply more supplies.

Her nostrils involuntarily flared when she smelled coffee, and she raised her head wearily to see a yeoman in her doorway. She was young, probably new to the ship, and they had not been introduced.

"You're an angel," Crusher said, accepting the cup.

"Commander Data's suggestion," the woman replied, all business. "He was noting how busy your department was and assigned a few of us to bring refreshments to your staff."

"I'm going to put that android in for a commendation," the doctor muttered between sips.

"I didn't know the CMO could do that."

"We normally can't, but I can certainly try. And you are . . . ?"

"Vasha Massaro."

"That's a lovely name," Crusher said with a warm smile.

"Thank you. When I came aboard Dr. Tropp did the medical workup," the yeoman explained.

"Not to worry, with so many to keep track of, I can't meet them all the first few months. Although I am sorry not to have met someone as thoughtful as you."

Vasha looked down for a moment and hesitated before replying, "I've been on board for a year, ma'am."

"My God, I'm so sorry," Crusher said quickly. A year and she hadn't met the woman. How was that possible? She prided herself on knowing the crew one way or another even if it took her some time to meet them. But a year was quite out of the ordinary.

"Well, I have been pretty healthy," the young woman said.

"That's still no excuse," Crusher quickly added. "Which department are you normally associated with?"

"Communications, but we're a pretty small group."

Crusher nodded, sipping at her coffee, which tasted nice and hot and came just in the nick of time. "I'd love to chat more, but patients await and it looks like there will be no end to them."

"I completely understand. After all . . ."

Her thoughts were interrupted by a shrill beep that alerted Crusher to another crisis. The doctor swiveled her desktop display to a better angle and activated it with her thumb.

"We have seventeen critical cases to beam aboard!"

Crusher rose from her chair. The medic's face was so grimy that it took her a moment to recognize him as the Bandi named Isthit.

"What the hell happened?"

"All we heard was a whistle, and then a building exploded near our position. It was an apartment complex. These people are the only survivors, and we can't help them because we're out of supplies."

"Transporter room, this is Crusher. Scan this transmission, lock on, and beam the injured in twos to sickbay. We'll clear bio-beds." She was out of her office helping to clear space for the new patients before the transporter chief had time to acknowledge her order.

"Seventeen incoming, get ready!" she snapped to everyone within earshot. Seconds later, the first two bodies materialized on the freshly cleared beds. One was a middle-aged Dorset woman, her right hand missing and blood trickling from the severed veins. The other was a corpulent older man, with something wedged into his abdomen—she couldn't tell from the blood and caked-on gore.

"Weinstein, with me," Crusher called as she looked at the stomach. The item was ceramic, a shard of something from within the man's apartment, no doubt. Her medical scanner was already probing the area while the man alternately groaned and whimpered. Weinstein waved a sterilization tool around the wound and additional abrasions farther up his chest. Her free hand was slowly peeling away shredded portions of the man's gownlike garment.

Massaro returned with her arms laden with gowns. She dumped them against a wall, grabbed two, and helped Crusher and Weinstein into fresh ones.

"How can I help?"

"Bring me the medical kit over there," she said, jerking her head toward a table. The yeoman was there and back quickly and opened the case. Crusher grabbed a hypo, checked the settings, and delivered a dose of painkiller to the man.

"I have multiple veins cauterized," Tropp called from the adjoining table.

"Seal the wound and dress it, then clear the bed," Crusher called. "What's with the girl?"

A meditech examined the body, waving a medical scanner again and again over the limp form, but he shook his head. "I have no idea!"

"I'll be there when I can," she called back. Her staff was competent, but there were times they seemed too new or too inexperienced to make the quick diagnosis that might be the difference between life and death. Could she do a better job training them if she were back on Earth? She angrily shook the thought from her mind, focusing on the here and now.

The transporter hum filled the room, and two more arrived. Her staff quickly took readings, and Crusher could hear them call back and forth for supplies and tools. She herself had been carefully probing the foreign object sticking out of her patient. The screen above the bed indicated a normal Dorset form, and Crusher figured she'd have to tend to damaged reproductive organs once the object was gone. With a snap, a sterilization field was activated and she gingerly stuck a finger into the wound, alongside the object. The man grunted in his sleep but didn't move.

"Yeoman, bring me the portable scanner from the next room. It's blue and boxy," Crusher called. "Weinstein, we're going to lift this directly up. Can you reach underneath when I lift it, and take the damned thing?"

"Absolutely."

"Good girl. Here we go." The object may have been firmly impacted, but with a little wiggling with her fingers, it moved. Blood and other fluids helped the doctor, although the damage would be extensive when fully exposed. The heavy foreign object moved incrementally, and she didn't dare go too fast for fear of dropping it and causing further damage. At that moment, she wished she had a Dorset doctor with her, or was performing this at a Dorset hospital where replacement organs might be obtained.

The object made a plopping sound as it finally cleared the belly. It dripped ichor on the deck before Weinstein's hands snatched it away. Crusher by then had already wiped her hands and grabbed the probe from the yeoman, who, to her credit, remained nearby. Quickly, Crusher used the probe to look deep into the wound to get a sense of the organ damage.

"I still can't find anything wrong with this patient," the doctor who was treating the unconscious teenage girl called out.

Crusher stifled a biting comment and then took a deep breath. She needed the best diagnostician besides herself, much as she loathed him. "Nurse Weinstein, have transporters reroute the remaining patients to Dr. Tropp. I'm calling the EMH."

There was a brief pause in sickbay as all work stopped and every pair of eyes turned toward their commanding officer.

"Knock if off," she said tartly. "Computer, activate the Emergency Medical Hologram."

In seconds, a balding humanoid form in current Starfleet uniform appeared.

"Please state the nature of the medical emergency," the hologram said in a clipped voice.

"The patient at bed five defies diagnosis. Please study and advise," Crusher called while removing the probe.

The EMH made a quick study of the body and checked the overhead display. As he did his work, Crusher returned her attention to the wound before her. Two organs were definitely pulped beyond repair. One was a secondary organ, and he could survive without it. The other was the sole kidney, and that needed replacement. She called for a portable dialysis machine, and Weinstein hurried for the item. Crusher then used her fingers to very carefully feel the surrounding organs and tissue. There seemed to be lacerations that could be closed and nothing else life-threatening.

"Yeoman, the blood infuser to your left, please."

Massaro grabbed the pistol-like device and handed it over without a word. Crusher was appreciating this woman more and more, and made a mental note to actually have a conversation with her when this was all over.

As Crusher worked methodically, sealing the lacerations and making sure the blood system worked, she called out to her other teams working on cases nearby. Despite drills and training, most of her staff had never seen anything quite like this. The *Enterprise* avoided the bloodiest battles during the Dominion War. Even the disasters on Dokaal weren't quite as insane as this. She'd have to make a study of their performance and figure out which ones would need additional drilling as time allowed. But first, she had to finish attaching the dialysis device. And she had to do it quickly since she was needed elsewhere in her domain.

"Neural stimulator!"

"I need more plasma!"

"Laser scalpel!"

"This one's ready to move out. Orderly!"

"I'm losing this one!"

At that, Crusher snapped the final connection and tapped a control, activating the dialysis machine. She hurried over, and from what she could tell, one of the people had a crushed head with bits of skull broken away. The brain was swelling faster than the medic could treat it, and the body could not take the strain. Nothing in sickbay could save this life. She slowly closed her eyes, and, taking the cue, Weinstein quickly covered the head with the sheet and snapped her fingers for an orderly. The bed had to be cleared, the body tended to in an adjoining room.

People moved, sometimes as blurs, other times gingerly. Crusher kept looking up and down, watching her room hum. The other sickbay, on deck twelve, was also keeping very busy, but Tropp was good and confident in his skills, and she appreciated having another experienced doctor down there. Once this patient was finished, she'd have to check in with them. In fact, unless she was specifically required, she was going to have to circulate. Seventeen-plus cases were just too many to juggle on top of the ones already in sickbay. She finished as quickly as she could, then joined the EMH at the bedside of the comatose patient.

He made irritating humming noises, rested his chin on his fist, and circled the body.

"The patient is suffering mental trauma," he announced. "Obviously," he added with typical unnecessary smarminess. Crusher gritted her teeth. Weren't there enough arrogant humanoid doctors in the universe? Did Starfleet really have to add arrogant holographic doctors to the mix?

"She has retreated within herself and won't come out until she gets the sense that everything is fine. If she recovers at all," the EMH continued.

Nice attitude, Crusher thought. She looked at the lithe, young body and found herself stroking the flowing dark hair. Then she glanced at the overhead monitor. Much as she hated to admit it, she was forced to agree with her holographic colleague. "An extreme defense mechanism."

"Absolutely."

"Let's get her out of sickbay into an unused area."

"Well, it's not likely we'll need the brig," the EMH suggested.

She frowned at the hologram, but acknowledged he probably had a point. Not that she was going to satisfy his ego by stating the fact. Instead, she signaled to an orderly and gave the instruction.

"Am I required further?"

"Please send yourself to deck twelve and see what you can do to help until I arrive," Crusher said, tired of seeing him.

"As you wish." He blinked once, and then his form vanished. Seconds later, the young girl was taken from sickbay, and the bed was immediately sprayed down to prep it for the next patient.

She knew there'd be someone along very shortly.

With the destroyed village now an hour behind them, Riker and Seer flew on. The protocol officer checked in with members of his staff and the news media, learning how bad things were getting. Riker, meanwhile, confirmed the official reports with Vale, who sounded breathless, exhilarated, and terrified all at the same time. A part of him wanted to work alongside her, do something more productive than fly over the devastation, but he had his own mission.

Riker and Seer were finally nearing the edge of the Tregor continent and were approaching the large islands that might be hiding Kyle Riker. They had hoped they would outrun the disturbances and find relative calm, but the cities and towns they had flown over on their way all reported troubles. Crusher had as much as confirmed that with her latest update, indicating that at least half the planet could be infected with . . . whatever it was.

Still, the sights were breathtaking.

The last city was behind them and they were flying over a thick forest that extended like a border for as far as Riker could see. The trees were an almost uniform shade of deep green, so thick he couldn't tell one from another. After a few minutes, they cleared the forest and were over plains that extended for maybe a hundred kilometers. He thought he spotted herds of animals grazing or running here and there.

And then there was the sea. It beckoned blue-green, gentle waves lapping against a distant sandy shore in parts, the land ending as cliffs in other parts. Not a person or animal in sight. It was as if they were the first explorers to the planet and nature was welcoming them in its glory. For a moment, Riker allowed himself a moment to enjoy the sight and its sheer beauty.

As they crossed from land to water, Seer changed course to northwest and added thrust. Within minutes, the first of several islands appeared, huge and brown with hills or mountains that were snow-capped. Seer pointed past Riker and identified a large animal with very long fur, a fish wriggling in its mouth.

"Riker to Data."

"Enterprise *here, Commander.*"

"We're currently flying over a series of islands to the north. Can you conduct scans for any Bader or Dorset life-signs?"

"One moment. We are detecting life-signs on three of the nine islands in the area."

The landmass directly beneath them was one of nine, or so Seer said. It formed a sovereign community and was inhabited primarily by Bader, although about a third of the people were Dorset. As one would expect, fishing was the mainstay of the economy. As they neared, Riker saw docks and ships of various sizes. A few were still out on the water, not far from the island.

"Fly over before we land," Riker suggested.

"Aye, aye, Commander," Seer replied.

They flew once around the island's perimeter, descending to get a good view. They spotted a rally near a dock, but it seemed small and generally peaceful. However the disease was being passed, Riker assumed that these people were protected by their relative isolation. How long that protection might last was unknown.

"Should we land?"

"Something doesn't feel right," Riker said, going with his instincts.

"What do you mean?"

"It's peaceful, they keep to themselves, and they're fisherfolk. I don't think he's here."

"You have an instinct about this?"

"I do. He'd been heading in this general direction, but this isn't his destination. I think he's looking for Alaska."

"Alaska. That's your home, right?"

"Yeah, and we need to find its analogous location here."

Seer thought for a moment and then asked Riker to call up information on Alaska on the tricorder. Riker complied and while the flyer hovered for a minute, the pilot studied the information, then compared it with navigational charts on the computer.

"I think I've got it. One place, not far, has what you want."

"Fly on," Riker instructed.

Something soothing and cool.

That's all Troi had on her mind as she walked into Ten-Forward. While things continued to churn on the planet below, Picard had decided Troi could get some rest. There was little more she could do with the Council, and the hours exposed to the harsh emotions had definitely worn her down. She doubted she was performing at her best as day wore on and was privately grateful for the respite. Even though it was late based on the capital's time, she figured she had been awake for nearly twenty-four hours.

The lounge was busy since much of the crew had little to do while the medical and security staffs were pressed into service. Department heads had granted additional leave time, which was no doubt appreciated by the crew. Chatter seemed light and felt comforting compared to the roiling feelings on the planet.

Jordan was bartending tonight, one of the few non-Starfleet crew these days. He was tall and handsome, though his good looks were marred by a prematurely receding hairline, giving him a sharp widow's peak. His laugh carried across the room as Troi saw him share a joke with three patrons. The laughter sounded good, and she hoped to hear a joke herself. Ten-Forward was a reflection of its manager, and while Guinan had served with the *Enterprise,* it was serene and hospitable. Under Jordan, it was a little rowdier, and the crew responded well to it.

As he spotted her, she gave him a welcoming smile. He was already reaching behind him for a glass. By the time she arrived at the bar, he was pouring something light green. He added two ice cubes, stirred the drink, and handed it to her.

Without a word, she took a sip and grinned.

"How did you know?"

"You looked like you could use a Talerian fizz," he said. "Well, actually, people were saying how tough it was down there, and I guessed."

"You guessed right," she replied and leaned against the bar. "It is tough down there, and I think it's going to get tougher."

"They find the commander's dad yet?"

"No."

"Dr. Crusher figure this out yet?"

"No."

"Want to come back to my cabin after you finish this?"

She smiled broadly. "No."

"Just making sure you knew what you were doing and your sanity remains intact," he said with a laugh. Almost every time he served her, it included an invitation back to his quarters, and while flattering, both knew it was harmless. Jordan was young for her, and the entire crew knew she and Riker had reunited. And he was wise enough never to ask her when Will was anywhere within earshot.

They chatted amiably about crew gossip, which she appreciated since it helped clear her mind. And, as ship's counselor, she needed to keep her finger on the pulse of the crew. Jordan was an invaluable resource that she consulted on many occasions. It was he who recently pointed out to her that the crew was feeling unsettled after the recent encounters. She started paying attention to corridor conversation and sure enough, the crew was expressing their apprehension over their reputations out loud.

The drink was everything she wanted and the conversation was diverting. As a result, she was acutely aware of her body relaxing, a sign of how tense things had gotten.

"Excuse me, Counselor, do you have a moment?"

The speaker was Dasan Malak, an unjoined Trill who worked in systems maintenance. They had spoken a few times in the past, usually about problems with his parents back home. He was stocky for a Trill and he wore his hair close-cropped, accentuating the dark brown spots that framed his neck and face.

Troi, inwardly sighed, gesturing him toward an empty table near one of the windows. As they sat, she looked at Delta Sigma IV and imagined where Picard, Riker, and Vale were, all working into the late hours. She knew she needed her rest and wondered when they would get their turn.

"How can I help you, Ensign?"

"Can you help me accelerate my transfer request? I just found out about an opening on the *Bonaventure* that's ideal for me."

"You've requested a transfer?" He was yet another one looking to leave a tainted ship—not at all surprising but disturbing nonetheless.

"Yes, filed it this morning and then I got a com from a buddy from the Academy. It's a senior technician spot that I would love to get."

"You've been doing exemplary work here, so why the desire to change ships?"

"Well, I . . . that is . . . well, with the ship hated by Command . . ."

"It's not hated by Command," she said emphatically. "We were cleared of all charges, as was Captain Picard. You're letting rumors affect your judgment, which I think is extremely unfortunate. Before you do anything rash, I think you should at least sleep on it, and we can schedule a meeting when this is over."

He fidgeted, his hands running over his thighs, and

he seemed ready to bolt from the chair. She sipped her drink, which suddenly didn't seem as satisfying as before. Her quarters and her soft bed seemed more in order.

"Reputation counts for so much, don't you think? There are hundreds of techs on starships across the quadrant, so captains have to look past service records. It comes down to the written evaluations and scuttlebutt. It's like Nafir, that troublemaker who transferred aboard a few weeks back. He's a misfit and they didn't know where to stick him so they gave him to the poisoned starship."

"And you think starship captains rely more on gossip than on a man's record?"

"And you don't?"

Troi paused. She wanted to give the official statement that of course only records mattered in such personnel decisions, but she'd lose his confidence by claiming something that no one believed. Of course scuttlebutt counted for a lot. She flashed back to the conversation she had with Riker regarding some of the crew transfers on and off the *Enterprise* and knew such gossip affected her impressions before meeting people.

"I'll admit it has a role, but every captain interprets such information differently. Captain Picard, for example, rarely lets such information affect his decisions."

"But doesn't Commander Riker make the majority of those decisions? He seems more likely to believe the gossip."

"If he believed all the gossip he's heard over the years,

I suspect we'd have a very different crew," she said confidently. "Instead, he's developed a strong filter and it has served him well."

The Trill paused, letting the conversation sink in, and he seemed to be considering his situation. Troi hoped she would prove effective because if more members of the crew bought into the belief that the *Enterprise* was an unofficially tainted ship, then it would become a disastrously self-fulfilling prophecy. As he considered, she thought back over Malak's service record—specifically why he left Trill to join Starfleet—and also what she knew of the *Bonaventure*'s upcoming mission.

"I can see why you'd want to take this transfer," she said, "given where the *Bonaventure*'s headed."

He snapped his head up, startled. "What do you mean? I thought they were exploring Sector 212-B."

"They've just finished that. Now they're being reassigned to Trill for the next nine months." She favored him with a pleasant smile. "You'll get to go home."

Not only did he not return the smile, but he looked downright depressed. "Uh, yeah, that's great."

"So, shall I expedite the transfer request? It is, as you said, a great opportunity for you."

"Maybe not, Counselor, I, uh, need to think about this some more."

Malak rose and moved away, letting Troi consider herself victorious. The ensign had joined Starfleet in part to get away from Trill, and she doubted he would greet spending nine months there with any enthusiasm. He might still request the transfer, but at least he would consider all the options, not just the fact that he'd be leaving the "tainted" *Enterprise*. That was the best she could hope for until the current assignment was concluded.

Reaching for the remainder of her drink, she glanced across the room and spotted Anh Hoang sitting by herself, looking out the window. The engineer was another cause that required her time and attention, but she was too tired to strike up another one-sided conversation. Instead, she watched Hoang's posture, the half-drunk glass on the low table, and the way she sat in public but clearly invited no contact. Disturbing as Troi found this, she needed to get to her cabin.

She nodded once, with thanks, to Jordan and strolled out of Ten-Forward, recognizing how much was left unsettled. It rankled her, but for a change, there was little she could do.

Standing alongside Morrow off to the side of the Council chamber, Picard sipped at a cup of bittersweet local tea and watched the Council inaugurate its new Speaker, Jus Renks Jus. Immediately after the ceremony Renks started taking notes and passing on instructions. There was nothing elegant about his style. Instead, it was perfunctory, almost cold. Then again, given the circumstances, he just might be what was needed at the moment.

"Population affected?"

"Forty-seven percent is the current estimate," an aide replied.

"When we tip sixty percent, we can give up," Renks said. Picard had no idea where the new Speaker came up with the number, but it made a certain amount of sense. By then, containing that much violence was going to be impossible, even if the full crew of the *Enterprise* were at the Council's disposal.

"Speaker," Councillor Cholan began, "given the difficulties caused by this disease, we need to mete out some form of justice to those behind it."

"You mean the Federation? We can't punish our own government," Renks replied.

"It's not our government," another councillor argued. "We are there by choice. This Council is your government. The Federation solved one problem and caused another."

"We still don't know what caused this," yet another councillor said.

"We know that it began when Riker brought the test subjects back here," Cholan insisted. "Riker must be responsible for this. Why else would he have fled?"

"But the doctor has demonstrated that Riker wasn't responsible when he arrived."

"He was, however, involved in the initial research to our problem," Cholan continued more loudly. "I want someone held accountable for this!"

Morrow looked at Picard with alarm. The captain remained silent, not willing to insert himself in the matter, content to let Renks lead. He suspected, however, the Council was not going to remain immune to the problem engulfing their world.

Fortunately, they had not yet found Kyle Riker, so the demand for his head was a pointless one.

"I think now might be a good time for us to retire for the night. Let them deliberate without us watching over their shoulders. You've had a very difficult day, Ambassador."

"Perhaps tonight I will take you up on your offer of a cabin."

Chapter Nine

"NOW THIS IS MORE like it," Riker said as the flyer banked around a snowcapped mountain. The snow covered much of the ground at the farthest northern edge, but as Seer brought the flyer around, the snow receded and brown tundra was revealed. There were scattered small villages, wild animals roaming, and to Riker it felt like he was home.

Or close enough.

"He's down there."

"I'll accept that," Seer said agreeably. "But where?"

"Good question. It'd have to some place he could have reached easily through some form of mass transit."

Seer checked the onboard computer and adjusted their course toward a small city. It was the most likely spot for a visitor to the region and from there, he could have headed in any number of directions. But they could start at the city and hunt from there. He requested permission to land at a small strip, and within minutes they were down.

"It's a little on the chilly side," Seer said, checking the onboard sensors.

"And you have no gear for it, right?"

"It's not like I woke up this morning, expecting to be this far north," Seer admitted.

"Of course not. We can purchase gear in town if we really need it, right?"

"Sure. The Council's credit is good everywhere."

"Everywhere but my poker table," Riker quipped. The two emerged from the vehicle and went to check in with the control tower. Seer showed his credentials and began asking questions, trying to learn if, by luck, anyone saw a human nearby. No one, of course, had, but they were directed to the local peace officers' headquarters.

On the short walk, Riker noticed the bite of the cold, crisp air, and while he enjoyed it, he recognized he'd need gear to stay on the hunt for long.

Inside the austere building, they were greeted with gruffness by the local officer in charge. The two men walked in and approached a small circular table with one uniformed woman behind it, who was engrossed in something on screen. She paid them no attention while the two stood silently. Seer clapped his hands loudly, generating enough noise to force the woman's attention from the screen.

"Help you?"

"I am Seer, protocol officer to the Council, and I could use some help in locating a man."

"Well, if he's single, he's mine first," she said, looking both men up and down in an appraising way. Riker returned the stare and decided she was too bony for his tastes, but would play along if necessary.

"He's a human . . ." Seer began.

"Well, then, he's yours first, they're too much trouble," she said. "He do something?"

"Now that's a good question," Seer said. "We're not sure, but he's doing a very good job convincing us he might have done something. Once we find him, I guess we'll find out."

"Well, haven't seen a human around here," she said, sneaking another look at her screen.

Riker snapped open his tricorder and had it flash her a picture of his father. She looked at it carefully, biting the tip of a finger.

"Nope, haven't seen anyone like this. Except you," she said to Riker.

"Well, I'm certainly not him," Riker said, suppressing his annoyance.

"Nope, beard's too full, jaw's all wrong," she said, and immediately Riker revised his opinion of her.

"He might be hiding up this way. Why aren't you monitoring the rally?"

"Got two of my people there already. They have all the right permits for the thing. Can't say I agree with their point."

"Which is?" Seer asked.

"Delta Sigma IV to withdraw from the Federation."

"Well then, I agree with you."

"Aren't you worried this will spiral out of control like so many others?" Riker asked, more than a little exasperated.

She bit her finger again, losing herself in thought.

"Why I've got two people there. We're a small place, so I'm here just in case."

At that, Riker nodded. He had to credit her with knowing her town better than he did. Still, he was concerned.

She slowly turned to her terminal, read a few lines on the screen, and sighed. "Ever read *Burning Hearts of Qo'noS?*" Neither man replied, their expressions telling her plenty. Silently, she wiped the screen clear, then accessed a database. Riker watched as she quickly and efficiently entered coordinates, crosschecked information, and scrolled through screens. He disliked her style, but her mind seemed quite sharp, and he knew better than to underestimate her.

"According to their latest report, the protest has drawn about fifty people. Lots of chanting, nothing violent at all."

"Maybe we should go see for ourselves," Riker said.

"We'll need gear then," Seer said, sounding less impressed than Riker. "Where can we go?"

"Head out the door, take a left, go about two hundred meters, and there'll be a really big, ugly building on your left. They have the best supplies. Happy hunting."

"You seem to be taking a very lax attitude, if you're really aware of the problems our world is currently facing," Seer said, barely hiding his contempt.

"And sir, you don't know what it's like dispensing law up here. So, I'll just do things my way and you can handle the protocol your way." She stared at him, holding the look for several seconds until Seer blinked and stalked out the door.

And as he left, he heard her mutter, "I gotta get me one just like him."

Troi was sitting down to breakfast when her door chimed. She was surprised since she had no appointments and her visitors were infrequent—beyond Will, of course.

"Come."

The door silently slid open and Crusher poked her head through the entrance. She was in full uniform, complete with smock, but seemed tired. Dark smudges were visible below her eyes, and the strain was evident in her posture.

"I was just about to eat, Beverly. Join me?"

"Thanks," she said, finally entering the cabin. Troi stood and brought over a chair for Crusher.

"Jean-Luc went to the planet early with Ambassador Morrow so I got stood up for breakfast," the doctor explained, taking the seat.

"Well, then join me by all means. Will is still down below. They're checking out some northern regions. He thinks his father is actually trying to guide him."

Crusher looked surprised and lowered her mug. "Is that possible?"

"I think so. Kyle is a brilliant tactician and could either totally go undercover or, if he wanted, see to it that only his son would find him."

"Why would he do that?"

"Now that's the question we can't fathom," Troi admitted. She took a mouthful of fruit and chewed thoughtfully.

Beverly poured herself a mug of coffee and breathed

in the fumes. "Do you think he's behind this outbreak of violence?"

"He's involved, that's for certain. But my guess is that he's involved in a way we can't imagine."

"Well, that's par for us," Crusher said.

"Indeed," Troi replied. They smiled at one another, each of them no doubt reviewing previous oddities. Troi finished another mouthful, not really tasting the food but concentrating on her friend. "Beverly, are you holding up?"

"I have to, don't I?"

"But these last few months have been difficult, and now you're dealing with a large number of casualties. It can't be easy."

"It never is, Deanna. The injuries are routine given what's going on down there, but there's no rhyme or reason to why. I can't entirely figure this out, and I've been distracted from the research to tend to the immediate problems."

"Well, for today, I suggest you delegate as much as you can to Dr. Tropp and return to the research," Troi gently suggested.

"I can try," Crusher said without enthusiasm. "I just know I'll get distracted."

"The others are good and competent; otherwise they wouldn't be on your staff. Remember that and then lock yourself in the lab."

"You make it sound so easy."

"Well, that's my job."

"And are you holding up?"

"Trying to, anyway," Troi said. "I miss Will. He's

been down there for over two days, chasing after his father and the phantoms associated with their shared past. I want to be there to help him and I can't. The captain needs me to help handle the Council."

"I heard about Chkarad's family. That was horrible."

"I've rarely seen a man so lost and anguished. To lose prestige, family, honor . . . all in a matter of hours is frightening."

"Did you talk with him?"

"He's kept himself isolated, and honestly, I don't know enough of the culture to be certain I could do any good."

"Has Jean-Luc been helpful to him?"

"I don't think so. It's not exactly a strength of his. Colt has actually been more useful there."

"It's all that diplomatic training," Crusher said. "You're right about Jean-Luc, though. He's come a long way since taking command of the *Enterprise,* but that's more to do with his crew. To the rest of the universe, he's perfectly pleasant and by-the-book polite."

Troi took another mouthful of fruit and chewed thoughtfully. "He's always tried to keep those emotions in check, using Starfleet's regulations as a guide, but I gather he wasn't always like that."

"Absolutely not!" Crusher said, her eyes going wide, mouth forming an O. "You know the story of how he lost his heart to a Nausicaan; it was just the most extreme example of the kind of outgoing person he was. But after that experience, he needed to reign in those impulses and now lets them out on rare occasions, like one of his fine wines."

"And you, of all of us, have watched most of those changes."

"Sure, from a distance at first. Most of my impressions were a result of Jack's messages from the *Stargazer*. And then, after I lost him, and Jean-Luc came to tell me . . . well . . . that seemed to affect him too. To lose crew and his ship, even if he was cleared at the court-martial, it could have destroyed a lesser man."

"The captain is anything but a lesser man," Troi added.

"Don't I know it," Crusher said with a wan smile. "I want him to be happy, I do. There are times I think he's finally ready to let go and there's always that hint it might be with me and then he gets involved with Anij or Vash or someone else."

"There's too much history between you and always will be," Troi said.

"And when Wesley came back, everything got stirred up again," Crusher said.

"The lack of family has weighed on you, hasn't it?"

"Very much so, Deanna." Crusher stopped talking, weighing matters in her mind and finally decided to raise the issue she'd been avoiding.

"All the things I expected to see my son do . . . graduate from the Academy or serve somewhere with distinction . . . gone. If he was meant for greater things, then fine, but I wish I was there to see it happen. Like so many of us, I use our friendships aboard the *Enterprise* to substitute for a real family."

"And when Wesley left, then Worf . . ." Deanna began.

"I saw that, yes, even this family will break apart.

We've been so very fortunate not to lose anyone really close since Tasha. Listen, there is something, no one else knows. Yerbi Fandau's retiring, and he's offered me the job."

Troi's eyes widened and she broke into a grin. "Oh Beverly, I think that's wonderful for you!"

"I don't even know if I want it," Crusher said carefully.

"Why not?" Troi asked, her tone deepening, getting serious herself.

"Because of the last time I tried it alone on Earth. Because I like what I do here. Because I don't want to leave Jean-Luc . . . or you and the others. Because, damn it, I just don't know."

"You certainly have been through a lot in a short time. Do you have to make any timely decisions?"

Crusher shook her head. "Yerbi's not retiring for a few months yet."

"Are you afraid that by being posted to Earth, you're less likely to see Wes again?"

"Maybe. I don't know," Beverly said. "And I am happy for him. Doesn't make me miss him any less. At least your mother is still alive, and there's always Will."

"Always Will . . ." Deanna repeated, letting the words drift into the air between them. She didn't feel like extolling the virtues of the romance and appearing to flaunt it to her friend, who was clearly dealing with her own personal pain and loneliness. "Obviously it's going to be first things first. Solve this problem and then you can decide about Starfleet Medical."

* * *

Aiken sounded worried, and that alone concerned Vale as she hurried to the transporter room to meet the team of reinforcements accompanying her to the surface. Aiken was first in his class at the Academy barely a year earlier. She actually pulled strings to get him assigned to the *Enterprise,* seeing in him the kind of spark she wanted in her corps. After his arrival, he was everything she expected from an ensign and then some. She thought he was ready for a true challenge, so she assigned him to work with Van Zandt, a veteran with the energy of a cadet. She pitied anyone trying to oppose these two.

But Aiken sounded worried.

The status board showed they were assigned to a port town on Huni, putting down a riot that led to the torching of several warehouses.

Vale had little to offer, but grabbed Floyd, Gonzalez, Perez, Simone, and Melo as they returned from a long shift. They needed rest, but it would have to wait. No sooner did they materialize than they spotted their leader and remained in place. She leapt onto the platform, calling for beam-down at the same time.

The moment she transported down she saw why Van Zandt's team needed help.

The warehouses threw off spectacular light, reds and yellows and, oddly, greens. Four or five tightly clustered buildings were fully engulfed. The flames served as a backdrop for the mob that was busily firing on the security personnel. They were hunkered down behind posts, storage units, and even small craft, wherever cover could be found. One body was prone; to Vale it looked like Bittan.

"Spread out, surround, and fire to suppress," Vale shouted, moving toward her squad leader.

The five officers followed her orders quickly despite their weariness. Vale ran, watching short, stocky Van Zandt scramble atop a box. He barely paused to aim, fired off three shots in as many directions, and leapt back to the dock.

Meanwhile the taller, thinner Aiken brushed a few unruly strands of hair away from his eyes, steadied his leader, and then fired a few shots of his own. All seemed to strike the same spot, a wall where part of the mob hid.

"How many are there?" Vale asked.

"I count at least fifteen," Aiken said, his voice high, the adrenaline clear. In the flickering light of the fire, he seemed even younger than usual.

"So we even the odds a bit," Vale observed.

Van Zandt's lower lip stuck out as he considered the situation, and Vale almost smiled at the comical expression.

"All right. We're gonna spread out and try to catch them in a crossfire," she ordered.

Within a minute, her people were signaling they were in position and ready to fire.

A loud sound distracted her before she could give the order. She felt the dock beneath her feet shudder. Quickly, she looked up to see if something in the buildings had exploded. Instead, she saw the boats behind her all go up in flames. Something had ignited at least a dozen service and pleasure craft.

"Look!"

At Aiken's call, she turned her head and saw that his

guess of fifteen people was wrong. She saw that there were at least four times that many, and they were on the move. Anything in their path was kicked, burned, or fired upon. The security officers, numbering just under a dozen, awaited instructions and refrained from firing on the advancing mass of people.

This mob was not going to get caught in anyone's cross-fire. Instead they had Vale and her people surrounded.

Picard and Morrow were updated by Councillor Cholan, the man who only hours before had demanded some form of retribution against the Federation. He was still glowering, but at least his tone was civil. Despite his advanced years, Cholan was the first councillor to awaken this morning. He had already checked in with the aides, none of whom looked like they had slept. One was passing around cups of tea and another had nearly fallen asleep at his terminal.

The captain declined an offer of the insipid-looking tea and let his eyes rest on the main map of the planet. The amount of violence marked on the map indicated that the number of affected people had climbed past fifty percent overnight. In another day they would reach the sixty percent mark, the point at which Renks declared all hope would be lost. Picard sincerely hoped Renks's estimate was wrong.

As Morrow and Cholan spoke, Picard walked to the front of the Council chamber and opened the wide double doors. Daylight, bright and beautiful, welcomed him. There was a hint of coolness in the dry air, the first sign of a seasonal change. The captain breathed in deeply.

He detected smoke in the first lungful of air. Quickly, he scanned the skies, but saw nothing against the cloudless blue. Carmona joined the captain and looked ready to give a report. Picard held up one finger, asking the man to wait as he took in another deep breath.

"Do you smell a fire?" he asked, knowing but still dreading the answer.

Chapter Ten

"IT'S GETTING a bit warm here," Van Zandt remarked.

The crowd had them surrounded, apparently ready to let the buildings behind them burn to the ground. Poor Aiken kept quiet, but he was looking a bit green around the gills. Or was that just the firelight?

"Well, this is going to take a little creativity." Vale said. A quick tap of her badge put her people on alert. All quickly acknowledged the plan. She grinned.

"Are you nits just going stand there and watch us burn? We could just beam back to the *Enterprise!*"

The mob remained silent.

"Is this the best you can do? I thought you were Dorset! I thought you were something to reckon with."

She heard some muttering from the crowd.

"I can walk out there and take on any five of you. Five? Maybe eight or ten!"

A male voice cried out, insulting Vale's parentage.

Other voices soon joined in, all demanding the privilege of knocking her block off.

"And here we go," she said to Van Zandt, who winked at her. Aiken watched, amazed.

Vale rose and strode forward, flexing her fingers in a show of readiness. Sure enough, five Dorset men broke off from the group. They started taunting her now, laughing between jests, a bunch of old friends out for some fun.

When ten feet separated them, a crimson beam cut between them, followed by another. The Dorset stepped back and yelped, almost in unison. Vale held firm. The men saw this and started forward again as a third beam lashed out.

Unable to stop their momentum, the men went crashing through the weakened dock. The now soggy contingent's fellow rioters stopped short, wisely avoiding their companions' watery fate. Those who persisted in firing were quickly stunned by wide-beamed phaser blasts.

When the last Dorset collapsed, Vale turned to Aiken, smiled, and said, "That's how it's done."

Her smile faded when she saw his eager eyes glaze over as blood spread across his uniform.

Picard's phaser was suddenly in his hand, instinct working faster than intelligence. The captain tensed.

Within moments, he heard the beginnings of a mob approach. There were yells and calls that he could not discern. However, Carmona seemed to recognize the tone and he jogged away, calling for his team. In seconds he returned, just as the new mob rounded a corner and was approaching the Council chamber.

"Evacuate the Council and their equipment," Picard ordered.

"I can't leave you out here, sir," the younger man said. His voice sounded strained.

"I'll be fine, get started," the captain insisted.

Carmona tapped his badge and started giving orders, then began yelling inside the Council chamber. Picard could hear the commotion behind him, but concentrated instead on the people approaching at a steady pace. Some held signs protesting the Council, others protested the Federation, while others held torches. The crowd was a true cross section of the population, men and women, young and old, Bader and Dorset. All were angry.

Morrow poked his head out from the door directly behind the captain. "They're all awake and moving. The equipment is being sacrificed, although the data is being downloaded."

"Excellent. Please accompany them and make sure you stay in touch," Picard said.

"I think I'd rather help you. You're a little short-handed," the ambassador replied.

"Ambassador, you are not at all trained for this sort of situation. My people are. Your training will help the Council maintain control of the planet. Please do as I say." Morrow opened his mouth to object, but closed it again when Picard shook his head. With that the door closed softly behind the captain, who watched with growing apprehension as the crowd drew closer.

A piece of brick sailed his way but fell short, some meters before his feet. Another, larger brick followed and flew to his right. Picard remained immobile, refusing to shrink from the mob, while at the same time not firing back.

The voices continued to cry charges and obscenities at the captain, but he ignored them. More pieces of debris flew his way, but none came near him. They were all being thrown from the rear of the crowd. Those in front seemed cowed by his immobile presence. Picard's strategy seemed to be working, and the seconds ticked by. Finally, Carmona signaled that the Council chamber was empty and the guards had the Council nearby. He begged the captain to withdraw. Picard knew the moment he turned his back on the mob, they would surge forward and he would be hurt. Instead, he stepped backward toward the doorway.

He groped behind him for the handle to open the door and reach relative safety, but before he could find it, the door opened and Morrow emerged.

"I couldn't let you—" he began, but froze when he saw the crowd.

Picard's attention wavered for a moment, and suddenly his spell over those in the front was broken. Someone shouted, a yipping sound like a call to arms, and debris began flying as the mob surged forward.

A piece of metal hit Morrow in the head while a brick buried itself deep in his stomach. He sagged under the attack, losing his breath. Picard reached out for him. Wrapping an arm around the injured ambassador, the captain tried once more to get through the door, but the crowd finally reached them. Hands grabbed at his legs and pulled him back.

The crowd was on them.

His arms punched, his legs kicked, Picard could feel the crowd all around his body. His grip on his phaser grew tighter as someone wrestled for it. Morrow lay still, under Picard's protective body, but that was not going to last for long. The screaming and accusations continued unabated.

The pummeling was getting to him, and he decided he would have to use his phaser to protect Morrow's life.

Then he heard a familiar whine.

The hands hitting him fell away, and Picard wasn't sure if he had accidentally squeezed off a shot.

Suddenly, people were being dragged off the captain and he was able to see the sky. He watched Christine Vale hauling a woman off his leg and toss her aside as though she were made of paper.

Picard scrambled to his feet, adjusting his duty jacket along the way. He pocketed his phaser and looked gratefully at his security chief. She nodded in his direction and then signaled for an emergency medical transport of Morrow directly to sickbay.

"Better late than never," Vale quipped.

"Bring down a fresh team to protect the Council and get your people some rest. They've more than earned it," Picard replied.

"Aye, sir," she replied. "Captain, we've begun to record . . . casualties."

Picard's gaze narrowed, then deepened into a frown as she relayed her recent experience and the loss of Aiken. He saw the pain in her eyes, but only for a moment. She was putting it aside for now, but he knew she would grieve.

As he felt the transporter take hold of him, Picard recognized how close to a true disaster he had come. The Council was once more on the run, a Federation ambassador had been hurt, and he seemed powerless to stem the tide.

Was Delta Sigma IV a lost cause?

Chapter Eleven

CRUSHER'S HEAD HURT. The headache arrived shortly after lunch and refused to surrender despite every fancy treatment she threw at it. *Some doctor I am,* she thought with disgust. How was she supposed to stop a plague when she couldn't even stop her own head from hurting? *Better not tell Yerbi I was defeated by a stupid headache if I'm even considering his offer.* She smiled at the thought of what he'd say: "Simple old-fashioned ailments respond best to simple old-fashioned medications." Maybe that was so, but at the moment she couldn't afford to succumb to the side effects of some primitive analgesic.

Sure, common, garden variety drugs tamed the pain, but they dulled the senses as well. And she couldn't get anything accomplished that way; sauntering around her lab relaxed, but muddle headed. *No one is very effective . . .* she thought. Suddenly Crusher raised her aching head from her desk.

. . . under the influence of common, garden variety drugs.

She had to talk to Jean-Luc. Now.

Crusher thought about it a moment and then gestured for Weinstein to sit at the guest chair in her office. Susan complied, a quizzical expression on her pretty face. "My head's swimming from the information, so much of it duplicative, from the Bader, Dorset, and Starfleet. It's given me a nova headache. Let me summarize for you out loud and tell me if I'm babbling."

"Shoot."

The doctor leaned back in chair and closed her eyes, forgetting about the padds and screens in her office. All she pictured was Delta Sigma IV and the damned liscom plant.

"The Bader and Dorset don't like each other. Don't even get along despite being neighbors, or maybe because of it. Within a short time, both find this gem of a planet and begin to study it for colonization. Miracle of miracles, they decide they'd rather build the planet together than fight over it."

"When was this?"

"Nearly one hundred and fifty years ago."

"Got it. Go ahead."

"Okay. It turns out this nice little plant emits a natural gas into the atmosphere which seems not to have any adverse affects on the people. Two generations later it turns out they were wrong. The gas had built up in the bloodstream, altering both races' genetic makeup and suddenly they're starting to age prematurely. Unchecked, the planet is uninhabitable in five more generations. You with me?"

"I'm fine, go ahead."

"Good. Okay, between colonization and this discovery, they petition for Federation membership and get it. So, they call us for help. Starfleet sends medical researchers, headed by Kyle Riker. They confirm the people's worst fears and return to Starfleet Medical to figure out a solution."

Weinstein nodded once more to indicate she was following the story. Crusher was ready to begin again when she snapped her fingers and announced, "Actually, the first series of studies were done by the Dorset and Bader and presented to the Riker team."

"Is that significant?"

"I have no clue," Crusher admitted.

"Time goes by and *voilà,* we find a counteragent to the problem. Five guinea pigs are tested for a year, and the buildup in the blood has dissipated. The genetic makeup seems back to normal. No one dies or grows a third arm, so, in time for the centennial celebration, they are returned home. Killing two birds with one stone, Riker is sent along with them, to help represent the Federation.

"Shortly after the celebrations begin, one test subject kills another. This triggers a few things. Riker running away is one, but that's thankfully not my problem. There are growing protests around the planet, protests that turn violent pretty quickly, and that's my problem. Something is causing it and the Federation is getting the blame and I don't even know the cause. These outbreaks of violence have now spread to nearly forty percent of the population."

"What's the nature of the violence?"

"Belligerence that can rapidly turn to fists or weapons," Crusher said wearily. "I've seen it happen and it's not pretty. There was one death, then another, and now carnage is planetwide." A thought snapped into focus in her head and she remained absolutely still. She turned over the information in her head, letting her brain process the notion before turning to the reports.

"Doctor? Did you fall asleep?"

Crusher's eyes snapped open and she grabbed a padd, discarded it, and grabbed another. "Help me find the report from the initial surveys."

"The Federation's surveys?"

"No, the original Bader and Dorset reports."

Weinstein flipped over two more padds before finding the one the Doctor wanted. Crusher nodded her thanks and called up a specific portion of the report. Her eyes rapidly scanned the information and then she turned her attention to the desktop display. Weinstein was wise enough to remain quiet, but also to stay put in case she was needed.

"Aha! There you are . . ." she muttered to herself. "Crusher to Picard."

"Yes, Doctor."

"Can we meet in private? I have something."

"Come to my quarters."

"I'll be there in five minutes. Crusher out." Turning to the nurse, she smiled widely and said, "Thanks for being here."

"Sure," Weinstein acknowledged. "Not that I did much. Want to clue me in?"

Crusher told her and was impressed when the nurse's

head bobbed in agreement. Her suspicions more or less confirmed, she headed toward the door and stopped. She turned to find a mirror and took a self-conscious look. *You look like hell,* she thought. *Tough.*

Donning the thick cold-weather garments took Riker back to a time and place he didn't really want to go. *Tough on me,* he thought as he straightened a bulky sleeve. That was the mission, to go back to Alaska, or its equivalent on this planet. To go back and find his dad.

As he and Seer walked shoulder to shoulder down the street, he heard sound followed by screams. The sound was muffled, almost like an explosion but not quite. It was coming from the general direction of a protest, so they broke into a run. Riker already had his phaser out, getting his gloved hand used to the feel.

The protest was in the center of town, in a wide rectangular park with benches and old-growth trees that provided shade. Sure enough, there were some fifty people now running away from the makeshift speaker's stand, which was engulfed in flames. Whoever had been standing on it was now rolling on the ground, trying to smother flames. One of the assigned peace officers was working with him, patting the man's burning clothing with gloved hands.

Emerging from the opposite angle came a group perhaps double the size of the protesters. Many carried signs that were not in support of the Federation but in opposition to the Dorset. That was always a bad sign, Riker reflected, when protests shifted from political to racial. He heard shouted epithets directed at the Bader. Some of the original Dorset protesters were drawn to the new mob, others continued to flee.

The remaining Dorset stopped running and took a stand, hurling back slurs of their own. Seer tugged Riker's arm to point out another section of the street. More people were showing up, some out of curiosity, others willing to join one of the sides. And these were not carrying signs but instead had lengths of chain, tree branches, or metal tools. There were enough crude weapons in both Bader and Dorset hands to insure that blood would flow.

Riker raised his phaser and took aim.

At the chime, Picard invited Beverly into his cabin. He was tired, frustrated, and concerned about the situation below. Vale and her team were pushed to their limit and she was down there now, caught up in another firefight. A part of him wanted to be there beside her, another part wanted to use the ship's phaser banks and stun the rabble causing the trouble on Huni.

As Beverly walked in, he noticed she looked tired, her hair unkempt, black smudges under her eyes. He'd like to suggest she sleep, but knew better. The captain knew everyone on his crew was working overtime to keep the planet stable until a solution was found. He was proud of them and made a mental note to commend them all when time permitted. But now Crusher was here with a report and hopefully a key to the solution.

"I'm sorry about Aiken," she began.

Picard nodded solemnly, showing a brief moment of

respect. He knew there would be more such moments in the days ahead. Then, he looked directly into her eyes, his own expression silently begging for some news.

"We've been entirely focused on the liscom gas's effects on the chromosomes and life expectancy," Crusher began. "What we've missed is how else the gas has been affecting the people."

Picard blinked. "I'm sorry, Beverly, but could you repeat that please?" he asked.

"Essentially the entire planet is drugged."

"The liscom gas . . ." he began.

". . . acts as a sedative. It turns out that the natural flora on the planet helped alter the biochemistries of both races, which had a catalytic affect. The effect was unique to the planet's ecosystem, so it couldn't be successfully replicated on either planet, according to Kyle Riker's report to the Federation."

"Why just them and not other races?"

"Given their location in the quadrant, I would say they ultimately came from the same root and don't get along because they're like and like, not opposites, but I'll worry about that later." There was a pause while Picard absorbed the information.

"Of course. I'm still not sure why the Federation tasked a senior man like Riker with solving a medical problem," he said.

"I have no idea. All I know is that the liscom gas was the source of their peaceful coexistence. It seems to have not only altered their chromosomes, but affected their brain chemistry as well. It wasn't a fresh start in a neutral place; it was the atmosphere that lulled them into loving one another." Picard nodded to himself and then nodded to Beverly to continue.

"The counteragent developed on Earth neutralized the liscom gas in the blood, which in turn should also readjust the chromosomes in a generation or two. But, it also neutralizes the peaceful effects, so both races' natural aggression is returning."

"But how is the counteragent spreading if it hasn't been mass produced?"

"Like the gas itself, it's in the atmosphere through close contact. It's acting like a virus and it's being passed on very quickly through a kiss, sweat, a cough, whatever."

"So, the people of this planet are suffering an epidemic of violence at the same time the races' lives are being saved." Picard seemed stunned and saddened by the news and fell silent, contemplating how this information would affect the mission.

"Vale hit it on the head when she observed that they've never done this before. They have never experienced their natural aggressive tendencies and don't know how to govern themselves."

Picard nodded again and seemed frustrated. When Beverly asked him why, he said, "Because all the time we've spent talking, all the peace I've tried to maintain has been useless. It goes against their true natures. And Morrow had no idea he was wasting his time. We all were." Picard rose and began pacing the room. "Beverly, I can help stem the violence, but you need to find a way to fix the counteragent."

"Captain, it took them two years to come up with the counteragent and a year to test it. At the rate the counteragent is spreading, the entire planet will be at war before I can fix it. If I even can."

He reached out, holding onto her arms with his hands. Sympathy filled his eyes, the look of one old friend to another. "You're my chief medical officer and one of the brightest diagnosticians in all Starfleet. There's no one better suited to step in and solve this."

"I'll do what I can, but medical miracles are hard to come by."

"I understand. Get back to work, and whatever you need, you will have. I'm going back down to help Vale."

Crusher frowned. What was left unsaid was that if things did spread planetwide, the *Enterprise* alone would not be powerful enough to maintain order.

She nodded and turned to go back to the lab. It looked like Yerbi would have to wait a while longer for an answer to his offer. Crusher had work to do right here.

Riker knew the standoff wasn't going to last long. Someone would grow anxious and throw the first punch or swing a club. Warily, he scanned the crowd, trying to pick which person would be the first.

The yelling seemed to intensify, and then there was a different sound. A rushing sound, not of wind but of water. Thick streams of water suddenly emerged from different portions of the town square's perimeter. Riker took a second to look to his right and saw that it all came from fire suppression equipment. The hoses were like cannon, striking one and all, quickly turning the field into a muddy mess. People dropped protest signs, others lost their grip on metal tools. The shouting was also drowned out by the gushing water, so the would-be conflict soon got rained out.

In a flash, Riker realized what had happened and let out a laugh.

Seer looked at him, unsure. "What is it, Will?"

"My father's here."

"How can you be sure?"

"Because he used the same water maneuver to defuse a civil war on Epsilon Canaris III."

Riker stopped laughing and scanned the perimeter near the fire hoses, hoping to spot his prey. There was no sign of him, but every fiber of the son's being knew the father was nearby.

"Seer, stay here and make sure things settle down. I've got to find him before he leaves town."

"Of course, but shouldn't I join you?"

"I'm better off doing this myself."

Without another word, Riker broke off into a jog and headed in the direction of the nearest field, which was where his father must have landed. His outerwear was necessary, given the temperature, but it encumbered him and made him sluggish. Couldn't be helped. He tried to control his breathing so the frigid air didn't hurt his lungs. If the cold could do this to him, then it would certainly also slow his father down. He had to count on that.

Will cleared the two blocks in less time than he estimated, his eyes always moving, seeking a human silhouette.

He didn't dare slow down to consult his tricorder. It was time to do this on his own, without help. Man against man, something he learned from his father in the anbo-jytsu ring all those years ago.

Turning the corner and starting east, Will could see several flyers on a field maybe seventy-five meters ahead.

There!

A figure was darting between two flyers and ducking under a third. It had to be Kyle looking for another aircraft to steal. But Will was on to him.

He scrambled around several flyers, nearing his father, who was still on the move. The gap was closing, but Will knew he had to be careful in case his father was armed or had already found time to lay a trap.

"Dad! Stop running! I've found you."

The figure was crouched beneath a ship, in front of an open panel with exposed circuitry. With his back to Will, the man raised both hands. He was breathing hard from the run. Frozen exhalation drifted about his head.

Will carefully kept the phaser before him, wary of a trap. He moved closer in a semi-circular pattern. Finally he was only a meter away.

His father seemed grayer than in the video image, his face more careworn. His kneeling posture made him appear foolish, but Will knew the old man was anything but that. Their eyes met, and there Will saw the steel he knew would always be a part of his father.

"You can get up," Will said harshly.

"Good. Cold ground's hurting my knees."

"I have to take you into custody, you know."

"I do. But first, you have to help me."

Will was surprised by that, and his expression must

have said so. His father looked at him appraisingly and then nodded in confirmation.

"My work here isn't finished. With your help, it can be."

"My help?"

"Yes."

"Are you behind what has happened to these people? Or the Federation?"

"Yes, but there's an explanation."

"I'm listening."

About the Author

Robert Greenberger wishes he were the last son of the doomed planet Krypton or was bequeathed an emerald power ring. Instead, he was born in a more mundane manner, surrounded by a loving family on Long Island. His parents encouraged him to pursue his dreams, which first led him to SUNY-Binghamton for his bachelor's in English and History and then into the world of publishing.

He has spent the majority of his adult life at DC Comics, joining them after a three-year stint at *Starlog* Press. At DC, he began as an Assistant Editor, rising to Manager–Editorial Operations prior to taking what amounted to a two-year sabbatical in the grownup world.

After ten months as a Producer at Gist Communications, he was lured back to comics, spending a tempestuous year as Director–Publishing Operations at Marvel Comics. He returned to DC as a Senior Editor in their collected editions department in 2002, where he continues today.

Along the way, he has written quite a number of articles, interviews, reviews, and a smattering of comics before turning to prose. He has collaborated with Peter David and Michael Jan Friedman on several *Star Trek* projects. Additionally, he has written several solo novels, including the one you have hopefully just completed. He has written two eBooks for *Star Trek: S.C.E.* and short works found in *Enterprise Logs, Star Trek: New Frontier–No Limits,* and *Star Trek: Tales of the Dominion War.*

He has also written many young adult nonfiction books on a wide variety of subjects.

He makes his home in Connecticut, joined by his patient wife, Deb, and his way-too-old children, Kate and Robbie. When not writing or working, he wants time to read and watch too much television, and prays for the day the Mets win another World Series.

The saga continues in July 2004 with

STAR TREK®

A TIME TO HATE

by
Robert Greenberger

**Turn the page for an electrifying
preview of *A Time to Hate*. . . .**

Kyle Riker got up from the ground, wiping the dirt from his hands. He didn't move with the same sureness Will always remembered. His father wore a bulky gray coat, not the same sort of flexible microweave jacket Will was wearing. His hands were bare because gloves would have prevented him from doing the delicate work that was necessary to steal a flyer. They were chafed and red from the cold, and scarred. Definitely the worse for wear, Will mused, watching without once lowering his phaser.

"I said, I'm listening," Will ordered.

Kyle looked over at him, pain in his eyes, something Will had not seen in his father since the one woman whose love they had shared, Will's mother, Ann, had died.

"You can put the phaser down, son," Kyle said.

"Right now, I can't trust you."

"Your own father?"

"Especially him," Will replied.

Kyle looked hurt for a moment but let it pass. "I

thought we tore that wall down a decade ago. I thought this was all past us."

"Funny thing about walls," his son said. "You can build them, tear them down, and rebuild them all over again."

"Is that what this is all about? My not being in touch? I've never been good about that."

"No, this is all about you leaving the scene of a crime and allowing yourself to become a fugitive. You need to come in and explain yourself."

Kyle gestured with his hands, palms up. "Can I at least put some gloves on? It's colder than a Romulan's smile."

Will gestured with the phaser. His father gingerly reached into his coat pockets, pulled out black gloves, and put them on. He rubbed his hands, trying to generate some friction to warm them faster. Will just stood there, sorting through the feelings that were conflicting in his heart and his head, trying to remain focused on the mission. While they had this reunion, a planet was falling apart, and he had to learn what role his father had played. Mixed in with it all was the dreaded feeling of guilt by association, and it nagged at him, fueling the anger he barely kept under control.

"Much better, thanks, son."

"Let's keep this professional, sir," Will said.

"Like we did on the *Enterprise?* What did you call it . . . your best Academy manners? Is the wall really that high and thick?"

Will did not reply, deciding to wait his father out. Get him to talk. Vale had taught him this trick some time back, and he liked using it. In the past he would have threatened or intimidated his subject, using his large physique to good advantage.

Kyle, no slouch as a negotiator, tried to wait him out too. Both must have felt the pressure of time, but Kyle seemed to think they both needed to settle their personal issues first. Will shifted his feet, sensing the cold seeping through his boots. He glanced up and saw the coming twilight. When the sun set, it was going to be a lot more uncomfortable standing in between parked flyers.

Finally, Kyle broke the silence. "Can we at least do this inside somewhere?"

Will stood his ground and started to reach for his combadge.

Kyle looked concerned and shook his head, saying, "No."

"*Enterprise* is a whole lot warmer than down here."

"My work isn't done. I have to finish, and you can be a part of it."

"You still haven't explained yourself."

"I will, but let's get out of the cold."

"How'd you get to Eowand?"

Kyle looked at the ground, almost like a child caught with his hand on the cookies. "I came on a flyer."

"Something you stole."

There was a spark of defiance in Kyle's eyes. "I intend to make reparations when this is done. But a stolen vehicle or two is nothing compared with the suffering these people are enduring." Some steel had also crept back into his voice, and Will tried to figure out just how broken a man Kyle was. Without answers, everything was conjecture. At that moment, he flashed on Deanna's face and wished she were here. She'd know what was in his father's heart.

"Is the flyer here?"

"Yes."

"Rather than compound your crimes, let's take that one. Do you have a destination in mind?"

Kyle gestured with his left hand toward a battered, pale blue and gold vehicle, somewhat haphazardly parked compared with the other ships on the ground.

"I wanted to change flyers, avoid possible tracking," Kyle explained, his frozen breath drifting around his head. "I've been doing it for days."

Will nodded and walked on the older man's right side, keeping out of arm's reach, his phaser on the side away from his father. A locking light blinked twice, and he heard a click. The hatch was a little wider than on Seer's ship, but the inside was much the same. He had to admit he was impressed by how easily his father slipped into the pilot's chair and began running through the preflight sequence. The flyer hummed to life, the engine sounding rougher than Seer's craft but more powerful. Kyle looked at Will and then at the piloting controls. Will nodded his consent, and Kyle's large hands struggled their way inside the two contoured holes that housed the controls. Within seconds, the engine's vibration grew a little rougher, and with a small shudder, the flyer began to lift into the air.

"I've changed flyers four times," Kyle explained as they traveled. "They're all built so damned consistently, it's a snap to master each new model." Will didn't reply, figuring the warming air would make his father more talkative.

Banking to the right, they swooped away, the town of Eowand rapidly growing smaller. The sky was now almost a royal blue before them, a golden haze behind them. They flew for several minutes in silence. The presence of two large men made the forward section of the flyer feel cramped, but Will made sure his right arm, which held the phaser, remained free to move. He rested the weapon in plain sight, certain that Kyle could do nothing as long as his hands were encumbered by the ship's controls.

"How'd you know where to find me?" Kyle finally asked.

"Someone was defusing things around the planet when no one else seemed capable. It didn't take a computer to figure out it had to be you."

"And here?"

"You seemed to stop following Bison; you followed the main path of the contagion. As I saw it head north, it became apparent you were heading for familiar climates."

Kyle nodded, a smile of approval on his features. He then narrowed his blue eyes, concentrating on a course correction that would take them directly toward the northern pole of the planet. "I lost Bison. Bet you did, too."

"Letting the magnetic field hide us?"

"If anything, it'll confuse the scanning and we can then go any direction we want."

"And this ship is shielded from the magnetic field?"

Will received a withering look from his father and he cursed himself for asking so naive a question. Was he an adult, or was he twelve again?

"We were never looking for Bison, to be honest. You didn't say, where are we going?"

"Next nearest mass concentration of people is here, on the Osedah continent. We'll check that out, make sure things are under control, and keep moving."

"What's your objective? What do you want my help for?"

KNOW NO BOUNDARIES

Explore the Star Trek™
Universe with Star Trek™
Communicator, The Magazine of
the Official Star Trek Fan Club.

Subscription to Communicator is
only $29.95 per year (plus shipping and handling)
and entitles you to:

- 6 issues of STAR TREK Communicator

- Membership in the official STAR TREK™ Fan Club

- An exclusive full-color lithograph

- 10% discount on all merchandise purchased at
  www.startrekfanclub.com

- Advance purchase preference on select items
  exclusive to the fan club

- ...and more benefits to come!

So don't get left behind! Subscribe to STAR TREK™
Communicator now at www.startrekfanclub.com

www.decipher.com

DECIPHER®
The Art of Great Games®

A VIACOM COMPANY
www.startrek.com
STFC